# Geek High

# Geek High

## Piper Banks

nal
jam
books

NAL Jam
Published by New American Library, a division of
Penguin Group (USA) Inc., 375 Hudson Street,
New York, New York 10014, USA
Penguin Group (Canada), 90 Eglinton Avenue East, Suite 700, Toronto,
Ontario M4P 2Y3, Canada (a division of Pearson Penguin Canada Inc.)
Penguin Books Ltd., 80 Strand, London WC2R 0RL, England
Penguin Ireland, 25 St. Stephen's Green, Dublin 2,
Ireland (a division of Penguin Books Ltd.)
Penguin Group (Australia), 250 Camberwell Road, Camberwell, Victoria 3124,
Australia (a division of Pearson Australia Group Pty. Ltd.)
Penguin Books India Pvt. Ltd., 11 Community Centre, Panchsheel Park,
New Delhi – 110 017, India
Penguin Group (NZ), 67 Apollo Drive, Rosedale, North Shore 0632,
New Zealand (a division of Pearson New Zealand Ltd.)
Penguin Books (South Africa) (Pty.) Ltd., 24 Sturdee Avenue,
Rosebank, Johannesburg 2196, South Africa

Penguin Books Ltd., Registered Offices:
80 Strand, London WC2R 0RL, England

First published by NAL Jam, an imprint of New American Library,
a division of Penguin Group (USA) Inc.

First Printing, November 2007
5  7  9  10  8  6

LIBRARY OF CONGRESS CATALOGING-IN-PUBLICATION DATA
Banks, Piper.
Geek High / Piper Banks.
p. cm.
Summary: Known as "The Human Calculator," fifteen-year-old Miranda is anything
but popular, and it seems that will only get worse when she has to move in with her estranged
father and his family, then is blackmailed into planning a school dance, where she will be
escorted by a freshman while her stepsister dances with Miranda's dream date.
ISBN: 978-0-451-22225-1
[1. High schools—Fiction. 2. Schools—Fiction. 3. Self-esteem—Fiction. 4. Stepfamilies—Fiction.
5. Popularity—Fiction. 6. Genius—Fiction. 7. Florida—Fiction.] I. Title.
PZ7.G2128Gee 2007
[Fic]—dc22          2007017340

Set in Bulmer MT  •  Designed by Elke Sigal
Printed in the United States of America

*For George, who inspired this story*

# Geek High

# Chapter 1

$$\|x + y\| \leq \|x\| + \|y\|$$

This is how pathetic my life is: My nickname used to be the Human Calculator.

I *know*. It's the dorkiest nickname in the history of nicknames. But it's pretty self-explanatory—I can do math in my head. Add, subtract, multiply, divide, fractions, even more complicated things like calculus. I don't know how I do it; I just do. When someone asks, "What's 52,652 times 95,737?" I just know that the answer is 5,040,744,524, the same way some people are musical, or good at languages, or know how to wear a scarf without looking stupid.

When I was eight years old, my weird talent landed me on the *Late Show with David Letterman*. I'd never seen the show before—it was on past my bedtime—so I didn't know that Letterman specialized in having freaks on, like grandmothers who can burp the alphabet or yodeling dogs. Or little girls who can solve math problems in their heads.

The studio was really bright and really cold, and Letterman kept making all of these weird faces, which the audience thought were hilarious. I wasn't at all nervous. Instead, I was happy, because my mom had gotten me a new pair of patent-leather Mary Janes for the occasion, and I liked the clicking sound they made when I walked onto the stage. Letterman asked me a few math questions, and I answered them all correctly—he verified the answers with a calculator, which the audience also found humorous, especially when he pulled on his tie and pretended he couldn't figure out how to make the calculator work—and then, when we were done, he said, "Ladies and gentlemen, give a hand to Miranda Bloom, the Human Calculator!"

And the name just sort of stuck, especially since my parents taped the show, and then insisted on playing it every year on my birthday. I'd beg my mom, Sadie, to at least wait until after all of the kids at my party had left before putting the video on. But Sadie would just shake her head and say, "Miranda, there's no shame in being special."

And so every year I'd be forced to sit through the mortifying spectacle of my eight-year-old self—the gap-toothed grin, the chipmunk cheeks, the swinging feet. And at the point where Letterman says, "Miranda Bloom, the Human Calculator!" all of the kids would smirk and nudge one another, while I sat there stewing in my humiliation. Then, on the first day of school after my birthday party, one of the kids—inevitably a boy with a buzz cut, whom I had been forced to invite, since Sadie insisted that I include everyone in my class—would start yelling, "Mir-an-da Blooooom, the Human Cal-cu-la-tor," in an annoying game-show-host voice.

And I'd always get in trouble for slugging him. This did not endear me to the school administrators, who were already tired of dealing with me when my teachers wrote me up for correcting them in class. As though it was my fault that Mrs. Brun misspelled the word *bellwether* when she wrote it on the chalkboard.

Or that I filled in my entire math workbook on the first day of seventh grade, and so whenever the appallingly lazy math teacher, Mr. Dyson, chose to assign us worksheets rather than teach—which was most days—I had a free period in which to entertain myself. Normally, I'd just pull out one of the racy romance novels I'd stolen from my mom's bookshelf. (She's a romance writer, and her publisher sends her piles of free books.) Hiding the book in my lap, I'd lose myself in stories of dashing buccaneers falling in love with beautiful heiresses. I did this with no guilt whatsoever—I figured the books filled in the gaping holes left by the cut-and-dried sex-ed unit we covered in health class.

But one day, I was so immersed in *The Rogue and the Lady*, I forgot to pretend to scribble in my workbook when Mr. Dyson walked up and down the aisles between the desks, and he caught me reading.

"What is this?" he asked, plucking the paperback out of my hands. He looked down at the cover, which showed a man with long, dark hair and an unbuttoned shirt leaning over to kiss the bare shoulder of a woman in an old-fashioned ball gown. When Mr. Dyson looked back up at me, his droopy basset hound–like face was thunderous.

"It's called *The Rogue and the Lady*," I said helpfully.

"I can see that," Mr. Dyson snapped. "The question is, why aren't you working on the math exercises I assigned?"

"I already finished them," I said.

"So move on to the next exercise."

"I did those, too. I've done all of them."

Mr. Dyson let out a snort of disbelief, and reached down to grab my math workbook off my desk. But then he thumbed through it, and saw that I'd been telling the truth. He stared at my workbook for a long time—I could tell that he was reviewing my answers to see if they were right (which, of course, they were)—before finally, decisively snapping it shut. He didn't seem happy that I'd done all of the work. If anything, it made him even angrier.

"Miranda, go to the principal's office," Mr. Dyson ordered.

"May I have my book back?" I asked, without much hope.

"No," he said, striding to the front of the room. He opened a desk drawer and tossed *The Rogue and the Lady* inside.

I never did find out how the story ended, and whether Slade and Lady Tilda ever made up after their fight over how Tilda's father, Sir Winston, had betrothed Lady Tilda to the evil Duke Harley.

Later, as I sat outside the principal's office, I could hear snatches of the conversation between Principal Scott and Sadie.

"... academically gifted, but socially immature ..." Principal Scott said.

"... should provide a more challenging curriculum ..." Sadie argued.

"... inappropriate reading material for a child ..."

"... her father and I divorced recently ... causing her to act out ..."

A week later, my mom pulled me out of public school and enrolled me in the Notting Hill Independent School for Gifted Children. To get into NHISGC, you have to take a test to prove that you have an IQ of at least 125, which I've always thought was harsh. What do they tell the kid who has a 124? "Sorry, you're smart ... but not quite smart enough"? It just seems mean.

Anyway, the school has grades K through twelve, but everyone calls the high school wing Geek High. And in a week, I'm going to be starting my sophomore year there.

Geek High was the first place I'd ever really fit in. Most of the students had ended up there after a usually disastrous attempt to fit in at a mainstream school, where we were misunderstood and frequently tormented by our classmates. But at Geek High, no one ridiculed you for being different; we were all outcasts.

And no one at Geek High had ever called me the Human Calculator. It was a definite improvement.

All of the kids who go to Geek High are smart, but just about everyone also has a special talent. My best friend Charlotte, aka Charlie, is a phenomenal painter. Lately she's been doing these huge, splotchy modern pieces, and after her latest show a local newspaper columnist said that Charlie's going to be the next Jackson Pollock. My other best friend, Finn, became a self-made millionaire at the age of twelve when he sold his computer game to a national distributor. Since then, he's created and sold a bunch more games, and basically will never have to get a real job for the rest of his life, unless he wants to.

Even the people I hate have special talents. Horrible Felicity Glen, aka the Felimonster, is an opera singer. Her best friend, Morgan Simpson, aka Toady, is a concert harpist who's played with the Miami Symphony Orchestra, and who is reason enough to hate all harpists everywhere.

So, basically, my mother was wrong: I'm not special, not when compared to the kids I go to school with. Sure, I can do math. And that might sound like it's special . . . for about five seconds. Right up until the point when you realize that in this age of computers and calculators, there's absolutely no benefit to being able to calculate sums in your head. It's a useless skill.

And you want to know what that makes me?

The least gifted kid in the entire freaking school.

But this year, I'm determined not to let my complete and utter inadequacy get me down. I know that you're supposed to make resolutions on New Year's Day, but I follow the academic calendar, so I'm going to make my resolutions now.

### In the New School Year, I, Miranda Bloom, resolve to do the following:

1. Stop obsessing over Emmett Dutch, aka My One True Love, and the most gorgeous, sensitive, brilliant guy at Geek High, and instead come to grips with the fact that he doesn't know I'm alive. Which is really sad when you consider there are only a little over one hundred kids in the entire high school;

2. Stop obsessing about the size of my nose. Yes, it's freakishly large, but since there's nothing I can do about that, it's time I came to terms with it;

3. Avoid mirrors, so as not to be reminded of my nose;

4. Not to let certain people—i.e., the Felimonster and her Toady, the Demon, and Demon Spawn—get under my skin. Instead, when they taunt me, I will raise my chin and smile at them coolly, which is sure to annoy the snot out of them;

5. Try to find a special talent other than the math thing. Maybe I'm really a brilliant sculptress or genius botanist, and just haven't realized it yet;

6. Not get exasperated with my mother, even if she is going through an annoying and seemingly interminable touchy-feely, New Agey phase, where she doesn't eat red meat, practices a lot of yoga, and dresses like Stevie Nicks, and instead accept her for who she is . . . even if she hasn't figured that out yet;

7. Remain calm and poised at all times, just like Audrey Hepburn;

8. Have an absolutely fabulous year.

# Chapter 2

$$\| x \| = (x , x)^{\frac{1}{8}}$$

"What do you mean, you're moving to London?" I shrieked, staring at my mother in horror.

We were sitting at our dining room table, which was lit by fourteen taper candles (Sadie has a thing for eating by candlelight, claiming that it's fabulously glamorous, although personally I think it has more to do with how she thinks candlelight is flattering to her aging skin), and I was poking at the inedible tofu-and-lima-bean unmeatloaf my mother made, and mostly thinking about the short story I'd been working on before dinner. It was about a teenage girl who wakes up one morning to discover that overnight, while she slept, she's sprouted a beautiful set of wings. She's torn between the glory of being able to fly, and fear that she'll be seen as a freak. I liked writing about the sensation of flying, and the beautiful swishing, beating noise her white-feathered wings made as she soared through the air. But at Sadie's startling announcement, I dropped my fork with a loud clatter, all thoughts of my short story driven from my mind.

"Miranda, why do you always have to be so dramatic?" Sadie replied, pursing her lips and rolling her eyes heavenward. "I'm not *moving* to London. I'm just going to live there for a bit."

"I'm not being dramatic," I said, stung.

If anything, my mother's the one in the family who has a monopoly on dramatics. But, then, Sadie's a romance novelist, so she comes by it naturally. She publishes under the pen name Della De La Courte. Which is about the dumbest pseudonym I've ever heard of, although her legions of fans think she's just wonderful. She gets a ton of e-mail telling her so.

> Dear Della (her readers write),
>    I just adored your latest book! That Admiral Duncan is so handsome and so virile! And I just loved that scene where Duncan realized that Fawn wasn't really a ship boy, but was actually a woman with her chest wrapped and her hair tucked up under her hat, and where he cut off her clothes with the tip of his sword! That Fawn is such a lucky girl!!!
>    I'm counting down the days until your next book comes out! I can't wait!!!
>    Love, Fran, Your BIGGEST fan!

I mean, really. How embarrassing is that?

Sometimes when Sadie's on a deadline, she pays me to respond to the e-mail.

> Dear Fran (I respond),
>    I'm so glad you enjoyed my book! A sequel is in the works, although I'm starting to run out of euphemisms for male and female anatomy.
>    XXXOOO, Della De La Courte

But then my mom caught me, and now she double-checks the "sent e-mail" folder before she pays me.

"I can't move to England. School starts next week," I said, reeling at this news.

"I know. That's why I'm going alone," Sadie said.

It took a moment for this to sink in. I spent the time gaping at Sadie, my mouth opening and closing silently.

"*What?* You mean you're deserting me?" I finally sputtered.

"Oh, sweetie, I'm not *deserting* you." Another eye roll. "I'm just going to stay in London long enough to research and write my next book. It shouldn't take longer than six months. A year at the most," Sadie said blithely, spooning the revolting unmeatloaf into her mouth.

"Six months to a year?" I repeated. I shook my head, not understanding. "But . . . but . . . *what about me?*"

This came out in a pathetic little bleat. But I couldn't help it. How could Sadie leave me?

"You'll be fine, darling, really. The time will go by so fast, you'll hardly even miss me," Sadie said.

And then a thought occurred to me that made the whole idea a bit more palatable.

"So, I guess I'll be staying here by myself?" I asked casually, trying to hide the flutter of excitement the idea gave me. Living all alone! The freedom! Rather than being known as the Human Calculator, I'd be That Really Cool Chick Who Lives by Herself and Plays the Guitar Just Like Jewel!

Or I'm sure they'd say that if I actually played the guitar. I've been meaning to take it up. Whatever. The point is, it'd be so cool. Everyone would want to hang out at my house, and we'd all sit around the living room on floor pillows and debate politics and world events and the demise of the boy band in pop culture.

But Sadie quickly put an end to that fantasy.

"Stay here alone? Don't be ridiculous. You're only fifteen; you can't live alone. No, you'll stay with your father," she said.

I felt as though something heavy had been dropped on top of my chest. I stared at Sadie, my breath choked off somewhere between my lungs and throat. Stay with my *father*? But that would mean . . . that would mean living under the same roof as my horrible, awful, terrible, evil stepmother.

*No.* No, Sadie couldn't be serious . . . she couldn't possibly mean it . . . she wouldn't do that to me. . . .

Would she?

Oh, no . . . she totally *would.*

"Mom," I said, aghast, forgetting for the moment to call her Sadie, as she prefers. She says that calling her Mother reinforces the stifling societal view of what the parent-child relationship should be. "I can't live with Dad and *Her.* I can't. Please don't make me. And, besides, what about Willow?"

Willow was our rescued greyhound, a tall and sleekly beautiful brindle. My stepmother hates dogs. Want to know what kind of a person hates dogs? I'll tell you: someone who lacks a soul.

"The thing is, sweetheart, that I'm at that age where I have to think of myself first. I need the room to grow, as a woman and as a writer. Someday you'll understand," Sadie said philosophically, waving her hand as she spoke. She was wearing a black tunic covered with sequins that winked and glittered in the candlelight. "Besides, your father was the one who wanted to run off and start a new life. I think it's time he remembered that he has just as much responsibility for raising you as I do. It's sexist for him to assume that I should do all of the mothering just because I'm a woman."

I was so angry that for a moment I was actually speechless. And that says a lot. Normally I'm quick with the smart-alecky response. It's sort of my thing.

"You're using me to teach Dad a lesson?" I asked. I was appalled. Hadn't she read any of the self-help books on how not to destroy your children during a divorce? I'd even left copies of them for her on her bedside table, marking the chapters I thought she most needed to read with Post-it notes.

My parents didn't always hate each other. I have happy memories of a childhood full of trips to the beach and family bike rides around our neighborhood. Every Friday we had a weekly movie night. My parents would rent *The Lion King* or *Mary Poppins*, and we'd all pile on the couch together with a big bowl of popcorn. And I remember my parents laughing, and my dad taking my mom's hand in his, while she leaned forward to brush her lips against his cheek.

But then came the fights. At first, it never seemed like they were fighting about anything important. My mom would be mad when my dad forgot to stop for milk on his way home from the office. My dad would get angry when my mom scheduled a book tour without running the dates by him first. But then the arguments grew louder and more frequent. When they started shouting, I'd zip myself into my purple sleeping bag and put my fingers in my ears, so that their raised voices would sound muffled, like the grown-ups on those old Charlie Brown cartoons. The fighting was awful . . . but, in a way, it was even worse when it stopped, and the house was filled with an awful cold silence.

They officially separated when I was eleven, and divorced when I was twelve. And less than a year later, my dad married Peyton, aka the Demon. And I'd hardly seen my dad since. He was too busy with his new life and his new family to make time for me.

And now my mother was proposing I move in with them.

"I won't do it. I won't go. I won't live there with Her. I won't, and you can't make me. I will not live with the Demon and her Demon Spawn," I announced.

My mother looked pleased at that. She and I may have different opinions on just about everything, but there was one subject we were in perfect agreement on: We both hated Peyton. She was *awful*. She was mean and snotty, and thought the fact that she was rich—her grandfather made a zillion dollars after he invented that mouthwash that's supposed to rinse all of the plaque off your teeth, but burns like crazy when you gargle with it—means that she can boss everyone around. And I'm not much fonder of Peyton's daughter, Hannah, aka Demon Spawn.

Hannah—who is my age—is stunningly beautiful and perfect at everything, which leads to all sorts of unfortunate comparisons, usually made by Peyton and usually at my expense.

"Can't I just come with you to London?" I asked. "Please don't leave me, Mom. Please."

I saw Sadie waver, read the uncertainty in her face, and I knew I had her. No parent could withstand such a guilt trip. I'd read all about it in biology class last year, during "The Human Mammal: Fact or Fiction" week. Parents are hardwired not to desert their offspring. A hormone is released when a woman gives birth that keeps her from running away, even when all the kid does is poop and cry and spit up. So I knew there was no way she'd be able to go through with her plans of deserting me. Even Sadie couldn't defeat Mother Nature.

# Chapter 3

$$| (x, y) | \leq \| x \| \| y \|$$

I stood on the doorstep of my father and Peyton's beachside mansion, holding Willow's leash in one hand and my wheeled suitcase in the other. Willow was sniffing around, extending her long neck and twitching her nose from side to side, like Samantha on *Bewitched*. It was early in the morning, and the sky over the water was still pink and hazy.

My dad, an architect, designed the house. It's how he and Peyton met. She hired him to draw up the plans, and by the time the construction was complete, they were married. The house was huge and modern, with long rows of square windows that faced out over the private curved driveway on one side, and huge floor-to-ceiling glass doors that took in the incredible view of the Atlantic Ocean on the other side. I knew the house was supposed to be impressive, and it had even been photographed for *Architectural Digest*. But I'd always hated it. It was just *too*—too big, too modern, too cold. The little Arts and Crafts cottage Sadie and I lived in was so much cozier and more comfortable.

My mother honked the horn suddenly, and when I turned to look at her, she waved wildly from behind the wheel of her zippy red convertible.

"Good-bye, Miranda! I'll call you as soon as I'm settled!" she called out the window before speeding off down the road.

I crossed my arms, and spun back around without returning the wave. I wasn't speaking to Sadie, aka the Child Deserter. Even if I'm not technically a child, I am fifteen, which everyone knows is a tender age. Teen girls are susceptible to all sorts of trouble—drugs, sex, Internet predators. Which reminded me: As soon as I got the chance, I was going to do some Internet research on how exactly you go about divorcing your parents. I know child actors are sometimes able to do that when their loser parents steal all of their money. Surely the courts would consider deserting your only child to be at least as bad.

I propped my suitcase up and rang the doorbell, feeling awkward as I did so. This was my dad's house, after all. But Peyton had never given me a key. Whenever I came to visit, she always stood stiffly at the door and said, "Welcome to our home." *Our* home. As in: *not yours*. She'd always made it very clear that I was just a guest.

Although now I wasn't just a guest. For the next year—or whenever Sadie decided to come back and rescue me—this was going to be my home, too. A cold burst of fear flooded over me.

A few minutes later, when no one answered the door, I rang again. And then again. My fear slowly turned into annoyance. Wasn't anyone going to let me in? What kind of a welcome was this? Willow let out a little whimper of impatience and looked up at me questioningly.

Finally there was a flurry of footsteps tapping down the white marble foyer. The door was flung open, and there stood the Demon in the flesh.

"Hello, Miranda. Welcome to our home," she said, stepping aside—ever so slightly—to allow me entrance.

"Hi," I said without enthusiasm.

I stepped inside, pulling my bag awkwardly after me, and immediately started to shiver. You can tell everything you need to know about Peyton from her house: It's always freezing cold and everything is white. The walls are white. The luxuriously thick wall-to-wall carpeting is white. The living room furniture is upholstered entirely in white leather.

Even the cat—a snotty Persian named Madonna, who looks like a cotton ball that's sprouted legs—is white.

Likewise, Peyton is pale with short, spiky white-blond hair, and she's so cold-blooded, I wouldn't be at all surprised to find out that she's secretly a contract killer for hire. She's also the thinnest person I've ever seen. She doesn't eat. Really: I've never actually seen even a morsel of food enter her mouth. She'll sit down at the table while other people are eating, but she just uses her fork to push the food around on her plate. Seriously, the woman is a freak. She should be locked up in a laboratory and studied by scientists.

Even though it was early, Peyton was already dressed in an ice blue T-shirt that was so tight, I could practically count her ribs; perfectly pressed white linen slacks; and tan pumps with high, needlelike heels and very pointy toes.

Peyton's nostrils flared when she saw Willow, as though something particularly unpleasant-smelling had just entered the room. Which was really unfair, since I'd just given Willow a bath the night before, and she was wearing her best collar, the pink one with the candy-colored rhinestones.

"The dog will have to stay outdoors," she announced.

I shook my head. "She can't. It's too hot outside. She might get heatstroke," I said, reaching down to pet Willow, who leaned against my legs like a cat.

"Well, perhaps we can put it in the garage," Peyton said, looking unhappy at the idea. As though Willow—beautiful Willow, who doesn't smell the least bit doggy—would foul up the stinky old garage.

"Willow's a 'she,' not an 'it.' And my dad said she could stay in my room with me," I said, trying very hard to keep my voice friendly. I didn't want to start off on the wrong foot, but I also wasn't about to let the Demon send Willow out to live in the garage. Willow would hate that. She's really very sensitive.

Peyton's eyes narrowed. "We'll see," she said ominously. Peyton crossed her arms and looked me up and down, her bony face pinched with disapproval. "Are those holes in your shorts, Miranda?"

I glanced down at myself. I was wearing my favorite old khaki shorts. I'd had them for so long, and they'd been washed so many times, that the material was comfortably soft and the seams had started to unravel in a few spots.

Peyton's white-blond eyebrows arched in disapproval.

"Your mother lets you go out with holes in your clothing?"

"Um, I guess," I said slowly, thinking that Sadie probably hadn't noticed. But, even if she had, I doubt she'd have minded. Sadie wouldn't care if I decided to go out wrapped up in a sheet, toga-style; she'd probably just applaud my creativity.

Suddenly I found myself missing Sadie fiercely, even though I'd just seen her moments before, and then I'd been so angry I hadn't spoken to her. So she wasn't the most dependable mother in the world . . . she was still *my* mother. The only mother I had.

"I see," Peyton said. "Well, while you're staying with us, I'd appreciate it if you dressed more . . . appropriately."

"Appropriately?" I repeated.

"Yes. Appropriately. I know you're used to living in a very . . . well, *bohemian* type of home, Miranda, but we have standards here," Peyton said. Her lip curled, making it very clear just what she thought of the bohemian home from whence I came.

My cheeks flamed hot with anger. As if it wasn't bad enough that I had to stay here with this woman who hated me, and my father whom I didn't even know anymore; now they were going to tell me how to dress, too? Outrage began to simmer inside of me.

*Don't tick her off*, I tried to warn myself. *It's not worth it. It's not worth . . .*

"You're not my mother!"

The words popped out before I could stop them. They echoed across the hard floors, sounding like a slap across the face.

*Uh-oh*, I thought.

Peyton stared at me, two spots of red rising on her pale face. When she spoke, her voice was frosty. "I am well aware of that fact, young lady."

Just then Hannah wandered in, yawning and tossing back her sleep-tousled hair, cradling Madonna in her arms. Despite her short pink pajamas emblazoned with VICTORIA'S SECRET in sequins across the chest, and a face that was still puffy with sleep, Hannah looked like a fairy-tale princess. She had long, platinum blond hair, sapphire blue eyes, a sweetly pretty face, and a perfect, slim body. Next to her, I always felt like a homely giantess—tall, gangly, big-nosed, and with an uncontrollable mop of brown curls.

"Oh," Hannah said when she saw me. Her lips twisted into a grimace. "It's you."

Peyton's face defrosted when she saw her daughter. "Good morning," she said in a singsong voice. "How did you sleep, honey?"

Hannah shrugged one elegant shoulder and yawned. "Okay, I guess. Until the *doorbell* woke me up." She shot me a dirty look.

Madonna stretched and raised her petulant flat face to blink at me with round yellow eyes. Then she saw Willow. The cat let out a loud hiss and leaped from Hannah's arms, landing on the floor with her tail straight up and all of her fur standing on end.

"Willow," I said warningly.

But it was too late. With an outraged yowl, Madonna turned and fled toward the kitchen. And Willow couldn't help herself. She is a greyhound, after all. They're genetically programmed to chase after small animals. Well, *hunt* small animals, actually, although I know that deep down in her heart, Willow is really nonviolent. Just maybe not when it comes to cats. Willow streaked off after Madonna in a blur of brindle. They skidded down the hall, around the corner, and out of sight.

"Madonna!" Hannah cried.

"Willow!" I yelled, and darted after my dog.

There was a loud crash in the kitchen, another hiss, and then the sound of glass breaking. I rounded the corner and sprinted into the gourmet kitchen, with Hannah and Peyton right on my heels. When I saw what awaited us there, I came to an abrupt stop, staring at the scene before me.

Madonna was sitting on the granite kitchen counter, looking pleased with herself as she twitched her fluffy white tail in the air. Willow was cowering on the slate-tiled floor, her face covered with strawberry jam, and surrounded by shards of glass that had clearly once been a jam jar. And there was jam everywhere—splattered on the cupboards, puddled on the counter, and a blob of jam was slowly oozing its way down the door of the stainless-steel refrigerator.

"Madonna, are you okay?" Hannah exclaimed. She grabbed the cat, pulling Madonna to her chest. "Did that big, mean, awful dog hurt you?"

I rolled my eyes at this. If anyone was hurt, it was obviously Willow, who was looking a little dazed. I wondered if the jam jar had fallen on her head. Willow extended a long pink tongue and licked at the jam dripping off her nose.

"Look at this mess!" Peyton shrieked when she saw the splatters of strawberry jam on the cupboards and floor and refrigerator door. She spun around and, with her hands planted on her bony hips, glared at me. "Look what your filthy dog has done!"

"Willow didn't break the jar," I protested. I wet a paper towel and used it to wipe Willow's sticky face. She quivered with fear, glancing nervously up at Madonna. "The cat probably knocked it over when she jumped up on the counter."

"Madonna's never broken anything before," Hannah said, still cuddling Madonna. The cat was looking smugly pleased with herself.

"From now on, the dog stays outside," Peyton ruled.

"But—"

"No buts. Outside," Peyton said. Her eyes glittered dangerously. "Hannah, once that *beast* is in the yard, please show Miranda up to the guest room."

Not *my* room, the *guest* room.

"Miranda!" My dad walked into the kitchen, a huge smile on his face. He was already dressed for work. My dad was tall, with thinning dark hair and the same too-big nose I'd inherited from him. He'd lost weight since he'd married Peyton, and he'd traded in his Dockers and golf shirts for designer suits and silk ties. These changes made him feel even more like a stranger, and less like the dad I'd known growing up.

"Hi, Dad," I said.

"Come here and give me a hug," Dad said, folding me into his arms and squeezing me tight. I stood there stiffly, not fighting him, but also not giving in. Just because I had to live there didn't mean I'd forgotten that he'd practically ignored me for the past three years.

"Let me look at you," Dad said, holding me back, while he looked me up and down, just as Peyton had back in the hallway. But, unlike Peyton, my dad beamed at me. "Don't you look pretty! And you're getting so grown-up!"

"Richard," Peyton said. "This . . . creature can't stay in the house." She pointed an accusing beige-lacquered nail at Willow.

"What? Oh, Miranda's dog? Of course he's going to stay inside! He's part of the family now," my dad said.

"She," I corrected him. "Her name is Willow."

"Right. Willow. Hannah, why don't you show Miranda and Willow up to their room," Dad suggested. "And then, once you're settled in, come down and have some breakfast with us, honey. Peyton and I can't wait to catch up with you."

*Yeah, right,* I thought, as I caught sight of the sour look on Peyton's face. *The only thing the Demon wants to know about me is when I'm moving out.*

That night I couldn't fall asleep. I just lay there in the unfamiliar bed, staring up at the unfamiliar ceiling, listening to the unfamiliar sounds of the house, while I thought about Sadie leaving, and school starting tomorrow, and how whenever Peyton looked at me, her lips pursed up as though she'd bitten into a Sour Patch Kids candy.

*This is what it must be like to be Charlie*, I thought, restlessly kicking at the bedsheets that were twisting uncomfortably around my legs.

My best friend, Charlie, has chronic insomnia. She goes through manic periods where she doesn't sleep for days—she just stays up all night painting. And then when she does finally sleep, she stays in bed all day long. She used to take medication to even out her moods, but she said it sapped her artistic creativity, and she stopped taking it. And her parents have this hippie, antimedication philosophy, so they let her do it. Although sometimes, when Charlie's been up for three days straight, and is talking so fast the words are tripping on their way out of her mouth, I have to admit I question her parents' judgment on that call.

Sadie's tried-and-true method for falling asleep is to wash down several peanut butter–smeared Ritz crackers with a glass of cold milk. It had always worked for me in the past, so I tossed the comforter aside, slid out of bed, opened the bedroom door, and padded down the hallway.

I reached the foyer and took a left. The marble tile felt cold and hard beneath my bare feet. I had just reached the door to the kitchen and was about to walk through it when I heard voices: Dad and Peyton were in there. I quickly stepped back before they saw me. I had no interest in another uncomfortable conversation with my dad, who seemed intent on pretending that we had a great father-daughter relationship, or enduring another of Peyton's narrow-eyed, nostril-flaring stares. I was just turning, about to retreat back to the guest room, when I heard my name.

"This must be hard on Miranda, what with her mother just up and leaving," Dad said. "I honestly don't know what Sadie was thinking."

I froze, listening intently.

"She obviously wasn't thinking. Face it, the woman is a flake," Peyton said.

Anger burned in my throat, and my hands clenched into fists. How dared the Demon call Sadie names? It was one thing for me to complain about Sadie's flakiness, but an entirely different matter altogether when Peyton did it.

"I don't see why, just because she decides to go tooting off to England, we should have to turn our lives upside down," Peyton continued. "For God's sake, she didn't even check with us first."

"I thought you were happy that Miranda was staying with us," Dad said.

*What on earth gave him that idea?* I wondered. Peyton practically hissed every time I walked in the room.

"Oh, I am," Peyton said, sounding completely insincere.

*Yeah, right,* I thought.

"It's just . . . Miranda . . . well, she's just a bit . . . odd," Peyton said.

My face flamed, and my stomach felt pinched and sour. I knew Peyton didn't like me and resented my living there, but having her call me *odd* was somehow worse. *Odd.* It made me sound . . . defective.

"Odd?" Dad asked. And I was glad to hear that he sounded almost angry.

"It's not that she's not a lovely girl," Peyton hurried on. "I'm sure she is. It's just that she's exactly the same age as Hannah, but she acts so much younger. Miranda's, well . . . less *sophisticated* than girls her age normally are these days."

I waited for Dad to tell Peyton off. After all, what kind of a parent could listen to someone make such catty comments about their kid and not get upset? And surely he wasn't buying that whole *I'm sure she's a lovely girl* crap.

But my dad didn't get mad. He just sighed and said, "Well, Miranda's always been young for her age. She's a late bloomer."

My jaw dropped at this. He was *agreeing* with her? Sure, *late bloomer* sounded a heck of a lot better than *odd*, but didn't it amount to the same thing? They thought I was a freak. An odd, late-blooming freak.

"I don't want Hannah to feel uncomfortable," Peyton said. "This is her home, after all."

"I think it will be good for Miranda to be around Hannah. Hannah could be a role model for her," my dad, aka the Traitor, said.

I heard a noise that sounded a lot like Willow does when she's hacking up a glob of grass—I always tell her not to eat grass, but she never listens to me—and only belatedly realized that the noise had come from me. Dad and Peyton fell quiet.

"Hannah, is that you?" Peyton called out.

I turned and fled, moving as quickly and quietly as I could, until I reached the guest room. I closed the door behind me and jumped into bed, pulling the white duvet up over my head. I was so angry, I was shaking.

Hannah, a role model? If the idea wasn't so offensive, it would be laughable. Hannah was the most shallow, the most materialistic, the most empty-headed girl I'd ever known. And *she* was supposed to be a role model for *me*?

A few minutes later, I heard a soft knock at my door.

"Miranda? Are you awake?" my dad said.

I didn't answer.

### My New Year's Resolutions, Revised, by Miranda Bloom:

1. Stop obsessing over Emmett Dutch, aka My One True Love, and the most gorgeous, sensitive, brilliant guy at Geek High, and instead come to grips with the fact that he doesn't know I'm alive. Which is really sad when you consider there are only a little over one hundred kids in the entire high school;

2. Stop obsessing about the size of my nose. Yes, it's freakishly large, but since there's nothing I can do about that, it's time I came to terms with it;

3. Avoid mirrors, so as not to be reminded of my nose;

4. Not to let certain people—i.e., the Felimonster and her

Toady ~~the Demon, and Demon Spawn~~—get under my skin. Instead, when they taunt me, I will raise my chin and smile at them coolly, which is sure to annoy the snot out of them;

5. Try to find a special talent other than the math thing. Maybe I'm really a brilliant sculptress or genius botanist, and just haven't realized it yet;

6. ~~Not get exasperated with my mother, even if she is going through an annoying and seemingly interminable touchy-feely, New Agey phase, where she doesn't eat red meat, practices a lot of yoga, and dresses like Stevie Nicks, and instead accept her for who she is ... even if she hasn't figured that out yet;~~

7. Remain calm and poised at all times, just like Audrey Hepburn;

8. ~~Have an absolutely fabulous year.~~ Somehow find a way to survive the year.

# Chapter 4

$$B(a; r) = \{x \in R^n \,/\, \| x - a \| \}$$

The next morning, Dad drove me to school. Kids come from all over town to go to Geek High—some commute as far as an hour each way—so the school doesn't operate a bus, which is just as well. I used to take the bus when I was in public school, and have not-so-fond memories of the smell—a combination of diesel gasoline, tuna fish sandwiches, and moldy sneakers.

I was still so angry about what I'd overheard the night before that I didn't talk to my dad on the way in. Instead, I folded my arms over my chest and stared out the window, as though the passing scenery of suburban homes and 7-Elevens were incredibly interesting. But my dad misread my silence.

"Are you nervous about your first day of school?" he asked.

"No."

"What classes are you taking this year?"

"The usual."

"What's the usual?"

"Math, English, science, history," I said in a bored monotone.

My dad fell silent for a moment before rallying.

"Did your mom call you when she got to London?" he asked.

"Uh-huh," I said, not bothering to add that I'd let her call go to voice mail.

My dad sighed and tapped his fingers on the steering wheel. "I know this must be hard on you," he said. "Your mom going, living in a new house, school starting up. It's a lot of change all at once."

"Nope. I'm used to having my parents desert me," I said flatly.

After that, he didn't say anything for the rest of the trip.

When we got to Geek High, Dad stopped a few car lengths back from the driveway that curves up toward the school. There was a line of cars in front of him, inching slowly forward. When the Notting Hill Independent School for Gifted Children first opened thirty years earlier, it was so small the entire school fit in a three-story Victorian-style house. But as the school's reputation grew, and more kids enrolled, the building expanded, too. The Victorian was still there, but was now used for the administrative offices and a dining hall on the ground floor, while the low modern wings that branched out from either side housed the classrooms. Kindergarten through eighth grades were in the east wing, and the high school was in the west.

"You can drop me off here," I said, unfastening my seat belt.

"I'll take you up to the front door," Dad offered.

"No, really, it's okay."

The only parents who wait in line to deliver their children right to the front door are the parents of the kindergartners. Oh, and Padma Paswan's mother, but she's from India and really, really strict. Padma once told me that her parents have already arranged a marriage for her, and I don't think she was kidding.

I opened the door and slid out before my dad could argue with me. I gave him a little half wave, hoping he'd just drive off. Instead, he rolled down the window.

"Have a great day, sweetheart! You look beautiful!" he called out.

He was lying, of course. I'm not at all beautiful. The best that can be said of me is that, other than my freakishly large nose, I'm perfectly ordinary-looking. I have boring brown eyes, boring curly light brown hair that has an annoying tendency to go frizzy, and a scrawny build, no matter how much I eat. I know thin is in, but I'm not sexy thin . . . I'm little-boy thin. No hips, no boobs, no butt. Last year in creative writing class, Mrs. Gordon assigned us to write an essay on our best physical feature. I chose to write about my feet. It's not that my feet are all that pretty; they, too, are perfectly ordinary. But since so many people have truly ugly feet, ordinary feet look good in comparison.

I flushed bright red and glanced around, hoping against hope that no one had overheard my dad's "beautiful" crack. But, sure enough, someone had.

I could hear Felicity Glen, aka the Felimonster, snickering behind me before I saw her.

"Miranda, do you think your father should be driving?" she called out as my dad pulled out of the car line, executed a three-point turn, and gave his horn a toot as he drove off. "He's obviously blind."

I sighed and turned to face her.

Why is it that the horrible girls are always so gorgeous? Felicity. Hannah. Every villainess on every television show about teenagers ever made. And the Felimonster was, annoyingly, the prettiest girl in school. She was petite and thin—sexy thin—with catlike green eyes, a perfect oval face, a little button nose, and Angelina Jolie lips. She had brown hair, too, but hers was dark with caramel highlights, and it fell in perfect shiny waves around her shoulders, seemingly immune to the humidity. And Felicity had such an extensive wardrobe, I'd once heard her claim that she had to keep a clothes diary in order to keep track of what she'd worn on each day, so that she didn't commit the cardinal sin of wearing the same outfit twice in the same semester, horror of horrors. Today she was wearing a white linen shift and strappy brown sandals, and looked like she'd walked off the pages of a fashion magazine.

Felicity had hated me ever since my first day at Geek Middle, three years earlier. Our social studies teacher, Mrs. Firestone, had asked a question about the Ais, a Native American tribe indigenous to this part of Florida before it was settled by Europeans. I raised my hand at the same time Felicity had raised hers, and Mrs. Firestone called on me. I'd read a book about the Ais the previous summer, so I was able to answer Mrs. Firestone's questions, for which the teacher praised me lavishly. And from that moment on, Felicity—who apparently saw me as a threat to her position as the teacher's pet—had loathed me, and did what she could to make my life miserable. Like making fun of my Minnetonka moccasins (which I thought were the height of cool when I was twelve). And spreading a false rumor that Sadie wrote erotic novels (romance is not erotica . . . they're entirely different genres).

Morgan Simpson, aka Felicity's Toady, was standing next her. Morgan wasn't nearly as pretty as Felicity, but she was every bit as vile. She was short and square, even though she was on a perpetual diet, and she wore her straight dirty-blond hair in an unflattering chin-length bob that made her round face look even rounder. Morgan's greatest asset were her dimples, which gave teachers and other adult authority figures the mistaken impression that she was sweet-natured.

Morgan was now laughing sycophantically at the Felimonster's joke. "Yeah, right, because no one who could see would think she's pretty," she said, trying to imitate Felicity's scornful tone.

"Hello, Felicity," I said, smiling over clenched teeth. "I see no one staked you in the heart over the summer. What a shame."

"I spent the summer at Yale, enrolled in a very selective fine-arts camp working with a voice coach," Felicity said. She twirled a lock of dark hair around one finger and smiled coyly. Felicity's a soprano, and, unfortunately, actually pretty talented.

"Wow. Better not tell me any more. I might pass out from the excitement," I said flatly.

I turned and started to walk up the sidewalk toward the school. The Felimonster and Toady followed me to continue our conversation.

"She met a guy there," Morgan said, her voice gleeful.

"Fascinating," I said in the same monotone voice, not turning around.

"An *older* guy. He's a sophomore at Yale," Morgan continued.

I stopped in my tracks, closed my eyes briefly, and then, with a sigh, turned to face them. "Morgan, why exactly would you think I'd be even remotely interested in Felicity's pathetic love life?"

"At least I have a love life," Felicity said, the smile fading from her face. "You've never even been on a date."

I could feel my cheeks burning again. Sadly, Felicity was right—I never had been on a date. The only guy who had ever asked me out was Danny Beck, a string-bean guy with an eye twitch, onion breath, and a photographic memory. He had been in our grade last year, and one day, in biology, had passed me a note asking me to go to the movies with him. Mortified, I quickly wrote back that I couldn't, shoved the note across his desk, and every time I saw him after that, I looked away, avoiding eye contact.

I still felt really bad about how I'd treated Danny, although his family moved to Tampa over the summer, so I'd missed out on my chance to apologize to him . . . and, possibly, my only opportunity to go on a date while in high school.

Suddenly, I remembered Dad and Peyton's conversation about me the night before: *Miranda's always been young for her age. She's a late bloomer.*

Great. So when exactly was I going to bloom? When I was thirty?

To make my dateless status even worse was the fact that Felicity spent all of last year going out with Peter Rossi, who's a grade above us and a nationally ranked chess player. Last I heard, Felicity and Peter were still going strong, and were even spotted making out in the back row of the Orange Cove multiplex.

"So what happened to Peter? Did he finally tire of having to wear strands of garlic around his neck when he took you out?" I asked.

"I thought you weren't interested in my 'pathetic love life,' " Felicity said, smirking. She made air quotes with her fingers around *pathetic love life*.

"Trust me, I'm not," I said.

"If you must know, I broke up with Peter ages ago. I didn't want to be tied down when I went to Yale," Felicity said airily. "But then I met Justin. And it was love at first sight." She sighed happily.

"And he's nineteen," Morgan broke in eagerly. She was so excited, she was practically panting. You'd have thought she was the one who had the older boyfriend.

"Great. Thanks for telling me. My life is now finally complete," I said.

"You're just jealous," Morgan said, trying to imitate Felicity's smirk, although it just made her look like she was constipated. Anyway, this was ironic coming from Morgan. She'd never dated anyone either, not even after she'd spread a rumor around school last year that she was easy.

Felimonster snorted in response. "If you want my advice on how to get a guy, Miranda, I've got two words for you: Frizz-Ease."

My perpetually frizzy hair is a particularly sore spot for me, and I scowled at Felicity.

"Hey." Charlie jogged up next to us. She was wearing black leggings and a diagonally striped shirt, a look that only someone as stylish as Charlie can pull off. Her short bright pink hair was pushed back in a black headband. She looked at my irritated expression, and then glanced at Felicity and Morgan, and immediately took stock of the situation.

"Hey, Felicity," Charlie said. She peered closer at my archnemesis, looking her over carefully. "You look different."

"Different how?" Felicity asked.

"I don't know. Just . . . *different*." Charlie frowned for a minute. Then, suddenly, her face cleared and she snapped her fingers. "I know! You've gained weight, right?"

Felicity paled beneath her golden tan. "No! I haven't gained a single pound," she said, looking nervously down at herself.

"Really? Huh," Charlie said. She shrugged. "Maybe you're just retaining water."

The realization that Charlie was just screwing with her dawned in Felicity's moss green eyes.

"Oh, ha, ha," Felicity hissed, and she and Morgan pushed past us, loudly saying, "Did you see what she was wearing? And what's up with her hair? I mean, pink? *God*. What a *freak*."

Charlie clapped. "Excellent comeback. Really stellar. I mean it; I'm wounded. Deeply wounded," Charlie called after them. She lowered her voice and turned toward me. "So what was that about?"

"Felicity has a new boyfriend, and couldn't wait to gloat about it," I said. "Supposedly, he goes to Yale."

"That makes sense. College guys are all lushes, and he'd pretty much have to be drunk to go out with the Felimonster. How else could he stand to be around her?"

I laughed. Charlie always knew just the right thing to say.

"How's the new pad?" Charlie asked as we started up the stone walk that led to the school.

"Total nightmare," I said. "Every bit as bad as I thought it would be."

"You can always stay with me," Charlie offered.

Which would have been the perfect solution. Charlie's parents, Mr. and Mrs. Teague, love me, and as soon as they heard that the Child Deserter was, well, deserting me, they offered to put me up. Only problem? Mrs. Teague is allergic to dogs. So allergic she breaks out in a red rash and her eyes run uncontrollably whenever she's in a confined space with one. So I was welcome to stay with them . . . but Willow was not. I suppose I could have tried to find someone to watch Willow for me for a few months, but I didn't want to put her through that. Willow needs me.

"Thanks," I said, nudging her affectionately.

"No problem," Charlie said, although she was yawning hugely, so it came out as *Nomenonon*.

"Tired?" I asked as we headed up to the school.

"I couldn't sleep last night. As soon as I got in bed, I had this amazing idea for a painting. It's an upside-down office building, only totally abstract, so that the lines are all blurred. I had to start working on it right away. I painted all night," she said.

Charlie was talking really, really fast, as she always does when she's on one of her manic swings. But she's sensitive about anyone pointing it out to her, so I never mention it.

"Cool," I said. "I can't wait to see it."

"Good morning, ladies," Finn said as we reached the stairs leading up to the school's entrance. He was standing in front of the ornate double wooden doors, oblivious to the students pushing past him, beaming down at us.

Finn was tall, even taller than me—which is saying something, because I'm five feet ten inches in my stocking feet—and thin as a rail. He's super pale, since he spends all his time indoors messing around on his computer (and by messing around, I mean inventing computer games that he then sells for millions of dollars) and is rarely ever out during daylight hours. He has shaggy brown hair, pale blue eyes, and a scar over his mouth, left over from the surgery he had as a baby to correct a cleft palate.

"Are we ready for another year of academic brilliance?" Finn asked.

Finn was a bit miffed that his parents had forced him to return to Geek High this year, considering that he earns about ten times what they—both orthodontists—make. But they insisted, and so Finn finally caved, only after they agreed to let him buy some really expensive computer thingy that he insisted he needed to have. (They make him put all of his earnings in a high-interest money-market account.) And even then, Finn said he's only coming back to be a subversive influence within the school. I had no idea what he meant by that, but I had to admit . . . it made me a little nervous. It's never wise to underestimate Finn. He's not the most morally centered person in the world.

"As always," Charlie replied, yawning again.

"My thoughts exactly," Finn said. "*Yawn*. But not for long!"

He looked smugly pleased with himself. Charlie looked at him sharply.

"What does that mean?" she asked suspiciously. "What are you up to?"

"Wait and see, grasshopper. Wait and see," Finn said, grinning deviously.

"Don't call me grasshopper. And whatever it is that you're planning, just make sure you don't get caught. You know that Headmaster Hughes is gunning for you this year," Charlie cautioned.

"Me? Get caught?" Finn asked, affronted. "It'll never happen. I'm far too wily."

"You're far too something," Charlie muttered as the three of us went into the school together.

As I walked into Geek High, I drew in a deep breath and felt a sense of calm for the first time since Sadie had announced she was leaving for London. Returning to the school was like coming home after a long trip away. It was the first place I'd ever felt normal. Sure, I might not like everyone I went to school with—Felicity and Morgan, for example—but this was the one place where I wasn't considered a weirdo or a freak for being smart. Everyone at the school was a genius, so here I was one geek among many. And, yes, many of my classmates could be a little odd at times. We were, after all, the square pegs who hadn't fit in at a normal school.

The three of us walked into the front hall, with its worn carpets and huge glass case featuring trophies won by Geek High students over the years. The awards were all for academics—the state science fair, writing contests, Mu Alpha Theta—with the exception of one small silver cup that a boy named Roger McNeil won in a local golf tournament in 1991. But, then, kids don't attend Geek High for its sports program.

Even though everything looked the same and sounded the same—the squeak of new sneakers, familiar voices calling out greetings—it took my nose a few minutes to adjust to the smell of the place—the mingling of old wood, ancient Oriental carpets, lemon oil, and hair spray.

Straight ahead was the dining room, filled with dark wood tables and chairs, and oil paintings of big-money donors hanging on the walls. We turned left just before reaching the dining room. The floor changed from hardwood to industrial tile, signaling that we'd entered the high school wing. It was one long locker-lined hallway where all of the upper classes were held.

"Hi, Miranda," Leila Chang called out as she passed by.

"Hey, Leila. How was your summer?" I asked.

Leila was a junior. She had a round, pretty face, and hair that she'd cut into a short bob like flappers wore in the 1920s. Purple-framed cat's-eye glasses were perched on her nose.

"Too short," she said with a grin. She gestured toward Mr. Gordon's classroom, which was just to my left. "Are you taking AP Calculus?"

"No, I took it two years ago," I said. "You?"

"Yup. Lucky me," Leila said, rolling her eyes. "Hey, did you hear that someone's started a blog about the school?"

"No. What kind of a blog?" I asked.

"It's all gossip! There're just a few items up now, but it's promising to dig up dirt on everyone. Students, teachers, the administration. Check it out—the URL is geekhigh.com," she said.

"I will," I said, intrigued.

"See you later," Leila said, ducking into the math room.

Finn and Charlie had been so immersed in their discussion of a French movie they'd seen the night before—I hadn't gone with them, since I refuse to watch movies I have to read—they hadn't noticed I'd stopped to talk to Leila. I sped up to catch them . . . and nearly careened right into a scrawny figure that suddenly loomed before me.

"Whoa!" I exclaimed, coming to an abrupt stop just in time.

"Hello, Miranda. How was your summer?" The voice was almost robotic in its monotone, and it belonged to Christopher Frost, a fellow sophomore. He had thin sandy hair and pale watery eyes that stared unblinkingly from behind thick glasses. Christopher wasn't a bad guy, although he lacked even the most basic people skills. Now he didn't wait for my response to his quasi-question. "I went to Arizona to visit my grandparents. They took me to see the Grand Canyon. Did you know that the Grand Canyon spans nineteen hundred and four square miles? And at its deepest point, it has a mile-long drop? And it's home to seventy-five species of mammals, fifty species of reptiles and amphibians, and more than three hundred species of birds . . . ?"

It was futile to wait for Christopher to stop talking; he wouldn't. He'd prattle on and on and on, listing off one statistic after another, until I stopped him.

"That sounds really great. I'm glad you had fun," I said. "I'll talk to you later, okay? I have to get to class."

Christopher blinked at me, his expression unchanged.

"Bye," I said, moving past him.

Charlie and Finn were now well down the hallway.

"Charlie," I called. "Wait up!"

I jogged to catch up with them. And that was when it happened: I tripped. For a long, terrible moment everything seemed to unfold in slow motion. My feet—which had been safely on the ground a moment earlier—were suddenly Scooby-Dooing under me. I pitched slowly forward. Up ahead, Charlie pivoted around as my voice reached her. I saw her mouth turn into an O as she watched me fall.

And just then—just as I was in a free fall, about to face-plant on the hard tile floor—that's when I saw him: Emmett Dutch. He was leaning against a locker, talking to Isaac Hanson, and looking every bit as beautiful as I remembered. The blond hair curling back from his handsome face had lightened over the summer, and he was sporting a golden tan. His sea blue eyes were vivid in his face, and his teeth flashed white as he grinned.

And then a moment later I was sprawled on the floor, feeling a sharp, stabbing pain in my wrist. Not to mention my pride. I was completely and utterly humiliated.

"Miranda, are you okay?" Charlie asked, hurrying back to help me up. Finn was a step behind her.

"Nice," he said. "A few points off for the dismount, but I'd still give you a solid seven-point-two."

"Finn," Charlie hissed, elbowing him in the side.

I was too mortified to speak. My fall had not gone unnoticed. The tittering was rising up around me as though I were a one-woman comedy act.

"Not used to the gravity on this planet, Miranda?" Felicity asked sweetly as she glided by with Morgan in tow. They both sniggered.

Charlie and Finn helped me to my feet, and the whole time, all I could think was, *Please don't let him have seen me, please don't let him have seen me, please please please please please . . .*

But when I finally got the nerve to glance in the direction where Emmett had been standing a moment earlier, he wasn't there. Relief coursed through me.

"He didn't see," I breathed.

"Actually . . . he did," Charlie said.

She knew exactly who I was talking about. I'd been in love with Emmett Dutch for the past two years, and Charlie's had to listen to me obsess over every last detail of our nonexistent relationship.

"Oh, no," I whispered. "Did he laugh? Please tell me he didn't laugh."

This was a disaster. A complete and total disaster.

"He didn't laugh," Charlie said. I felt marginally better. Charlie never lies, not even to make me feel better.

"Who didn't laugh?" Finn asked. Finn was as clueless as Charlie was perceptive.

"Nobody. Nothing. Never mind," I gabbled. "Come on; let's get to class. We're going to be late for astronomy."

# Chapter 5

$$f(x, y) = \frac{xy}{x^2 + y^2} \quad \text{if } (x, y) \neq (0, 0), f(0, 0) = 0$$

I spent all of astronomy with my head down, reliving the fall over and over again. I tried to pry some more information out of Charlie on Emmett's reaction—did he smile? look concerned? disgusted? repulsed?—but she clammed up and refused to say anything other than, "I will not enable your unhealthy obsession," in an annoyingly superior voice. All the while Finn—who was ignoring us while he checked his e-mail on his laptop—would occasionally glance up with a confused expression, and say, "Who are you guys talking about?"

Our astronomy teacher, Mr. Keegan—who wore socks with his Birkenstocks and insisted that we call him "Doug"—gave us an overview of the syllabus, and then got into a long and incredibly boring debate with Tate Metcalf, whose life ambition is to become a nuclear physicist, on a new five-dimensional theory of gravity that some researchers at Duke were working on. It wasn't until the end of the period, when my fingers were cramping from how fast I'd had to type to take down all the information, that Mr. Keegan told us that none of what we'd covered in class that day would be on the final.

"I thought astronomy would be heavier on the time-space continuum stuff," Finn said after the period ended. We left the classroom and joined the tide of students moving down the hallway. "Doug didn't even mention the Prime Directive. Isn't that supposed to be the cornerstone of mankind's philosophy on space travel?"

"I think maybe someone's watched a little too much *Star Trek*," I said.

"Just you wait and see. *Star Trek* will help me ace that class," Finn said confidently.

"I should have taken advanced physics," Charlie grumbled.

"Why didn't you?" I asked.

"Because Forrester is teaching it," she said. No further explanation was necessary. I got stuck with Forrester for biology last year, and had to chew chocolate-covered espresso beans all period just to stay awake. He's just that boring.

"What do you have next?" Charlie asked.

I consulted my schedule. "Modern literature with Mrs. Gordon."

"Cool. Me too," Charlie said.

Finn was too busy texting someone on his BlackBerry to respond—he was in the middle of selling a game he'd developed called *Terrorist X*—but he followed us down the hall to Mrs. Gordon's room, so I assumed he was probably in our class, too.

We filed into mod lit and sat down at desks arranged in a horseshoe formation. There were seven other kids already there. Felicity and Morgan were in the class—gag—as were Tate Metcalf, Padma Paswan, Sanjiv Gupta, Christopher Frost, and Tabitha Stone. Tabitha has a long, angular face, dark skin, super-short hair, prominent teeth, and takes herself very, very seriously. She's the school's resident English lit prodigy. Last year she published a book of cryptic post-postmodern poetry, none of which I understood, but it was a huge deal around the school.

"Miranda, we need to talk about Mu Alpha Theta. Mr. Gordon scheduled the first meeting two weeks from Wednesday," Sanjiv called across the classroom.

Mu Alpha Theta was our school's math team, and it competed against other schools across the state. I'd been on the team ever since I started at Geek Middle. In fact, at twelve, I was the youngest student in the school ever to compete on Mu Alpha Theta.

"Actually . . ." I hesitated, knowing that my next words were sure to send Sanjiv into a tailspin. ". . . I'm not going to be on the team this year."

Sanjiv gaped at me as his eyes widened in shock. "You're not going to be on the team? But *why*?" he stuttered.

Mrs. Gordon came in then, saving me from having to respond.

"Welcome back!" she said, beaming at us.

Math may be my best subject, but English lit was by far my favorite . . . and Mrs. Gordon was my favorite teacher. She's short and sort of dumpling-shaped, with wispy brown hair that's always falling out of a messy bun. We sometimes joked that she looks like the quiet spinster secretary on one of those cheesy cable movies, who all of a sudden takes off her glasses, shakes out her hair, and turns into a sex goddess in order to seduce her boss. When, really, nothing could be farther from the truth. Besides, Mrs. Gordon was married to Mr. Gordon, the math teacher, and I'd lose all respect for her if she tried to seduce Headmaster Hughes.

We pulled out our laptops while we waited for the bell to ring. And then just a minute before it sounded, the door opened again . . . and Emmett Dutch walked in. I inhaled quickly, sucking my breath in loudly enough that Charlie shot me a sidewise glance.

I'd never had a class with Emmett before. He was a junior, and so mostly took advanced-level courses. But the Geek High curriculum is like a college—every course is open to anyone who has the prerequisites for it. So it wasn't at all uncommon to have an upperclassman or two pop up in an elective course.

Emmett slid into the seat that was at the end of the horseshoe closest to the door, just as Mrs. Gordon began to speak: "Welcome to modern literature! We're going to have a very exciting year reading some of my favorite books of all time," she said happily.

I tried to listen to her; I really did. But I couldn't pay attention, not when Emmett Dutch was sitting *just over there*. I kept pretending to look out the door, as though idly seeing who was passing by (nobody), so that I could secretly admire him. Today, Emmett was wearing a green Lacoste shirt, threadbare chino shorts, and Tevas, for the preppy boho look he favored. Tall, and broad-shouldered, with strong arms and a narrow waist, Emmett was the least geeky-looking guy enrolled at Geek High. And, best of all, he was *brilliant*. He'd won the state science fair three years in a row, and placed second in nationals last year for developing a technique for purifying water in third-world countries. He was, in short, a god.

"Miranda!" It was Charlie, hissing in my ear.

"What?" I whispered back.

"Stop. Staring. At. Him."

I turned bright red and began fumbling with my laptop, quickly opening up Microsoft Word to start taking notes on *The Stranger* by Albert Camus, the first book Mrs. Gordon was assigning us. But even as I began typing away about the background she was giving us on Algiers, where *The Stranger* was set, I could feel someone's eyes resting on me. I looked up, my heart pounding, wondering if it was . . . could it possibly be . . . ?

But, no. Emmett was busy typing away on his own laptop, seemingly transfixed by Mrs. Gordon's intro to *The Stranger*. I glanced to my left, and then to my right . . . and right into Felicity Glen's soulless green eyes. She cocked her eyebrows at me, and then looked pointedly at Emmett before flashing me with what can only be described as a truly evil smile.

*Oh, no,* I thought. *Oh, no no no no no no.* The Felimonster knew I was interested in Emmett. And I knew her well enough to know that she'd somehow use this knowledge against me.

Technically, we're not supposed to use instant messaging during class. But since we're all supposed to be super-students obsessed with academics, no one ever bothers to monitor it. So I quickly pulled up my IM, and tapped a message to Charlie.

| MIRABLOOM: | felimonster knows! |
| BLANKCANVAS: | knows what? |
| MIRABLOOM: | about YOU KNOW WHO!!! |
| BLANKCANVAS: | i have no idea what you're talking about |
| MIRABLOOM: | E.D. |
| BLANKCANVAS: | Ohhhhh . . . that's not good |
| MIRABLOOM: | TELL ME ABOUT IT! WHAT SHOULD I DO? |
| BLANKCANVAS: | inhale, exhale |

Suddenly Finn popped into our conversation. I have no idea how he does this. He could probably hack into the CIA's secret computer files if he wanted to. In fact, he probably already had.

| PINKFLOYD: | check out www.geekhigh.com |
| MIRABLOOM: | FINN! don't DO that! |
| PINKFLOYD: | what's your damage, heather? |

Finn's favorite movie was the cult classic *Heathers*. He idolized Christian Slater's character, J.D. Charlie and I both found this more than a bit disturbing, considering that J.D. was a homicidal crackpot.

| MIRABLOOM: | don't break into our conversation like that! what if we were talking about something important??? |
| PINKFLOYD: | like the insidious effects of socialism on western culture important, or the difference between a latte and cappuccino important? |
| MIRABLOOM: | GO AWAY |
| BLANKCANVAS: | ignore her, f, she's in the middle of a freakout |
| PINKFLOYD: | just check out the Web site |

In the trauma over tripping, I'd forgotten all about the Geek High blog Leila had told me about. I closed out of my IM program and clicked on the icon for my Firefox Mozilla browser—Finn is very anti-Microsoft, and starts to lecture me whenever I use Explorer—and then surfed over to geekhigh.com.

Just as Leila had said, it was a blog written anonymously by someone who signed him- or herself *Sam Spade*. There were only two entries up so far, but *Sam Spade* promised daily updates.

The first entry was a blind item:

*HOOKING UP*

*What dramatic pairing is doing more than reading lines together? HE says that they're just friends, and SHE says her boyfriend is still in the picture, but GEEKHIGH.COM has learned that the pair was seen canoodling at Reef Beach last week. Developing . . .*

"Do you know who's writing this?" I whispered to Finn.

"Ms. Bloom, did you have something you want to share with the class?" Mrs. Gordon asked loudly.

*Argh.*

My face turned the color of a ripe tomato. I was actually going to have to speak in front of Emmett. I desperately tried to think of something—*anything*—I might know about *The Stranger*, but I'd never read the book. I have enough existential angst in my own life without including it in my recreational reading.

"No, no. I'm just really excited about reading *The Stranger*," I lied. "Big fan of the Cure."

"What is she babbling about?" Felicity asked loudly to the room at large.

"The Cure did a song back in the seventies called 'Killing an Arab' that was based on *The Stranger*," I said.

"Very good, Ms. Bloom. And next time we meet, I'm going to play the song for you," Mrs. Gordon said, twinkling with pleasure. This is why I loved her. I don't know anything about the stupid book, other than that the Cure wrote a song about it, but Mrs. Gordon still managed to make me feel like something other than a complete moron.

Plus, it's always fun to know something that Felicity doesn't. At Mrs. Gordon's praise, Felicity's mouth twisted into a pout. I sneaked a glance at Emmett, but he was intently typing away on his laptop.

Mrs. Gordon turned to write, *Example of an Absurdist Theme* on the blackboard. When she turned back around, Tabitha raised her hand.

"Yes, Tabitha," Mrs. Gordon said, nodding to her.

"Is it true that Camus was deliberately copying Hemingway's style when he wrote *The Stranger*?" Tabitha asked in her most serious voice.

I used the opportunity to IM Finn.

| MIRABLOOM: | saw the Web site . . . who's behind it? |
| --- | --- |
| PINKFLOYD: | it's a mystery |
| MIRABLOOM: | do you know? |
| PINKFLOYD: | *twirls mustache fiendishly* |
| MIRABLOOM: | tell me tell me tell me |
| PINKFLOYD: | can't . . . sworn to secrecy |
| MIRABLOOM: | at least tell me who the hookup is |
| PINKFLOYD: | alex bendell and guy parkinson |
| MIRABLOOM: | yawn . . . old news |
| PINKFLOYD: | buzz kill |
| MIRABLOOM: | hoping for something a little more . . . newsworthy |
| PINKFLOYD: | it's only the first day of school . . . give it time |

I clicked back to the Web site and read the second entry.

**DIRT DISHING**

*Sources deep inside the administration of GEEK HIGH have informed GEEKHIGH.COM that the school cafeteria came*

*perilously close to failing its health inspection last spring.*
*Bugs? Fecal contamination? No one can—or will—say for sure.*
*But take my advice and bring your lunch until the matter is*
*cleared up.*

Ewwww, I thought.

# Chapter 6

$$f'(a; y) = \lim_{h \to 0} \frac{f(a + hy) - f(a)}{h}$$

Charlie's mom, Mrs. Teague, dropped me off at my dad's house after school. She offered to wait until I got inside, but I insisted that I'd be fine, so Charlie and her mom said good-bye and drove off back down the sandy road, while I waved from the front steps.

I turned and opened the door. Or, at least, I tried to. As it turned out, the door was locked. I reached into my knapsack, rooting around for my Hello Kitty key chain (it's meant to be ironic), when I remembered—I didn't have a key. Peyton still hadn't given me one. Her cleaners had a key to the house, and the caterers, and the woman who came once a week to water the plants. But me? No key.

I sighed, closed my knapsack, and rang the doorbell. No one answered, although I heard the scrabbling of nails on marble as Willow bounded joyfully toward the door. Willow doesn't bark, so she just stood there, her body wriggling with happiness as she peered at me through the glass panels that flanked the front door.

"Hi, Willow. Any chance you can grow an opposable thumb and let me in?" I asked.

She just wriggled some more.

"Great," I said. The driveway was deserted, and there were no sounds of life inside the house, so chances were good that there wasn't anyone home. I dropped my knapsack and sat down next to it, wrapping my arms around my knees as I waited.

It was a typical Florida August afternoon: steaming hot and blindingly sunny, and the air was thick with the late-summer humidity. I was slick with sweat within a matter of minutes, and I could feel my hair growing frizzier by the minute.

*At least we're on the beach,* I thought. *If it gets any hotter, I can always go jump in the water to cool off.*

I'd always hated the heat, and considered it a true tragedy that I was born and raised in Florida, rather than somewhere cold and snowy, where I could wear cozy wool sweaters and curl up with a pile of good books in front of a roaring fire. In fact, one of the ironies of my current situation—i.e., Sadie deserting me to wing off to London—is that I'd always fantasized about living in England. Or, at least, the England that was featured in all of my favorite childhood books, from *The Little Princess* to *The Wolves of Willoughby Chase* to *Paddington Bear*.

But no. I was stuck in hot, humid Florida, living in a house with a stepmother and stepsister who didn't want me there, and a father who thought I was a late bloomer, and making a fool out of myself by falling in front of everyone at school, and basically everything was bleak and grim and not looking as though it was going to get any better anytime soon.

*Oh, well,* I thought gloomily. *At least it isn't raining.*

Which was precisely the moment when the first boom of thunder sounded, followed seconds later by a crackling flash of lightning that made the hair on my arms stand up.

A dark gray cloud that I swear hadn't been there a moment earlier suddenly appeared overhead, and raindrops began to fall. First it was just a scattering, a drop here and a drop there. But then there was another crack of lightning and another boom of thunder . . . and it began to pour. I let out a yelp and backed up on the stoop, trying to get as much of me under the narrow overhang as possible. But it barely offered any protection from the downpour. And the whole time I was sitting there getting drenched, Willow stood on the other side of the door whimpering.

The rain was finally starting to taper off when a sporty red Jetta turned into the driveway. By this point I was completely soaked. My T-shirt stuck uncomfortably to my skin, and my hair was plastered to my scalp. I didn't have a mirror, but I had a pretty good idea that the average drowned rat would look positively glamorous compared to me.

The driver's door opened, and a girl slid out from behind the steering wheel. She had a thin face with narrow eyes and a pointy chin. Her black hair was cut into an edgy pixie that suited her catlike features. I didn't recognize her, nor the identical twins who emerged a moment later from the backseat.

Hannah, who had occupied the front passenger seat, got out and slammed the door shut behind her. She gave me a hard stare, as though I were a Jehovah's Witness waiting on her doorstep to convert her.

"Who's that girl?" the driver of the Jetta asked Hannah, as though I weren't standing ten feet away and couldn't hear every word she said.

"She's nobody," Hannah said, with an eye roll. "Just my step-sister."

"You have a stepsister?" one of the twins asked her. Both of the twins were tall and lanky, with creamy dark skin, braided hair, and open, friendly faces. They wore identical short denim skirts, although they varied their tops. One was wearing a clingy pink tee, the other a blue baby-doll rugby shirt.

"Unfortunately," Hannah said. She turned to look at me, swishing her pale blond mane back from her face as she did so. Hannah is the master of the hair swish. She does it so frequently and so perfectly, I've long suspected that she practices the gesture in front of the mirror.

"What are you doing?" Hannah asked me.

"I don't have a key," I said through clenched teeth.

"Oh." Hannah stepped past me and unlocked the door. "Try not to track water in the house," she said to me over her shoulder.

Willow was so excited that we were finally being reunited that she pushed past Hannah to greet me, sticking her long nose in my hand.

"Ewwww," one of the twins said, cowering back. "That dog is so weird-looking."

"Tell me about it." Hannah sniffed.

"She's a greyhound," I said with dignity. "And she's beautiful."

Unfortunately, Willow chose that exact moment to let loose a noisy and particularly stinky fart.

"Ewwww," all of the girls said in unison, as they pushed past us to get into the house and downwind of Willow.

I had no interest in hanging out with Hannah and the Barbie Squad—and even though it was only the first day of school, I already had a pile of homework—so rather than follow them back to the living room, I started to turn left down the corridor that led to the guest room.

"I don't recognize you. Do you go to our school?" the driver of the Jetta asked me. I had no choice but to pivot back around.

"She goes to Geek High," Hannah said before I could answer.

"Wow," one of the twins said, looking impressed. "You must be really smart."

At this Hannah looked annoyed.

"What's your name?" the driver asked, looking at me with more interest. Her heavily made-up eyes were an unusual color: hazel brown and flecked with gold. I got the feeling that she was the leader of their little group.

"Miranda," I said.

"I'm Avery," the girl said. She bobbed her head in the direction of the twins. "And they're Tiffany and Britt."

"Hey," the twins said in unison. I had no idea which was which, and probably never would, unless they started wearing name tags.

"So you're living here now?" Avery asked. She glanced sideways at Hannah, as though questioning why this important nugget of information had been kept from her. An inner conflict began to rise within me.

I instinctively didn't like Avery—there was a hard, almost mean glint in her eyes—and it really wasn't any of her business why I was staying in the House of Demons. On the other hand, I was enjoying Hannah's obvious displeasure.

"I'm just staying here while my mom is out of town," I explained.

"Oh-hhh," Avery said, drawing the word out into two syllables. "So we're going to make some popcorn and watch a movie. You want to hang out with us?"

Hannah looked horrified at this suggestion, and I toyed with the idea of accepting Avery's invite just to torture my stepsister. But since that would mean hanging out with the Demon Spawn all afternoon, I shook my head.

"Thanks, but I really should start my homework."

"You got homework on the first day of school?" Britt—or maybe it was Tiffany—asked, her jaw dropping open.

"Yup," I said, shifting my soggy knapsack up to my shoulder. "Have fun."

"Why did you ask her to hang out with us?" I heard Hannah hissing at Avery as they headed to the kitchen.

"Are you kidding? She could totally get me through chem. I'm going to need all the help I can get in that class," Avery replied.

I shook my head, glad I'd followed my instincts not to hang out with them. Hannah's friends were as awful as her. Big surprise.

# Chapter 7

$$\nabla f(a) = (D_1 f(a), \ldots, D_n f(a))$$

To celebrate our first day of school, and my forced confinement in their home, my dad announced he was taking us all out to dinner. Hannah and Peyton didn't seem any happier about the idea than I was, but Dad insisted.

"I want to show off my girls," he said.

And despite everything that had happened with my dad, and that I'd hardly seen him over the past few years, I still felt a twist of jealousy. Dad considered Hannah to be one of his "girls"? But I was his daughter, his *real* daughter. Hannah was just a step. Didn't genetics count for anything anymore?

Besides, Hannah already had a father of her own. A really glamorous dad who was an investment banker in Manhattan. Hannah went to visit him two or three times a year, and spent those trips eating out at swishy restaurants and shopping with her impossibly chic stepmother, who—unlike Peyton did with me—treated Hannah like a daughter.

Life? Totally unfair.

We went to Swordfish for dinner, a steak-and-seafood restaurant with a huge window along one wall overlooking the Intracoastal Waterway that winds past Orange Cove. My dad had reserved a table right next to the window, although Peyton and Hannah grabbed the seats with a view, while my dad and I had our backs to the water. The waitress took our order. Dad and I ordered steaks, while Hannah and Peyton, after moaning about the calorie content of each and every entrée, ordered salads.

I couldn't help feeling a little smug. As much as I moan about my scrawny frame—I'm about as curvy as a plank of wood—it does have an upside: I can eat whatever I want, and I never gain weight. Sadie always tells me to enjoy it while I can. Apparently all of the women in our family are skinny right up until they hit thirty, at which point their metabolisms crap out on them.

"So, girls, tell us all about your first day of school," Dad said brightly. Clearly he wanted this dinner to be Quality Time. I felt another stab of resentment. Did he really think one lousy dinner was going to make up for three years of neglect? Because if so, I had news for him: It *wouldn't*.

"Yes, Hannah, how were your classes?" Peyton asked, as though I didn't exist.

I thought I saw my dad frown at her a moment.

Hannah shrugged one pretty bare shoulder. "Fine, I guess. Boring mostly. I can't believe I got stuck with Meloni for English. He's the *worst*. He has waxy ears, *so* gross, and he wears the same pair of pants to school every single day." Hannah snorted. "We call him 'Same-Pants-New-Shirt Meloni.' "

Peyton let out a tinkly little laugh of appreciation for this witticism, but my father's frown deepened.

"I'm not sure—" he began.

But Peyton cut him off before he could complete his thought. "How are your friends, honey?" she asked Hannah. "Did Avery have a nice summer? She was in Maine, right?"

"Yeah. Her parents have a summer house there. Well, her mom does, anyway. Her parents are in the middle of a divorce, and I think her dad is under court order to stay away from Maine," Hannah said.

Peyton's eyebrows shot up. "*Really*? The divorce is that contentious?" she asked, clearly eager to get all of the dirt.

Hannah nodded. "They were getting along for a while, but then Avery's dad piled all of her mom's shoes in the front yard, doused them with gasoline, and set fire to them."

Peyton gasped in horror. "How is poor Avery handling it?" she asked.

Hannah rolled her eyes. "She's *thrilled*. Her parents are both totally sucking up to her, hoping she'll take their side in the divorce."

Hannah launched into a detailed description of the car Avery's dad had given her for her sixteenth birthday to one-up the Prada handbag her mother had gifted her with. Having lost interest in this conversation, I glanced around at the other diners, wondering if any of them were as miserable as I was.

And that's when I saw him: *Emmett Dutch*. He was sitting two tables away, eating dinner with his parents. My mouth gaped open in surprise. And just then, just as I was ogling him, Emmett turned and looked right at me. As our eyes met, my heart lurched and then began to skitter around in my chest as though someone had just shocked me with CPR defibrillating paddles. We were actually making eye contact!

And then—I could hardly believe it—*he waved at me*. Okay, so it was more of a raised hand than an actual wave—he didn't waggle his fingers, for example, although I maintain that the finger waggle is highly overrated—but, even so, for the first time ever, Emmett Dutch was actually acknowledging my presence.

There were many things I could have done at that moment. The normal reaction would have been to smile and wave back. Or to mouth the word *hi*. Or to wink saucily. But did I do any of those things? No, I did not. Instead, I blushed . . . and looked away.

Emmett Dutch waved at me, and I *looked away*.

I sat there, staring down at the half-eaten crust of butter-smeared sourdough bread on my plate, feeling completely traumatized. Peyton was right . . . I was hopeless, so socially backward I shouldn't be allowed out in public to mingle freely with normal people.

"Miranda, are you all right?" my father asked me, interrupting Hannah's transparent attempt to talk her mother into buying her a car for her upcoming birthday. Not that it was taking much work. Peyton was happily discussing the pros and cons of having a beige leather interior versus chocolate brown leather.

"Fine," I muttered.

When I finally had the nerve to look back up at Emmett, he was engrossed in a conversation with his parents. I don't know what they were talking about, but they were all laughing and chiming in, and looking like a typical happy family. If there was such a thing as a typical happy family. I certainly didn't have one. But then, it didn't look as though Emmett had an evil stepmother and stepsister to deal with, nor a mother who had deserted him.

"You have a sixteenth birthday coming up, too, Miranda," my dad said.

I blinked up at him. Why were we talking about my birthday? "Not until February," I said.

"That's not so far away." My dad smiled at me. Apparently he was still trying to pretend that he was an interested, committed parent. I wondered how long he'd be able to keep up that act. "Is there anything you'd like for your sweet sixteen?"

"I don't know," I said, shrugging. "I hadn't really thought about it."

Actually, I had, and what I really wanted was a new laptop—mine made a weird grinding noise when it started up—but I didn't want to sound grabby. Then again, Hannah was angling for a new car, so compared to that, a laptop seemed like an almost modest request.

"How about a nose job?" Peyton suggested.

It took a long beat for her words to sink in.

"What?" I asked, sure I had misheard her.

"A nose job," she said, enunciating the words.

"Peyton," my father said warningly.

"What? Lots of girls get them. And I think it would do wonders for your face if your nose was a bit shorter, Miranda. And maybe they could do something about that bump." She pointed vaguely at my nose.

I stared at her. I had been right all along . . . Peyton really *was* evil. And not just a little evil, but impressively evil. Like, so evil she probably had a dark altar hidden away somewhere in the house on which she sacrificed puppies to Satan.

But on the other hand . . . as awful as she was to suggest it, I *had* always secretly wanted a nose job. I know that it's superficial to fixate on your looks, and that surgically altering your appearance to comport with the rigid and narrow standards of modern beauty is a copout, but still. I've always hated my nose. It's just way, way too big for my face. In fact, my nose was so freakishly large, it apparently prompted people to spontaneously suggest I get plastic surgery.

"Peyton," my father said again, and this time he sounded really annoyed. I glanced over at him, and was surprised to see he had that pinched-up expression he always gets when he's around my mom. "Miranda is *not* getting a nose job. She doesn't need one, and anyway, she's far too young."

"No, she isn't. I had my nose done when I was sixteen," Peyton argued.

Wait . . . Peyton had a nose job? I stared at her nose, which had always seemed a bit too pointy, and had a tendency to flare when she was angry. I wondered what it had looked like before, and had a sudden vivid image of Peyton with a hooked, wart-covered witch's nose. I quickly took a sip of Coke to cover my snort of laughter.

"Well, Miranda is too young," my father said firmly. "Besides, her mother would never go along with the idea."

*Hmph,* I thought. Why should Sadie have any say? I think there should be a law that when a parent deserts her offspring to go live in Europe, she immediately surrenders any right to have input in decisions involving minor cosmetic procedures.

"Actually, I think I might like a nose job," I said. A bit too loudly.

Which wouldn't have been a big deal . . . except for the fact that Emmett Dutch had chosen that exact moment to appear at our table, standing just behind me.

"Hey, Miranda," he said.

I spun around and stared up at Emmett. I had no idea that he actually knew my name. Discovering this delicious nugget of information was almost worth the mortification of him hearing my announcement that I wanted to have a nose job. Almost . . . but not quite. Because surely now every time Emmett saw me, all he'd be able to think about was my freakishly large nose. It's true. Finn said that whenever he tells someone he was born with a cleft palate, from then on they always stare at the surgical scar just over his mouth, as though trying to imagine what the birth defect must have looked like. So now Finn just tells everyone that the scar was caused by a freak fly-fishing accident.

I suddenly realized that Emmett was waiting for me to say something.

"Oh. Um. Hi," I gabbled nervously. "You know my name?"

*Oh, no. Please tell me I didn't just say that out loud,* I thought miserably.

"I'm here with my parents," Emmett said, nodding over toward his mother and father's table. They were watching us with friendly interest, and so I waved feebly at them.

"Oh . . . cool," I said. An awkward pause followed, during which I couldn't think of a single thing to say.

"Miranda, aren't you going to introduce us to your friend?" Peyton asked in her most fakey-nice tone. It was how she used to talk to me back when she and my dad were first dating, and she felt it was important to pretend to like me . . . a pretense she dropped as soon as they got married.

"Oh! Right. Sorry. This is, um, Emmett. And this is my dad, and my stepmother, Peyton, and that's Hannah," I said, pointing to each in turn.

"Hi," Emmett said, looking right at Hannah.

"Hey," Hannah said. She tipped her head coyly to one side and began to wrap a sleek tendril of platinum blond hair around one finger.

Wait . . . why was Hannah looking at Emmett that way? Almost as if she were interested in . . . *Oh, no. No no no no no no no.*

"Where do you go to school?" Emmett asked, still not taking his eyes off of Hannah.

"Orange Cove High," Hannah said. She smiled, flashing her perfect white teeth. "Do you go to Miranda's school?"

"Yeah. Notting Hill," Emmett said, nodding.

"That is *so* cool," Hannah said. "You must be really smart."

I couldn't help rolling my eyes at this. Hannah had never once let the subject of Geek High pass without making a comment about how only dorks and freaks go there.

But neither my dad nor Payton caught my eye roll. They were too busy beaming up at Emmett. Who, in turn, was beaming down at Hannah.

*Oh, no no no no no no no!*

But, I realized, my stomach sinking, there wasn't a chance that Emmett would ever look at Hannah and me standing side by side and choose me. She looked like she'd walked straight out of a shampoo commercial, whereas I was the girl who possessed a nose so large, it inspired discussions of rhinoplasty. Well, okay, *one* discussion, but still. Surely no one had ever told Hannah *she* needed plastic surgery.

"I almost sent Hannah to Notting Hill, but then decided that I'd prefer she have the experience of a more traditional school," Peyton said.

I turned to stare at her. For one thing, I'd never heard this before. And for another, just that afternoon I'd overheard Hannah informing her friends that Chicago was (a) a state, and (b) located next to California. There was no way she'd ever have gotten into Geek High.

Wait . . . unless that was just it. Had Hannah applied to Geek High and not gotten in? It would certainly explain a lot of Peyton's hostility.

She was the most competitive woman alive. It wasn't enough that Hannah was prettier than me, and had a killer body, and was insanely popular . . . of course Peyton would want her to be smarter than me, too.

But as I looked up at Emmett, who was beaming down at Hannah while she giggled up at him and flirtatiously tossed her hair over one shoulder, I started to feel a little sick.

People say that it's who you are on the inside that counts, and that being smart and thoughtful is far more important than being pretty. But that just isn't true. The pretty girls always beat out the smart girls. Always.

# Chapter 8

$$\frac{\partial h}{\partial s} = \frac{\partial f}{\partial x}\frac{\partial x}{\partial s} + \frac{\partial f}{\partial y}\frac{\partial y}{\partial s}, \qquad \frac{\partial h}{\partial t} = \frac{\partial f}{\partial x}\frac{\partial x}{\partial t} + \frac{\partial f}{\partial y}\frac{\partial y}{\partial t}$$

I told Charlie about the horrible Emmett/Hannah flirtation the next day before mod lit began, keeping my voice low so that nobody—particularly the Felimonster—would overhear us.

"Wait . . . go back to the part where your stepmonster said you needed plastic surgery," Charlie said, outraged on my behalf.

"That's not the important part of the story," I said. Which was saying something, since normally I'm more than happy to run Peyton down. "The important part is where you-know-who was totally into the Demon Spawn."

Charlie just shook her head sadly and gazed at me with the sort of pity she normally reserves for contestants on *The Bachelor*.

"Miranda, I think you really need to take some time to work on your self-esteem," she said.

"Are you even listening to me?" I asked. "This is a nightmare. A total nightmare."

"Perspective time. A guy whom you hardly know, and yet have somehow persuaded yourself that you're in love with, spoke to Hannah. I don't think that quite reaches nightmare proportions," Charlie said.

And even though deep down I knew she was right, her condescending tone still irritated me. Just because Charlie has never truly fallen for anyone, and so has never experienced how it throws your entire life into chaos, she thought she was above the whole thing.

"Hey, Miranda," a voice said.

I'd been so distracted by Charlie's annoying armchair psychoanalysis, I hadn't noticed that someone was hovering just in front of my desk . . . and, more important, that the somebody was Emmett. For the second straight day in a row, he'd crossed a room to talk to me! Had I been wrong to assume he was interested in Hannah? Was it possible . . . could it be . . . that maybe, just maybe, he'd been nice to Hannah only for my sake? After all, Emmett didn't know that Hannah and I despised each other.

"Oh. Um. H-hi, Emmett," I stuttered, wondering if he could actually hear my heart galloping away at full speed.

"How was your dinner last night?"

"My steak was too rare. I had to send it back."

*My steak was too rare? I had to send it back?* What was I saying? I sounded like an idiot. Why was it that my supposed genius-level IQ seemed to drop to that of a not-very-bright shoe whenever I was around Emmett?

"I was wondering . . . that girl you were with," Emmett began. "Hannah, right? So . . . is she seeing anyone?"

And just like that, the galloping skittered to a stop. I don't know what a broken heart is supposed to feel like, but for me it felt as though I'd been frozen clear through. I went numb and cold at the same time.

"Miranda," Charlie murmured. She surreptitiously poked me in the side, causing me to jump in my seat. I realized only then that I hadn't answered Emmett.

"She probably has a boyfriend, huh," Emmett said.

"Um . . ." I said. I could have said, *Yes, she does have a boyfriend.* I could have said, *She's dating the hottest guy at Orange Cove High, and oh, by the way, he also happens to be a black belt in jujitsu.* But I have my pride, even if it was now currently hanging about me in tatters. "No, I don't think she does," I finally said.

Emmett grinned at me. His smile was just the tiniest bit crooked, and there was a small dimple in his right cheek. I'd spent hours fantasizing about him smiling down at me like that. Never once did I ever imagine that it would hurt this much.

"Cool. So, um, would you mind giving me her number?"

Numbly, I wrote the beach house phone number down on a slip of notebook paper, tore it off, and handed it to him.

"Thanks, Bloom," Emmett said. He winked and sauntered off, flushed with happiness.

"He's calling me Bloom," I said miserably. "When they start calling you by your last name, all hope is lost."

"Actually, I think when they ask you for your stepsister's phone number, all hope is lost," Charlie said.

I looked at her reproachfully. This was heartless, even for someone as unromantic as Charlie.

"Sorry," she said, immediately contrite. "But you know what I'm going to say."

"I know, I know. You're going to say that anyone who would choose Hannah over me is an idiot, and not worth getting upset over," I said. I was trying not to cry, which made my voice sound unnaturally creaky.

"No. I was going to say that anyone who would ever be interested in such a vain, shallow, self-centered little brat like Hannah isn't even worth knowing," Charlie said.

"Maybe he doesn't know she's vain, shallow, and self-centered," I said wistfully, watching Emmett as he pulled out his copy of *The Stranger* and opened up his laptop. "Maybe once he realizes it, he'll lose interest in her."

"Oh, no," Charlie said, shaking her head. "Don't even go there. Life is not one of those feel-good teen movies, where the nice girl triumphs over the horrible popular girl in the end. Just forget about him, Miranda. Seriously."

I knew the sort of movie she was talking about. The protagonist is always beautiful, but everyone around her pretends that she's plain because she wears clunky glasses, dresses in overalls, and keeps her hair pulled back in a ponytail. And then at some key point in the movie—usually at the prom—she puts in contact lenses, wears a slinky dress, and shakes out her hair, and suddenly everyone realizes for the first time that she looks *exactly* like Lindsay Lohan. It's because of those propaganda films that every smart but plain girl secretly believes that one day she'll shake out her hair and the hot guy in school will suddenly see her for the beauty she really is.

But I don't wear my hair up, or have glasses. And my clothes are pretty much the same ones from the Gap that everyone else at school wears. And so far, no one's ever confused me with Lindsay Lohan. I slumped forward over my desk and stared at the glowing screen of my laptop.

"Why so sad, Miranda?" Felicity asked so loudly, she was practically yelling.

I ignored her, which was usually the best plan of action when it came to Felicity.

"I would have thought you'd be excited that a certain someone crossed a room to talk to you," Felicity continued, in the same too-loud voice.

And suddenly, my eyes widening with horror, I realized what she was doing. Felicity was talking so loudly, everyone in the room could hear what she was saying. In fact, conversations about whether MIT or Stanford had the better engineering program, or the best extracurricular activities to have on your college applications, were coming to a rapid halt as our classmates looked up, their expressions curious.

"Unless, of course, he was telling you that he's taking out a restraining order to keep you from staring at him during class," Felicity continued.

She'd timed it perfectly—everyone heard her. They looked from Felicity's smug face to my white-with-shock one, and then the whispering began.

"What is she talking about? Who is Miranda staring at?" Padma Paswan asked, gaping at me across the room. I like Padma, but she can be such a gossip.

"I'm not sure. But Felicity said something about a restraining order," Tabitha said gravely, regarding me with her big, solemn eyes.

"Really? Someone got a restraining order? Against Miranda?" Padma asked eagerly. She was sitting on the edge of her chair.

It was like a car accident. No, worse than that. It was like a multiple pileup on the highway. It was a big rig jackknifing in the middle of rush-hour traffic and turning the roadway into real-life bumper cars.

Charlie made a noise that sounded like a snarl. "Felicity, were you raised by a wire-monkey mother?" she asked.

"What are you talking about?" Felicity asked, narrowing her eyes.

"You know, the wire-monkey baby experiment. It was a research project where they took away a baby monkey's mother and gave it a fake mother made out of wire instead. All of the monkey babies who were raised by wire-monkey mothers became vicious and eventually went crazy. Which sort of reminds me of you," Charlie finished.

Padma tittered appreciatively at this. I stole a look at Emmett. He alone was ignoring the conversation.

"Oh, ha, ha. You're so funny," Felicity snarled.

"I think so," Charlie said serenely.

"They were rhesus monkeys," Christopher chimed in unexpectedly in his robotic voice. "Harry Harlow of the University of Wisconsin–Madison conducted the experiments in 1930. He separated the infant monkeys from their mothers to study the effect of deprivation on emotional development—"

Charlie glanced at me. She must have read the misery in my expression.

"Thank you, Christopher, you're exactly right," Charlie said, hastily cutting him off.

Finn slipped in just before Mrs. Gordon walked into class, brandishing her notes.

"Thank you for joining us, Mr. Eggers," Mrs. Gordon said to him.

"My pleasure, Mrs. G," Finn said, grinning at her. "You know there's nowhere I'd rather be than right here in mod lit."

Mrs. Gordon loves Finn, so she just laughed.

"What did I miss?" Finn whispered to me as he slid into his seat.

I just shook my head numbly.

"Good morning. I'm assuming everyone had time to read the first three chapters of *The Stranger*, and came to class prepared to discuss them," Mrs. Gordon said.

I considered making a run for it. I could plead cramps or a sinus infection, and spend the rest of the morning in the nurse's office curled up on a cot. And while there, I could figure out a way to escape from my life. Maybe I could run away to Alaska and get a job on a fishing boat. Because clearly things weren't going so well here . . . in fact, it was hard to imagine they could get much worse.

But Charlie—who I could sometimes swear has the ability to read my mind—whispered, "Stay where you are. If you run away, you're just letting her win."

And so I stayed. Even though at that moment, I didn't really care if Felicity won or not.

# Chapter 9

$$D_{1,2}f(a, b) = D_{2,1}f(a, b)$$

After the interminably long mod lit class, during which I sat marinating in my humiliation, Charlie insisted I go to Latin, too.

"Keep your head high and your shoulders back," Charlie kept hissing in my ear, sounding like a beauty pageant coach. I kept waiting for her to whip out a tube of Preparation H to zap the puffiness under my eyes. "Don't let Felicity or anyone else know that she got to you."

And I kept soldiering on, trying to look serene and unbothered, even though what I really wanted to do was to lock myself in a toilet stall and never come out again.

But Charlie's approach seemed to work. The story fizzled and died out before lunch, which was nothing short of a miracle, considering that people still occasionally talk about how Olivia Malkin fell asleep in Advanced Physics last year after pulling an all-nighter to finish up her science fair project, and drooled all over her desk. Gossip does not die an easy death at Geek High.

"I have something that will cheer you up," Finn said at lunch. He, Charlie, and I had staked out our favorite table in the corner of the dining room. Lunch is included in the tuition, although we don't have the typical cafeteria lunch line. Instead, platters of sandwiches, crudités, fruit, and cookies are put out on each table, and we help ourselves, family style. We'd all been careful to grab turkey sandwiches before they ran out (trust me, you don't want to get stuck with the egg salad), although I wasn't eating today. Being humiliated in front of one's peers has a way of ruining the appetite.

"I seriously doubt that," I said morosely.

Two tables over, the Felimonster and Toady had their heads bent close together as they whispered excitedly. It wasn't too hard to figure out whom they were talking about, as they kept darting sly looks at me and then tittering behind their hands.

"Keep smiling," Charlie hissed, and I obediently curled up the corners of my mouth, even though it felt like I was baring my teeth rather than smiling.

"See for yourself," Finn said, and he pushed his open laptop toward me. He had the Internet up, and set to the same weblog he'd shown me yesterday: geekhigh.com. At the top of the page, the newest entry read:

*GEEK HIGH STUDENT FAKES IQ TO GAIN ADMISSION*
*GEEKHIGH.COM has learned that one of its students—sophomore opera aficionado Felicity Glen—forged her IQ test in order to gain admission to Geek High. Allegedly, Glen has an IQ of only 115—ten points below the requisite 125 IQ needed to gain entrance to the school. Apparently, the rules do not apply to all students . . . especially those with rich fathers who have bestowed significant financial gifts to the school. In not completely unrelated news, Morris Glen, the prominent local criminal defense attorney and father of Felicity Glen, has announced his intention to donate fifteen thousand dollars toward a new library for Geek High. Developing . . .*

"Is this true?" I gasped.

"Absolutely," Finn said with satisfaction.

"How do you know?" Charlie asked suspiciously.

Finn smiled enigmatically at her. "I just do."

"Who's writing this?" I asked. "Oh! Do you think it's Megan Reilly? I overheard her saying she was trying to get an internship at *Entertainment Weekly* next summer, and this is just the sort of stunt she'd pull to get it."

"I think Finn knows who's writing it," Charlie said, fixing him with a beady stare. "Don't you, Finn?"

Finn shrugged, trying—and failing—to look modest. "I may."

Charlie snorted.

"What?" I asked, looking from one to the other. I had the feeling I was missing something.

"It's *him*," Charlie said. "*Finn*. He's the one writing it."

I looked at Finn for confirmation, but it was immediately obvious from his expression, which was a cross between smug pride and sheepishness.

"How did you know?" he asked Charlie.

She shrugged. "I know everything," she said.

Finn tossed a sweet-potato chip at her.

"Hey! Don't! Okay, fine, I saw you writing it in mod lit. You should be a little more discreet, you know. It was pretty obvious you weren't taking class notes—you were typing way too fast," Charlie said.

"Thanks for the tip," Finn said. He popped a chip in his mouth.

"But *why* are you writing it?" I asked.

"I'm an anarchist," Finn said nonchalantly.

"Writing a snarky tell-all blog counts as anarchy these days?" I asked, arching my eyebrows.

"I'm starting small," Finn said. "I'm slowly working up to overthrowing the school administration."

"Did you make this up about the Felimonster?" I asked, looking back at the salacious blog entry. It was written in bold white type against a black background, for dramatic effect.

"Of course not," Finn said indignantly. "That wouldn't be ethical."

"So how'd you find out about it?" Charlie asked.

"A journalist never reveals his sources."

"Please," I said dismissively. "It's a blog, not the *New York Times*."

"Let's just say I have an in within the administration," Finn said mysteriously. He drew a circle in the air with his fingers as he said it.

"Mrs. Boxer," I said, snapping my fingers and pointing at him. Finn looked crestfallen.

"How'd you figure that out so fast?" he asked.

Mrs. Boxer's official title was executive administrative assistant to the headmaster, but that was just a fancy way of saying she was the school secretary.

"Because (a) she's a gossip, and (b) she adores you," I said. "What did you do, bring her a latte and then, once she was hopped up on caffeine, wheedle it out of her?"

"I did no such thing." Finn actually looked affronted at this. "I just . . . overheard her talking. She didn't actually know I was there."

"Did you hide in the coatroom by her office again?" Charlie asked.

"Again?" I asked.

"That's where he hid last year when he was trying to find out if they'd figured out who was behind the rash of toilet paper thefts," Charlie said.

"That was you?" I asked, stung that I'd been left out of this scheme, too. "You guys don't tell me anything."

"We wanted you to have plausible deniability," Finn said.

"Gee, thanks," I said crankily.

Although, still, I had to admit this was good gossip. I don't normally subscribe to the politics of personal destruction, but Felicity Glen really did have it coming to her. I glanced over at Felicity's table. She, clearly unaware of the piece Finn had posted about her, was still giggling with Morgan, and smirking in my direction. I knew I should tell Finn to take down the piece, and that no matter how much Felicity might torture me, we shouldn't sink to her level. But I didn't.

Which, as it turned out, was a big mistake.

# Chapter 10

$$f(a + y) - f(a) = \nabla f(a) \cdot y + \frac{1}{2!} yH(a + cy)y^t$$

**F**elicity found out about the blog in Twentieth-century History class. She was sitting at her desk, legs primly crossed at the ankles, skimming over the reading assignment Mr. Aburro had given us the day before, when Morgan came skittering into the room, looking both traumatized and titillated. She was clearly torn between wanting to appear upset on Felicity's behalf, and overcome with the bounty of good gossip. Morgan bent over, and, cupping her hand over her mouth, whispered into Felicity's ear.

I watched as Felicity's expression morphed from surprise to shell-shocked horror. She wheeled around in her seat and began to type furiously at her laptop. I couldn't see what was on her screen, but I had a pretty good idea of what Web site she'd just surfed over to. Felicity leaned forward toward the screen, her shoulders bunching up to her ears. She turned to Morgan, who was doing her best to control her excitement and look sympathetic.

"Don't worry; it's totally bogus," Morgan said soothingly.

But Felicity just shook her head and looked back at the screen. She whispered something to Morgan that I couldn't hear, although I could figure out the substance of it, since they both then turned to look at me. Felicity looked wounded, and her moss green eyes had filled with tears. Morgan's lips were pressed together into a tight, angry line.

What were they . . . Wait just a minute. Did they think *I'd* written the blog?

I looked over at Finn, who sat next to me (Charlie had opted to take History of the Renaissance instead). He was engrossed in a conversation with Tate Metcalf about some online role-playing game they were both hooked on.

"Dude, you have got to try playing as an evil wizard. It's the only way you can get the Wand of Asb'el. That wand kicks ass," Finn was advising Tate.

"Really? I always play as a paladin," Tate said. "You get the good armor that way."

"True, but paladins are such boring do-gooders," Finn said with a dismissive wave of his hand. "Think of all of the henchmen you can recruit if you're evil."

"Finn," I hissed, tugging on his shirtsleeve to get his attention.

"Just a sec. I have to illuminate Tate on the beauty of evil-aligned characters," Finn said. He started to turn back to Tate, but I grabbed his arm.

"Listen to me; this is important! She thinks I wrote that blog," I said.

"Who?" Finn asked. He looked at me blankly, blinking like an owl. I suppressed the urge to take him by the shoulders and shake him. Honestly, if you met Finn when he's acting like this, you'd be shocked to learn that he's a genius.

"Who do you think? *Felicity*," I said through gritted teeth.

"Huh?" Finn asked. And then he finally got it. "Ohhhhh," he said, drawing out the word.

"Right. *Oh*," I said, and turned to look back at Felicity. She suddenly stood and bolted out of the classroom, pushing past Mr. Aburro just as he was walking in with a model of a World War I German U-boat tucked under his arm. Mr. Aburro is nearly as wide as he is tall. I was actually a little surprised Felicity could squeeze by him.

"Miss Glen, class is about to start," Mr. Aburro called after her. But Felicity didn't stop. Mr. Aburro looked startled. "What was that about?" he asked no one in particular.

"I think she just read about herself on the Geek High blog," Padma said helpfully.

So everyone had found out about Finn's blog. That hadn't taken long.

"Geek High blog?" Mr. Arburro repeated slowly. His brow wrinkled in confusion. "What's a blog?"

Morgan hurried out of the room after Felicity, calling out, "Felicity, wait!"

As I watched her go, I felt uneasy. I knew I should feel vindicated, especially after Felicity's blatant attempt to humiliate me in mod lit that morning. But I didn't. Instead, I actually felt a little sorry for her.

"It was during the First World War that truly practical submarines emerged. Germany used their fleet of twenty-nine U-boats to great effectiveness as the war began. Within the first ten weeks, the Germans had used their subs to sink five British cruisers. And on September fifth, 1914, a German U-boat was successful in sinking a British warship for the very first time," Mr. Arburro enthused. He was just getting into his zone when there was a knock at the door.

"Come in," Mr. Aburro called out.

A small girl with blond ringlets and a snub nose shuffled in. I recognized her: Cecilia Bendell. Her older sister, Alex, was a senior. Cecilia couldn't have been older than ten, and she looked traumatized at having to stand in front of our class. She handed over a note to Mr. Aburro, and then fled. Mr. Aburro put on his reading glasses and frowned down at the note.

"Ms. Bloom, you're wanted in the headmaster's office," he said.

I looked up, surprised. Me? I never got called to the headmaster's office. Sure, I'd had my share of trips to the principal's office back when

I was in public school, but not since I'd transferred to Geek Middle. But this I know—no matter what school you go to, getting called to the main office is never a good omen.

"It says that you're to go immediately, and not to wait until the end of the period." Mr. Aburro pursed his lips, clearly not pleased with the interruption. "I'll send an e-mail out with the homework assignment," he continued, folding the paper and tucking it into his pocket.

I gathered my books and stuffed them into my knapsack, and then closed my laptop and pushed that in the bag, too. I could feel everyone's eyes on me as I stood and self-consciously walked out of the class.

The headmaster's office was located on the third floor of the main building, and could be reached only by hoofing it up six flights of narrow, twisting, creaking stairs. By the time I reached the tiny reception area, manned by the school receptionist, Mrs. Boxer, I was out of breath. Mrs. Boxer was a large woman—tall and broad-shouldered, with wispy gray hair that she wore up in a beehive, adding even more height to her already towering figure. The first time I saw her, I thought she was a man in drag.

Mrs. Boxer was typing with two fingers when I came in. She started when the door opened, and lifted a hand to her heart.

"Goodness, you frightened me," she said, in a breathy, Marilyn Monroe–esque voice.

"Sorry, Mrs. Boxer," I apologized. "I was told to come and see the headmaster."

"Why? What did you do?" Mrs. Boxer asked interestedly. She was a notorious gossip, which Finn had frequently and shamelessly used to his advantage.

"Nothing! Or, at least . . . nothing that I know of," I said.

"I'll tell him you're here," Mrs. Boxer said. She picked up the phone and pressed a button. After a pause, she said, "Miranda Bloom is here to see you, sir. Yes, of course." She set the phone back down and looked at me. Her plucked eyebrows arched like two sideways commas over her turquoise-lined eyes. "He said to send you right in. And I should warn you . . . he doesn't sound happy."

"Really?" I asked. I started to feel uneasy. Just what had I done to warrant getting called into Headmaster Hughes's office? It was only the second day of school. I hadn't been back long enough to get into trouble.

"You'll have to stop and tell me all about it when you're done," Mrs. Boxer said eagerly. "Felicity Glen was in earlier, and looked as though she'd been crying, but she rushed by me so quickly I couldn't get a word out of her."

There was an unpleasant prickling on the back of my neck. I had a good idea why the headmaster had pulled me out of class. I took a deep breath and walked past Mrs. Boxer. The door to the headmaster's office was just behind her desk.

"Good luck," she whispered, and gave me an encouraging thumbs-up.

"Thanks," I whispered back, and then I pushed the door open.

Headmaster Hughes's office was enormous. It occupied half of the third floor of the central building. The room was lined in bookshelves, which were crammed with framed photographs and heavy leather-bound books, and the furniture was old-fashioned—a pair of cream settees, a fussy little coffee table, a decorative globe on a wooden stand. Past the sitting area there was a desk so large it looked like an island in the middle of a sea of Oriental rugs. And behind the desk sat the headmaster of Geek High: Mr. C. Philip Hughes.

Headmaster Hughes's head looked very much like an egg. Other than his caterpillarlike eyebrows, there wasn't a hair anywhere on his head—his scalp was shaved clean, as was his face. He had dark, unblinking eyes, a square jaw with a cleft chin, and he never displayed his teeth when he smiled. Instead he'd draw his lips back in a tight, close-lipped grimace, pulling the outer corners of his mouth down instead of up.

"Good afternoon, Miss Bloom," Headmaster Hughes greeted me in his deep, slow voice. He sat with his elbows resting on the leather blotter, his hands arched together as though he were about to start playing *Here is a church; here is a steeple.*

"Hello, sir. You, um, wanted to see me?" I said uncertainly.

"Yes. Sit down," he said, gesturing toward the pair of navy blue damask wing chairs lined up in front of his desk.

"Thanks," I said, and sat on the edge of one chair. I rested my knapsack on the ground next to my feet and waited.

Headmaster Hughes was unnervingly silent. He fixed his stern eyes on me, his hands folded in front of him, and sat as still as a statue. A statue of a bald gargoyle. I did my best not to squirm. Just sitting there, being watched like that, made me feel guilty, even though I knew I hadn't done anything. He was quiet for so long that when he finally did speak, I jumped in my seat.

"How are you, Miranda?" he asked.

This surprised me. I'd been sure he was going to start right off interrogating me about the Geek High blog.

"Fine, I guess," I said.

"You're adjusting to your new home?"

*My new home* . . . Wait, how did he know about that?

"Um . . . sure," I said.

"Your mother was concerned about how you'd handle the transition," Headmaster Hughes continued, still staring at me. He didn't seem to have any need to blink. It freaked me out.

"My mother?" I repeated. When had he talked to Sadie?

"We've been in touch," he said.

"But . . . she's in London," I said.

"Yes, I know. We spoke just yesterday. She's quite an extraordinary woman, your mother," Headmaster Hughes said, his lips quirking down into his frown-smile.

*Extraordinary woman?* Was that what they called child deserters these days? And why was the headmaster talking to Sadie anyway? I hadn't even talked to her since the morning she'd flown to London. Well, actually, to be completely accurate, I didn't talk to her then, either. I simply sat in the car with my arms crossed and tears of anger burning in my eyes, while Sadie drove me to my dad's house. She, on the other hand, had nattered away about how excited she was to leave on her big adventure, as though we were best friends and not a mother and daughter in a fight. I think she finally figured out that I really was angry at her only when I didn't bother to return any of the messages she'd left on my cell phone's voice mail. If there's one thing Sadie hates, it's being ignored.

But since I didn't have anything to say, I just sat there quietly and stared at the Newton's Cradle perched on the edge of Headmaster Hughes's desk. It's the game that has five marbles hanging from strings, and which demonstrates the conservation of momentum and energy. You pull back one marble and then let it go so it hits the resting marbles, causing the marble on the far side to swing up and then back down again into the resting marbles, and so it continues until you stop it.

I had an almost irresistible urge to reach out, pull back the nearest of the hanging balls, and start the Newton's Cradle swinging. Seriously— my hands were practically twitching. But the unblinking eyes were still boring into my forehead, and so I managed to keep my hands folded in my lap.

"Sometimes children who are dealing with a disruption at home are more apt to act out at school," Headmaster Hughes said.

He waited, and I had the feeling I was supposed to respond.

"Uh-huh," I said.

"It's a way of trying to attract attention . . . a cry for help, of sorts."
Another pause.

"Mm-hmm," I said, nodding encouragingly.

"And although it's sometimes tempting as a parent or educator to let the disruptive behavior pass by, that doesn't benefit anyone. Especially not the child, who is undoubtedly craving boundaries."

"Well . . ." I said, feeling a twinge of discomfort. Where was he going with this? And was I supposed to be the child he was talking about?

"Which brings us to the matter at hand," Headmaster Hughes continued. "Specifically, the blog entitled 'Geek High.' It has been alleged that you are the author of it."

"I'm not!" I said quickly.

Headmaster Hughes raised one furry eyebrow at me. It was a pretty cool trick. If I could raise one eyebrow at a time, maybe I'd shave off all of my hair, too.

"I am aware that you and Felicity Glen had a conflict this morning," he said.

A conflict? Was that what he called her attempt to humiliate me in front of Emmett Dutch? But I couldn't exactly tell him that, could I? Not without admitting that I was infatuated with Emmett, and that he'd developed a crush on my evil stepsister, with whom I was currently being forced to cohabit because my mother—who, according to Headmaster Hughes, was *extraordinary*—had deserted me so that she could live it up in London.

So instead I just shrugged and nodded.

"And just a few hours later, a derogatory piece about Miss Glen appeared on the Geek High blog. That's quite a coincidence, don't you think?" Headmaster Hughes asked.

I shook my head vehemently, so that my ponytail slapped me in the face. "I didn't write it," I insisted.

This prompted more skull-penetrating stares. I had to admit it was an effective interrogation technique. I almost confessed to everything, just to get out of there and away from his creepy unblinking stare. But I held fast, and stared right back at him. Only I couldn't help blinking. In fact, the more I tried not to blink, the more I blinked.

"I think you're aware that we have an honor code in place here at Notting Hill," Headmaster Hughes said slowly.

"Yes, sir, I am," I said.

"And that all of our students have pledged that they will remain truthful in all matters," he continued.

I nodded and tried not to tap my foot nervously, worried that it might make me look guilty.

"So I have to accept your word that you didn't write the blog," Headmaster Hughes concluded.

At this I perked up, hope swelling like a balloon in my chest. "Really?" I said too quickly. "I mean . . . thanks."

"However"—another stern stare—"I have reason to believe that if you are not the party responsible for this blog, you know who is."

The hope quickly deflated. I looked away. The thing was . . . we did have an honor code at Geek High. So technically I *couldn't* say I didn't know who wrote the blog.

"Do you know?" he prompted.

I swallowed, and, after a painfully long moment, I nodded.

"Who is it?" he asked.

"I can't tell you," I said in a small voice. Honor code or not, I wasn't going to turn Finn in. He'd be expelled for sure.

"Are you telling me that you're refusing to answer the question I have directed to you?"

I hesitated, and then nodded. "I'm sorry, sir, but I can't tell you."

Headmaster Hughes sighed and leaned back in his chair.

"That," he said, "is very unfortunate."

*Oh, no.* He was going to suspend me. And I was going to be forced to go to Orange Cove High School with Hannah and her Barbie posse, who would shun me for not knowing what Hilary Duff's favorite lip gloss was.

The long silence, during which time Headmaster Hughes seemed to be deliberating my fate, stretched on forever. At least he'd stopped staring at me, instead fixing his unblinking gaze on some point behind me.

"The Snowflake Gala," he finally said.

Whatever I'd been expecting him to say, that wasn't it.

"It's been waning in popularity over the past few years," he continued, rather cryptically. "Do you know why that is?"

This was such an odd turn in the conversation that I hesitated. I did have a fairly good idea why the Snowflake Gala was waning in popularity. Although I actually doubted the *waning* part, since the event was so incredibly lame, it couldn't possibly ever have been popular in the first place.

Every year the school put on the Snowflake Gala the weekend after fall exams, and just before winter break. Geek High students were all forced to dress up and come to school on a Saturday night, eat a gelatinous chicken dinner, and listen to speakers talk about the importance of accelerated education programs. And then the tables would be pushed aside to make room for a dance floor, and Mr. Sanchez, the foreign languages teacher, would act as deejay, while everyone sat around and watched the teachers embarrass themselves dancing.

But Headmaster Hughes didn't wait for my input on the Snowflake Gala, and instead continued to speak as though he hadn't just asked me a question.

"I think that part of the problem is the lack of student involvement in the event. If a student were in charge of planning the Snowflake Gala, enthusiasm would naturally filter through the rest of the student body."

Actually, it wasn't such a bad idea. And maybe whoever they put in charge could hire a decent deejay. And cancel the speakers. And get the teachers to stay home . . . or at least not strike John Travolta–style disco moves while on the dance floor.

"I think that's a really good idea, sir," I said supportively.

"Excellent. I'm glad you agree."

We smiled at each other. And then suddenly I realized that there was something going on. . . .

"Wait. Why are you glad I agree?" I asked cautiously.

"Because I'm putting you in charge of planning the Snowflake Gala," Headmaster Hughes said.

"No!" I yelped.

He stopped smiling and frowned at me.

"I mean . . . I can't . . . I couldn't possibly . . ." I gibbered.

"I think it's just the sort of direction you need, Miranda," Headmaster Hughes said with finality. "Unless, of course, you tell me who is behind the Geek High blog."

So that was it: He was blackmailing me. I sighed.

"Which will it be, Miranda? Truth or consequence?" Headmaster Hughes asked.

I decided I really didn't like Headmaster Hughes. You'd think a guy who shaves his head would be somewhat cool. It was disappointing to learn otherwise.

"I'll take the Snowflake," I muttered.

"As you wish," Headmaster Hughes said gravely, inclining his head. "Why don't you start brainstorming ideas for the gala and get a committee together, and we'll meet . . . shall we say"—he paused while he flipped through his old-fashioned desktop calendar—"on October third to discuss your ideas?"

I nodded dejectedly.

"Have a nice rest of your day," Headmaster Hughes said. I stood and was about to slink out of the office when he continued. "Oh, and Miranda? Try to stay out of trouble. I'd hate to have to tell your mother that you're not living up to the high standards we set for our students here at the Notting Hill Independent School for Gifted Children."

# Chapter 11

$$\int f \cdot d\alpha = \int_{a}^{b} f[\alpha(t)] \cdot \alpha'(t) \, dt$$

"So I'll just go to Hughes and tell him it was me. You'll be off the hook," Finn said later that afternoon.

Finn, Charlie, and I were hanging out at Grounded, a coffee shop located just around the corner from school. The space used to belong to a pizzeria, and there was still a hand-painted mural of Venice along one wall. But the booths with the red vinyl benches that had been there during the pizzeria days were long gone, replaced with sleek round aluminum tables and café chairs. The counter doubled as a display case for the pastries for sale, and behind it there was an enormous hissing espresso machine.

Charlie and I were sipping iced lattes, and Finn was drinking black coffee. He leaned back in his chair, long legs crossed in front of him, trying to pretend he wasn't thrilled with the opportunity to get kicked out of school once and for all.

"No," I said, shaking my head. "Absolutely not. You're still on probation for the loudspeaker stunt last year."

On the last day of school before summer break, Finn had uploaded a computer program onto the Geek High mainframe that caused Alice Cooper's "School's Out" to play at the end of every period instead of the regular bell.

Finn smiled happily at the memory.

"Good times," he said. "But they couldn't prove it was me."

"Which is why you didn't get expelled," Charlie said. "But remember what the headmaster said—you're one prank away from being kicked out."

"That's the whole point," Finn said. "I *want* to be kicked out, remember?"

"You can't drop out of school," Charlie said.

"And why not?" Finn demanded.

"Because you have to graduate from high school," she said severely. Charlie may look like she's alternative, what with the pink hair and the free-to-be-you-and-me parents and all, but she's surprisingly rigid and narrow-minded when it comes to issues like school and recycling.

"No, I don't," Finn said.

"Yes," Charlie said, "you do!"

Finn shrugged. "I can always take one of those equivalency test thingies to get my degree."

"It's not the same. If you drop out of school, you'll spend the rest of your life regretting it and feeling like you missed out on something important," Charlie said. "It's out of the question."

Finn sighed heavily. He obviously didn't agree with Charlie's assessment of the situation, but had learned from prior experience—as had I—that arguing with Charlie is a lost cause.

"Forget it. I'm already stuck organizing the Snowflake," I said with a wave of my hand. "And it won't be that big a deal. Really."

"Finn will help you," Charlie said.

"No, I won't," Finn said.

"Yes, you will." Charlie frowned at him.

"Are you crazy? I'm not going to be involved with the Snowflake in any way, shape, or form. I still hope to lose my virginity someday," Finn said.

Charlie rolled her eyes. "Lovely," she said.

"You think it's really that bad?" I asked tremulously.

Finn nodded, his face uncharacteristically solemn. "Everyone hates the Snowflake. You know that. If people think you're the one responsible for making them come to school on a Saturday night to be bored half to death by speakers, well . . ." He trailed off ominously and shrugged. "I wouldn't want to be in your shoes."

"Ummm," I said. I'd thought that organizing the Snowflake would just be a huge pain in the butt, but now I was starting to feel a bit panicky. I really didn't want to alienate large portions of the Geek High student body.

"Finn, you idiot," Charlie said furiously, "it's your fault that she's stuck with this thankless job in the first place. Do *not* make it worse than it already is!"

"Hey, I'm just keeping it real," Finn said, raising his hands in mock protest. "Don't shoot the messenger."

Charlie began to mutter dark threats about just what she'd do to the messenger if there weren't laws in place to prevent it. Plus, she wanted to get into the Rhode Island School of Design, and I suspected they'd frown on admitting students with criminal records.

"What if he's right?" I asked, mournfully slurping at my iced latte through a red-and-white-striped straw. "The Snowflake probably is going to suck. It always does. And I really, really don't want everyone to hate me."

I thought, but didn't add, that I was feeling unpopular enough, considering how unwanted I was at my new home. Geek High was my last safe haven, the only place where I felt I truly belonged. I didn't want to lose that sense of security.

"Don't worry," Charlie said bracingly. "Finn and I will help you with the Snowflake. We'll think of something. It will be the least lame Snowflake ever. I promise."

I smiled gratefully at her.

"Hey, I've got an idea," Finn said.

"What's that?" I asked.

"One word," Finn said. *"Karaoke."*

Charlie and I looked at him blankly.

"Karaoke," Finn said again.

"We heard you," Charlie replied. "We just don't know what you're talking about."

"That's how to spice up the Snowflake. Rent a karaoke machine, and then sit back and watch as the whole school rocks out," Finn said, looking pleased with himself.

"Karaoke," I repeated. "That's what you come up with? *Karaoke?*"

"That's the worst idea I've ever heard," Charlie said with a derisive sniff.

"No, it's not. It's an amazing idea," Finn said, affronted. "In fact, it's so amazing, you're just jealous you didn't think of it yourself."

"Yeah, that's it," Charlie said, rolling her eyes. "And just when are people supposed to sing karaoke? In between the speakers?"

"Why not? And if any of the speakers decide to sing in lieu of giving their talk, well, all the better," Finn enthused. "Trust me: It's a *brilliant* idea."

"No," Charlie said, "it's not."

"And why not?" Finn demanded.

"If you don't automatically know the answer to that question, there's nothing I can do to help you," Charlie said sadly.

Finn flicked his plastic coffee stirrer at her, and Charlie began to tell him off for splattering coffee on her favorite shirt. And I just slumped back in my chair, and, between sips of iced latte, tried to convince myself that things would get better. Eventually.

They had to, right?

# Chapter 12

$$\int (af + bg) \cdot d\alpha = a \int f \cdot d\alpha + b \int g \cdot d\alpha$$

I avoided Peyton and Hannah at the beach house as much as I could. Peyton was always click-clacking off in her insanely high-heeled pumps to a work meeting, or a fund-raiser, or possibly to see her plastic surgeon for another Botox injection, which meant that she wasn't around too often. Hannah was harder to dodge. The house had become a default clubhouse for her Barbie posse. Every day after school they'd appear, nonfat lattes in hand, and spread out all over the living room with copies of *Vogue* and *Allure* and *InStyle*. Their conversation revolved around clothes, makeup, and celebrity gossip. If the SATs covered what color eye shadow was hot this year or which starlet was dating the guy on that television show, these chicks would ace it.

After school on Friday, I hung out at Grounded with Charlie and Finn, and then Charlie's mom dropped me off at the beach house. (I would never think of my dad and Peyton's house as "home.") Avery's little Jetta convertible was out in front, along with two other cars I hadn't seen parked there before—an old station wagon with wood panels on the sides, and a small, boxy SUV.

I sighed. Obviously Hannah was having a larger crowd over than usual. I never felt comfortable around her friends. They always treated me like I was a freak, an exhibit at a museum labeled TEENAGE NERD.

At least I had a key now, so I was able to let myself in. Hopefully I'd be able to sneak back to my room without being seen. But Willow had other ideas. As soon as she heard the door close behind me, she came skittering out into the hallway and ran straight at me, her long tongue hanging goofily out the side of her mouth.

"Hi, Willow," I said, glad that someone was happy to see me around this place. But then my eyes widened. "Wait . . ." I began, but that was as far as I got.

Just as Willow tried to slow down and skid to a showy stop right in front of me, she lost control on the marble floor. Her paws flailed beneath her, and I could see the panic in her eyes . . . but it was too late for her to do anything about it. Eighty pounds of greyhound knocked right into me, bowling me over. My backpack went flying, while I hit the ground with a sickening thud. A second later Willow slammed into the door, letting out a whimper as she bounced off it and fell over. For a long moment both of us just lay there, too stunned to move. Willow's head had hit me in the stomach like a well-aimed punch, and nausea now rippled through me. I could distantly hear the sound of voices getting closer.

"What *was* that?"

"I thought I heard someone at the door."

"Ohmigod, what if someone's breaking into your house?"

"Don't be an idiot, Britt; no burglar would make that much noise."

The last voice I recognized: Avery.

And then Britt spoke again, sounding hurt. "Well, I saw on *Oprah* once that sometimes criminals do all sorts of things to try to trick you into letting them in."

"No one's breaking in," Hannah said in an annoyed voice. "It's just my stepsister."

"Ohmigod, is she okay?"

"Why is she lying on the floor?"

And then a male voice from somewhere very close by me: "That was quite an entrance."

He sounded amused, which irritated the snot out of me. Why do people find it so hilarious when someone falls? What if I were seriously hurt? What if I had a concussion or a spinal-cord injury? Would that be funny? Huh? Would it?

I opened my eyes and attempted to focus them on the owner of the mocking voice. He was cute. Which wasn't a surprise, since I doubted Hannah would hang out with anyone who didn't look like they were about to pose for a Tommy Hilfiger ad. He had red hair that curled back from his face, the sort of pale, lightly freckled skin that doesn't tan, and light blue eyes that were currently narrowed with humor. His smile was crooked, and his face wore a sardonic expression. Cute . . . but not my type. I've never had a thing for redheads. Besides, if he was a friend of Hannah and the Barbies, that meant he was a walking, talking Ken doll. Probably the quarterback of the football team, or something similarly clichéd.

"Do you always laugh at people who've been knocked down?" I asked, not bothering to keep the hostility from my voice.

"Only the ones who look so cute sprawled out on the ground," he said, his grin growing wider.

Cute? The Ken doll was calling me cute? It was a sacrilege of the Laws of Barbiedom. Only blondes with snub noses and big boobs were cute. Girls with frizzy hair, big noses, and no boobs? Definitely *not* cute.

He bent over and extended a hand out to me. I paused for a moment. Was this a practical joke? Pretend to help Geek Girl up, only to let go of her hand at the last minute and watch her fall down all over again? Raucous laughter all around? But he waited patiently, and since I couldn't think of a graceful way to get around it, I finally took his hand. And then something weird happened—when his hand touched mine, I actually felt a zing pass between us.

Willow had gotten up on her own, and was now indulging in a good shake. Willow is the master of the shake. She starts with her head, lets it move down her body to her tail, and then finishes up with one last full-body shake for good measure.

"Thanks," I said gruffly, once I was back on my feet. I knew I sounded ungracious, but the zing had unsettled me.

"No problem. I'm Dex," he said, still holding on to my hand.

"Oh," I said.

"No, you see, this is the part where you're supposed to tell me your name," Dex said patiently, although I could tell from the glint in his light blue eyes that he was teasing me.

"Thanks for the tip," I said, withdrawing my hand.

And at that, Dex chuckled softly. "Tough crowd," he said.

"Dex, you don't have to talk to her," Hannah said, marching over and grabbing the sleeve of his faded blue T-shirt. "She's just my stepsister. She's temporary."

"I didn't know you had a sister," Dex said. Even though Hannah was pulling on his sleeve, he continued to look at me.

"Stepsister," Hannah corrected him.

"I normally stay in the kitchen, scrubbing the pots and pans," I said.

"Until the prince arrives with your glass slipper?" he asked.

"That's right," I said.

Hannah didn't get the Cinderella reference. She frowned, so that three vertical lines appeared just over her nose. "Come on, Dex. *TRL* is coming on. And Avery needs you to open a soda for her," Hannah said to Dex.

"She can't open her own soda?" Dex asked.

"God, no. It'd ruin her manicure," Hannah said seriously.

Dex glanced at me.

"Don't let me keep you. It sounds like you're needed, and besides, we can't have you missing *TRL*," I said.

If Dex was put off by my mocking tone, he didn't show it. He just grinned at me in a way that gave me the same tingly feeling I get when I eat cake frosting straight from the can.

"One does have to keep up on pop culture," Dex said.

And then he pivoted and followed Hannah down the marble hallway. Just before they took the left-hand turn that led into the den, Dex glanced back at me. I blushed, embarrassed that I was caught watching him, and I immediately looked away, down at Willow. She still seemed a little dazed.

"Come on, girl," I said, and looped my fingers under her collar to lead her back up to my bedroom. When I took one final glimpse back down the hallway, Dex and Hannah were gone.

That evening I had to sit through yet another uncomfortable dinner of takeout with my dad, Peyton, and Hannah. As usual, my dad was trying to pretend that we were one big, happy family, Peyton was doing her best to ignore me, and Hannah was yammering on about her favorite subject: herself.

"Can we go to the mall this weekend? I was looking through *Marie Claire* and saw the cutest denim corset skirt from Bebe. I *have* to have it," Hannah said.

Hannah was a bottomless pit of material need. There was always something—a skirt, a sweater, a bracelet, a bag—that she *had* to have. And Peyton never, ever said no to her.

"Sure, we'll go tomorrow and pick it up. Oh, wait, I can't tomorrow. I'm playing tennis. Why don't you go with your girlfriends?"

"Okay," Hannah said with a pleased smile. Now that the skirt had been promised to her, she was—for the moment, at least—satisfied.

"Miranda could go with you," my dad suggested.

I could? Hannah, Peyton, and I stared at him.

"What?" Hannah said, which pretty much summed up what we were all thinking.

"I don't like going to the mall," I said quickly.

Hannah found this news so startling, she stopped gaping at my father and began to gape at me. "You don't like the mall?" she asked, as though I'd just announced that I'd decided to grow a pair of fish gills, and from now on would be breathing underwater. "But . . . where do you get your clothes?"

"The Gap mostly," I said. Sadie had always dragged me there twice a year so I could stock up on essentials.

Hannah shook her head slowly, as though she couldn't reconcile my lack of interest in shopping with her consumer-driven life philosophy.

"Come on; it'll be fun," Dad said. He was like Willow when she got hold of a used Q-tip, and then clamped her mouth shut and refused to let me pry it from her jaws.

"Richard, I don't think you should force it," Peyton said.

"I think it would be good for the girls to spend some time together," Dad said. He looked hopefully from me to Hannah. "You go to different schools and have different friends, after all. Wouldn't you like to get to know each other better?"

*No*, I thought. *No, I do not want to get to know Hannah better. And what's more, just because you decided to marry Peyton doesn't mean that I should have to make friends with her insipid, balloon-headed daughter.*

But I couldn't say that, obviously. And besides, my dad was looking so hopeful. And even though I was still really angry at him for being absent from my life for the past three years, there was a small part of me that couldn't bear to disappoint him.

"Okay," I said reluctantly. "I'll go."

Hannah looked at me, her eyes round with horror.

"Well, I suppose, if the girls want to . . ." Peyton said, with a shrug. "And Miranda, you could use Hannah's help picking out a few new outfits. She has excellent taste. And you could use a makeover."

Dad rewarded Peyton with a huge grin. "That's right. You can do a makeover. It'll be fun."

"But . . . wait," I said. I didn't *want* a makeover. I *liked* my boring Gap clothes.

"Mom," Hannah said in protest.

Peyton looked at her daughter, eyebrows raised and mouth pinched.

"And you can pick up a new pair of shoes while you're there, too," Peyton said, in a transparent bribery attempt.

Hannah sighed, and slumped back in her chair.

"Fine," she said. She could be bought with new shoes, but that didn't mean she had to be happy about it. Hannah picked up an egg roll, took a bite out of it, and then made a face. "Gross. It's cold." She dropped the egg roll, pushed her plate away, and then crossed her arms irritably.

I really, really hoped I'd be able to think up a reason to bail on the shopping trip by tomorrow morning.

# Chapter 13

$$\int_c f \cdot d\alpha = \int_{c_1} f \cdot d\alpha + \int_{c_2} f \cdot d\alpha$$

"So are you coming, or what?" Hannah asked the next morning.

I looked up. I was sitting cross-legged in the middle of the modern platform bed in the guest room, working on a short story I was writing. Willow was sacked out on the floor next to the bed, lying on a white flokati rug. The room also contained a spare modern dresser and a low, boxy white chair that looked like it had never been sat on. I hadn't done anything to make the room my own, other than set out two photographs in plastic frames on the dresser. One was a snapshot of Charlie and Finn that I'd taken at SeaWorld the previous spring. We'd been standing in line for the Kraken ride, and they were wearing sunglasses and smiling cheesy grins. The second photo was of Willow at the dog park being chased by a tiny little Yorkie. The picture of Sadie and me in our faux-diamond tiaras and sucking our cheeks in like beauty contestant pageants—taken last year at the book party Sadie's publisher had thrown for her when *The Gentleman Pirate* was released—was squirreled away in the top drawer, under my favorite sock-monkey pajamas.

Hannah was standing in the doorway to the room, wearing short shorts, a pink hoodie, and pink leopard-print Dr. Scholl's sandals. Her blond hair cascaded down over her shoulders in a glossy sheet, her makeup was cover-girl perfect, and her toenails were painted a sparkly shade of lilac.

"Is that what you're wearing?" she asked, looking me over critically. Her lips quirked into a frown.

I glanced down at myself. I was wearing a pretty typical out-fit for me—khakis and a white T-shirt from the Gap. It seemed pretty inoffensive.

"Yeah. Why?" I asked, puzzled.

"Never mind," she said with a sigh. "Come on. Avery's going to be here any minute."

"Wait . . . Avery's coming?" I asked.

"Of course. Why?"

"Nothing. I just. . . ." I just needed to think of an excuse to get out of this. Spending the day with Hannah was bad enough. Adding Avery to the mix made it just that much worse. But what excuse would work? *I'm not feeling well, cough-cough?* Or, *My school just started having classes on Saturdays?*

Something told me Hannah wouldn't buy it, so I just shrugged and nodded. I slipped on my Jack Purcell sneakers—Hannah wrinkled her nose when she saw them—and then followed her out the front door. Avery was just pulling up in her sporty red Jetta. Hannah waved before turning back to look at me with a swish of pale blond hair.

"Oh, I forgot to tell you. That guy called," she said.

"What guy?" I asked, although I already knew from the sinking feeling in my stomach exactly whom she was talking about.

"You know. That cute guy you introduced me to at dinner the other night," she said. "We're going out to a movie tonight."

And then she opened the front passenger door of the Jetta and slid gracefully inside. I stood there, gaping down at her while the blood pounded in my head. Hannah and Emmett were going out. On a *date*. I felt dizzy, almost sick. And my mouth was suddenly dry, feeling just like it does when the dentist fills a cavity and packs your cheeks with cotton.

I mean, I knew Emmett was going to call her. Obviously. He had asked me for her number, after all. But a small part of me was hoping that he wouldn't really, that he'd somehow figure out that Hannah was too vain and shallow for someone as amazing as him.

"Are you getting in?" Avery asked, leaning across Hannah and peering up at me.

I nodded, and, feeling as though my limbs had turned to wood, I climbed into the backseat.

"Are Britt and Tiff coming?" Hannah asked as Avery peeled out of the driveway, narrowly missing the mailbox.

"Nope. No room. The backseat is only big enough to seat two," Avery said. And even though neither of them said anything, I knew what they were thinking—it was my fault that the twins weren't accompanying them on the mall trip. Well, I wasn't any happier about it than they were.

"I have a date tonight," Hannah announced. "So I have to find something *amazing* to wear."

I felt another stab of pain, although it wasn't quite as pronounced. Maybe if Hannah brought up her date with Emmett another four hundred times, it would stop hurting altogether.

"With who? Not Matt!" Avery gasped.

Hannah snorted. "As if. After what he did at Parker's party, I'm not even speaking to him." She turned back to look at me. "Matt's a guy I was sort of seeing over the summer."

I was surprised that Hannah was addressing me directly. Ever since I'd moved in, she'd gone out of her way to ignore me, other than the occasional eye roll when Willow bounded in the room or an exasperated sigh if I exceeded my four allotted minutes in our shared bathroom. Not that I was all that torn up about it. As far as I was concerned, the less direct contact I had with the Demon Spawn, the better.

I hadn't liked Hannah from the first time I'd met her. We were twelve, and I was going through an awkward phase made worse by the horrible short haircut I'd insisted on getting after seeing Audrey Hepburn in *Roman Holiday*. Unfortunately I failed to realize something that in retrospect seemed obvious: Audrey Hepburn didn't suffer from frizzhead. I did. The haircut was a big mistake. Hannah—looking perfect, as I would come to learn was her usual state—had stared at me, and then turned to her mother and said, "Who's that boy? I thought Richard said he had a daughter?"

My father's vision of Hannah and me turning into Best Friends Forever was pure fantasy. I'd agreed to go on this shopping trip only to please him. So I was surprised—pleasantly so—that Hannah was making an effort. Well, if she was going to be on her best behavior, I would try, too.

"What happened at Parker's party?" I asked.

Avery giggled, and Hannah rolled her eyes dramatically. "He got wasted and hooked up with Melanie Carmichael. Like, five different people saw them," she said.

And I actually felt sorry for her for a minute. Even a girl as gorgeous as Hannah had guy trouble now and again . . . it made me like her a little more to know this.

But then she ruined the effect by continuing. "He was totally beergoggling. Melanie is such a freak. She has these huge lips. . . ."

"Oh, I know!" Avery squealed. She stuck out her lips in an exaggerated O shape. "Like this," she said.

"And she's so annoying," Hannah continued. "She's freaking obsessed with cheerleading."

"Cheerleading is *so* passé." Avery sighed.

"Oh, I *know*," Hannah agreed.

And the conversation pretty much continued like this all the way to the mall. One of them would bring up someone and think of awful things to say about them, while the other would exclaim, "Oh, I *know*!" Over and over and over again.

For my part, I was too busy worrying about staying alive to pay much attention to their conversation. Avery seemed to do everything but look at the road as she drove. She talked, fiddled with the radio, answered her cell phone, ran her fingers through her hair, text-messaged the twins, touched up her lip gloss . . . all while tooling along at fifteen miles per hour over the speed limit. She ran two stop signs and came close to side-swiping a Jaguar.

"Why are you screaming?" Avery asked, turning all the way around in her seat to look at me.

"That was a red light!" I said.

"No, it wasn't. It was definitely yellow," Avery said with a shrug, although she did look back at the road, which was a definite improvement. "So, Melinda . . . I wanted to ask you something."

"It's Miranda," I said.

"Sorry," Avery said, although she didn't sound particularly sorry. "*Anyway*, what exactly did Dex say to you yesterday?" Avery kept her voice casual, but undermined this by peering intently at me in the rear-view mirror.

"Dex? Oh, that guy who was over at the beach house?" I asked.

"Yeah. Wasn't he talking to you?"

"Sort of," I said, remembering the mocking glimmer in those star-tlingly pale blue eyes. No, that wasn't right. He hadn't been mocking me. . . . It was more as though he and I were in on a joke together.

"Did he say anything to you about me?" Avery asked.

"No," I said. And then I caught on. "Oh! Are you two dating?"

"I wish." Avery sighed.

"I think he's totally going to ask you out," Hannah assured her. "Now that he and Wendy have broken up." She looked back at me to explain. "Dex was going out with Wendy Erikson for, like, two years, but they broke up over the summer."

"Wendy Erikson?" I asked. I had no idea who she was talking about.

"Wendy," Avery pronounced, "is freaking gorgeous. She's a model. She was in a commercial for Lever 2000. She was totally naked except for a towel. I could never do that. Well. Maybe I could if I had her body. Here, look. I have a picture of her."

Avery rooted around in her purse and pulled out a page that had been ripped out of a magazine. It was an advertisement for zit cream, and featured a beautiful girl with the sort of creamy skin that a pimple wouldn't dare mar.

"This is her?" I said. "Dex's ex-girlfriend?"

"Uh-huh. She's gorgeous, right?" Avery said.

"Um . . . yeah," I said. Because the girl was, indisputably, gorgeous. She had a mane of golden blond hair, enormous chocolate brown eyes, full, rose-colored lips, and perfectly straight, white teeth. It was almost painful to look at her—*that's* how beautiful she was.

"There's not an inch of fat on her anywhere," Hannah said enviously.

"I would kill to have her body," Avery moaned.

I found it hard to believe that Hannah could envy anyone for her looks, considering she herself was certainly pretty enough to model. And Avery, while not as classically beautiful as Hannah, was no slouch herself. With her dark hair, striking features, and golden-flecked eyes, she was glamorous and exotic-looking.

"And she was really dating Dex?" I asked. Because Dex was cute, sure, but he didn't strike me as the date-a-model type. He seemed a little too . . . well, grounded for that. But then, it wasn't like I knew him. I'd talked to the guy for only two minutes.

"Well," Hannah said, twisting around in her seat to look at me, "the story *I* heard was that Wendy broke up with Dex because she's going to drop out of school and move to New York to become a professional model."

"Really? I heard *Dex* broke up with *her* because he thought she was distracting him from lacrosse," Avery said.

"He plays lacrosse?" I asked. *Aha!* I knew I'd gotten a jock vibe off him.

"Oh, yeah. Dex is, like, the star player at OC High," Avery said. She looked at me in the rearview mirror again. "So you saw him yesterday. Isn't he gorgeous?"

"Well . . ." I hedged. Because he wasn't, really. I mean, sure, Dex was appealing, and had the whole sparkling eyes and easy grin going for him. But he was also a bit quirky-looking, what with his pale, freckled skin and curly hair. No, not gorgeous. Emmett was gorgeous—Prince William gorgeous. Dex was more like William's kid brother, Harry.

But thoughts of Dex and Emmett and their relative states of gorgeousness were momentarily chased from my consciousness by the garbage truck looming ahead that Avery was about to crash into. I let out a terrified yelp. "Look out!" I squeaked.

"Whoops!" Avery said. She swerved at the last minute and averted a collision with the truck, and then took a scarily sharp right-hand turn into the mall parking lot.

"I totally thought Dex was going to ask you out yesterday," Hannah said, and my breath caught in my throat . . . right up until I realized that she'd been talking to Avery, not me.

"No," Avery said with a rueful shake of her head. "I gave him, like, three different chances—I even mentioned that I wasn't doing anything tonight—but all he said was, 'The library's open late on Saturday.' "

This made me laugh, although I had to disguise it with a cough. Hannah glanced back at me.

"Sorry, I have allergies," I said apologetically.

"I don't even know what that means. Do you think he meant that he wanted to *meet* me at the library?" Avery asked.

"I don't know," Hannah said, frowning. "Wouldn't he have said that?"

"You're probably right," Avery said as she pulled into a parking spot and slammed on the brakes. "But maybe I should buy a new outfit. You know. Just in case he calls."

"Good idea," Hannah said supportively. "You should always be prepared."

I'd fully expected the day at the mall to be as bad as spending hours on end sitting in an airport terminal, trying not to make eye contact with the crazy guy who smells like baked beans and talks to himself, but it actually wasn't all that bad. Mostly I just tagged along after Hannah and Avery while they attempted to max out their Visa cards in an all-out shopping blitz. Hannah bought the Bebe skirt, as well as two pairs of shoes, a mini-handbag, three bejeweled T-shirts, and a cascade of barrettes and hair clips from the accessory store. Avery was a bit more restrained, limiting herself to a new pair of Seven jeans and ridiculously overpriced rhine-stone flip-flops.

By the time they finally agreed to break for lunch, I was exhausted and weak with hunger. We headed to the food court, where Avery and Hannah ordered diet sodas and salads. I had a burger, fries, and a Coke, and after I wolfed that down, went back for a Cinnabon. Avery looked at the gooey, sticky pastry longingly as I pulled it apart.

"That looks so good," she said, sighing.

"Want some?" I offered, holding a piece of my Cinnabon out to her.

"I wish," she said. "I'm getting fat just looking at it. How do you eat that and stay so thin?"

"I don't know," I said with a shrug. I'd always been thin. Honestly, I never thought it was so great. I'd much rather have Hannah's curves, or Avery's big boobs. I was flat as a plank, with skinny boy legs.

"You're lucky," Avery said. She stretched her arms up over her head and looked around to see if anyone—i.e., any cute guys—was watching her. A couple of Goth guys wearing Black Ice T-shirts and dark nail polish who were sitting a few tables down from us eyed her with interest, but Avery just curled her lip and rolled her eyes. Chastened, they quickly looked away.

"So why haven't you bought anything?" Hannah asked me.

"I don't really need anything," I said. And I didn't. Also, I didn't have a credit card. Sadie thinks they're bourgeois and encourage consumerism.

Which reminded me: Sadie had called me again the night before. She sounded hurt in her message.

"I was hoping to talk to you. I wanted to see how school is going," she said.

But I'd just erased her message, and hadn't called her back . . . which was now causing me no small amount of guilt. I tried to shrug it off. After all, *Sadie* was the one who left, not me. I was still really ticked off at her for that. Although . . . this was the longest we'd ever gone without speaking. And the void that had suddenly come up between us—my anger, Sadie's departure, the Atlantic Ocean—had left me with a sick feeling in my stomach.

"Of course you need something!" Hannah said. She stood and picked up her tray with its still half-full plastic container of salad. "Let's go find a new outfit for you. Come on. It'll be fun."

Avery stood up too, shouldering her pink patent-leather handbag.

"That's okay," I said. "I didn't bring enough money with me to get a new outfit anyway."

"So charge it," Hannah said.

"I don't have a credit card," I said.

At this Hannah looked horrified. "You don't? Oh, my God, I'd *die*." It took her a few moments to rally from this shock and form a new plan. "I know. We'll just put it on my credit card."

I looked dubious at this, and she shook her head impatiently. "My mom won't care," she said. "She never even looks at the bills."

"Hey, then you should totally buy me that key fob we saw at Coach.

I *have* to have it, but my dad will freak if I spend any more money this month," Avery said excitedly.

I was appalled. I couldn't believe that Avery was actually asking Hannah to buy her a sixty-dollar key chain. Hannah hesitated. I could tell she didn't relish the idea of saying no to Avery, but she was also clearly uncomfortable with the idea of letting Avery use her credit card.

I saw a flash of annoyance pass over Avery's face, but a moment later she was laughing. "I was totally kidding, Hannah. God, you should see your face. Did you really think I was serious?"

"God, no," Hannah said, looking relieved as she laughed too.

But this exchange had left me feeling ill at ease.

"Look, maybe we should just get going," I suggested. "Your mom might get angry if you buy me clothes."

"No. My mom told me to do a makeover on you. I'll just tell her, and she'll get Richard to pay her back for your stuff," Hannah insisted.

"She said that? That Miranda needs a makeover?" Avery asked, her eyebrows raised. "That's really rude."

For a moment I loved Avery.

"Although, Miranda, you would look a lot better if you wore cuter clothes and maybe some makeup," Avery said, looking at me critically.

And the moment of loving Avery ended.

"No, that's okay. Let's just go home," I said, shaking my head.

"Come on; it'll be fun," Hannah coaxed me.

"Well . . ." I hesitated.

I really didn't want the makeover. Avery was right—it *was* insulting. But I had to admit, I was touched that Hannah was making such an effort to bond with me. And who knew? Maybe makeup and clothes were the only way she really knew how to reach out.

"Okay," I said with a resigned sigh. "Make me over."

# Chapter 14

$$\int_C \varphi \, ds = \int_a^b \varphi[\alpha(t)]s'(t) \, dt$$

It was my own fault. After all, I volunteered for the makeover. So I really couldn't blame the fact that I came home from the mall with a bag full of short skirts and tight tops I would never wear in public on anyone other than myself. My cheeks sparkled with powder, and my lips were sticky with a gloss that smelled like fake raspberries.

"You look amazing," Avery had assured me as she tamed my hair into two low pigtails while I was sitting at the makeup counter in Sephora.

"You really do. Better than I've ever seen you," Hannah gushed.

But I didn't feel amazing. I felt like someone else . . . someone who wore too much makeup and not enough clothing. And I really wasn't digging the pigtail thing. I looked like a girl-band wannabe. And not in a good way . . . if there *was* a good way.

But, I thought grimly as Avery dropped us off at the beach house before squealing out of the driveway, I had bigger problems to deal with.

"What time is Emmett picking you up?" I asked Hannah as she waved good-bye to the departing Jetta. I tried to keep my voice casual.

She turned and looked at me blankly. "What?" she said. Her voice wasn't unfriendly so much as it was completely devoid of feeling. If anything, she looked a little surprised I was talking to her.

Which, considering we'd spent the past four hours together talking and even laughing as though we might actually be almost friends, was more than a little weird.

"Your date?" I prompted her.

She tossed her hair back with a well-practiced swish and turned to walk into the house.

"Later," she said vaguely.

I stared after her. What was going on? Did Hannah have multiple personalities? Was there a friendly Hannah and an evil Demon Spawn Hannah? Why had she made the effort to be nice to me earlier if just to act cold now? I mean, from the moment we climbed into Avery's Jetta, Hannah had gone out of her way . . . Oh, wait. *From the moment we climbed into Avery's Jetta* . . . Did that mean . . . Was Hannah being nice to me only on account of Avery? But why? Then I remembered Avery's snarky comment about wanting to cultivate a friendship with me so that I'd help her get her grades up. But she'd only been kidding, right? No one was that mercenary . . . were they?

Feeling vaguely disappointed, I followed Hannah into the house and headed up to my room to get Willow. She sprang up off her round pink bed and danced around me, wriggling her long, sleek body. I kicked off my sneakers and tossed them into my closet.

I slipped a martingale leash over Willow's head, and together we padded back down the hall, took a left at the foyer, a right into the kitchen with its pale wooden cupboards and gleaming stainless-steel appliances, and headed for the sliding glass back doors.

Although I still wasn't happy about being forced to live in the Demon's Lair, the house did have one thing going for it—it was right on the beach. There was a gorgeous view of the ocean from the kitchen and living room, both of which were equipped with soaring glass windows and doors to take full advantage of the scenery. And every afternoon Willow and I took a long walk along the water. The gentle roar of the waves as they crested against the shore relaxed me, and Willow liked finding dead fish to roll in.

We were almost out the back door when my father walked into the kitchen. He was wearing khaki shorts and a white button-down shirt, and his hair was still damp from the shower.

"Hi, honey," he said. "What are you doing?"

"Taking Willow for a walk," I said.

"Great! I'll come with you," Dad offered.

"Oh," I said. "Um, okay."

I still hadn't forgotten about my dad agreeing with Peyton that I was odd, although the anger had faded a bit, leaving behind a dull hurt. And while I knew I should be happy that my dad was making the effort to reconnect with me, it still felt weird spending time alone with him after how distant he'd been for the past few years. I knew he wanted a second chance; I just wasn't sure I wanted to give it to him.

Dad followed me out the door onto the back deck and then down the tall wooden stairs that descended to the beach. The sand shifted and felt hot under my bare feet. Willow let out a happy woof and dipped her nose down low to investigate a clump of dried seaweed. I gave her leash a gentle tug, and Willow abandoned her sniffing to prance happily at my side as we made our way down to the firmer sand at the shoreline. Occasionally the waves would lap up all the way to our feet, and each time Willow would jump to one side and reach down to nip playfully at the water.

"She seems like a nice dog," Dad remarked.

I felt a rush of pride, and stroked Willow's head behind her ears, just the way she likes it. "She is."

"Did she race?" he asked.

I nodded. "For two years. But she didn't win enough races for them to breed her. If the greyhound rescue group hadn't saved her, they would have put her down," I said.

My dad looked surprised. "Really? They destroy the dogs when they're done racing them?"

"Yes. It's criminal. They kill perfectly healthy, amazing dogs. The greyhound rescue groups save as many as they can, but they can't save them all," I said, and shook my head angrily. "It's so unfair and so irresponsible that the racing people breed so many greyhounds, and then throw them away as soon as the dogs aren't turning a profit for them."

"You sound very passionate on the subject," Dad remarked.

"I am. Every year Mom and I drive down to West Palm to go to a fund-raising picnic for Great Greys, the rescue group we got Willow from. They have games, and a costume contest, and a silent auction. Last year Willow and I won second prize for our Dorothy and Toto costumes—I was Toto; she was Dorothy. This year I want to dress up as—" But then I stopped abruptly and looked down at the wet sand. I was going to say Calvin and Hobbes, if I could figure out how to make a tiger suit for Willow. But then I remembered: We probably wouldn't be going to the fund-raiser this year.

"As what?" Dad asked.

"Actually . . . nothing. I don't think we're going to go this year."

"Why not?"

"The picnic is in November, on the first Saturday after Thanksgiving, and Sadie probably won't be back in time to go," I said. I shrugged. "It's not a big deal."

"I'll take you," Dad offered.

"That's okay. You don't have to," I said.

"I want to," Dad insisted.

"Okay . . . maybe," I said, trying to stay as noncommittal as I could.

The truth was, I didn't want to get my hopes up that he'd remember. After all, he hadn't come to any of my Mu Alpha Theta competitions last year, and he'd completely forgotten about parents' night at school, even though Sadie had called him twice to remind him.

"So how was your shopping trip?" Dad asked.

"Fine," I said.

"Your hair looks cute," Dad said, giving one of my pigtails a tug.

I remembered my girl-band hair and makeup, and blushed. I was going to wash my face and shake out my hair as soon as we got back to the house. "Just so you know, Hannah charged some clothes for me on her credit card. She said Peyton wouldn't mind," I said.

"I'm sure she won't," he said. "But don't you have a credit card of your own?"

"No," I said. I was going to add, *Sadie doesn't believe in credit cards*, but I knew from experience that this would probably lead to my dad muttering something under his breath about Sadie being a hippie, and then I'd yet again be put in the middle and feel weird about it.

"Well, we'll have to get you one," Dad said. "I'll call my bank this afternoon and have them issue you a card on my account."

"Oh ... thanks," I said awkwardly. And I knew that this was supposed to be the ultimate teen fantasy—parent-funded shopping sprees—but agreeing to it felt like I was betraying Sadie.

"I'm just glad that you and your sister can spend some time together and get to know each other," Dad continued.

"Sister?" I repeated, confused. "Do you mean Hannah?"

"Who else?"

"It's just ... she's *not* my sister," I said, probably a little more emphatically than necessary. But just because he decided to remarry didn't automatically mean that Peyton and Hannah became my family, too. It didn't work that way.

I glanced at my dad to see if my reaction had angered him. But he didn't look mad. He was quiet for a moment, and then he said, "I know this is all new and unfamiliar to you now. But I had hoped that your coming to live with us would be a chance for us to get closer. All of us."

And since I didn't have a response for this, I just stared down at the sand in front of me, which turned out to be a good thing, since I was able to sidestep a beached jellyfish.

We walked a bit farther, passing onto the public beach. I looked up to see if the lifeguard was on duty—dogs aren't technically allowed on the beach—and was glad to see that the guard shack was closed up.

"Wow, look at that," Dad said. He stopped and pointed out toward the water.

A parasurfer was deftly moving through the waves, riding one as it crested and then jumping easily to another. His blue-and-yellow parasail soared high overhead. A burst of wind came along, picking the surfer right up off of the water. He flew through the air, and then landed gracefully back on another big wave. A crowd had gathered on the beach to watch him, and they broke into applause. I doubted he could hear them, though. He was too far out, and the thrum of the water too loud.

"Wow," Dad said. "Do you think I'm too old to try that?"

"Yes," I said so quickly and so authoritatively that we both laughed. It was the first time we'd laughed together since I moved in. I could feel some of the tension that had been there between us break away.

The parasurfer glided gracefully onto shore and leaped off his board, pulling down on the sail as he did so. The parasail rippled in the wind before it succumbed and dove down into the sand. The crowd cheered some more, and then turned their attention to two teenage boys with long hair and baggy shorts who were attempting to surf on the high waves. They weren't as skilled as the parasurfer, and neither was able to stand for more than a few seconds before wiping out.

"Maybe I should stick to surfing," Dad mused, watching as one of the surfers rose unsteadily on his board and almost instantly crashed back down into the surf.

But I continued to watch the parasurfer, who had begun folding up his sail. He looked familiar, and I squinted at him, raising a hand to shield my eyes from the sun. And then my heart gave a jolt. It was Dex! I recognized his hair, which glinted coppery red in the sun. And just then, as I was staring at him, he looked right at me and raised a hand in greeting.

*Does he remember me?* I wondered. Maybe it was Willow he recognized; she was very distinctive, after all. I waved back and then turned away, not wanting him to think I was lusting after him, like Avery was.

Because I wasn't. Really.

Although I had to admit . . . the parasurfing? Very cool.

"You want to walk down a little farther?" Dad asked.

"Sure," I said. I gave Willow's leash a gentle tug—she'd grown bored and flopped down on the sand, resting her head on her front paws—and she stood, panting.

Dad started down the beach, his feet leaving tracks in the wet sand. Willow and I trailed after him. I glanced back once at Dex. He'd turned to talk to another wet suit–clad surfer, who was standing holding a board under one arm. But just before I turned back, I could have sworn that Dex had swiveled his head to look over at me . . . and that he had the same sardonic smile I'd seen on his face the day before, when he'd helped me up after my fall.

When we got back to the beach house, Dad asked me to grab the mail. So Willow and I walked around to the front of the house, through the side gate, and down the driveway to the mailbox. As I collected the usual bunch of circulars and bills, a Jeep pulled into the driveway and slowed to a stop. My stomach gave a lurch. I'd immediately recognized the Jeep; in fact, I'd been in the habit of scanning the school parking lot for it every morning. The Jeep belonged to Emmett. He'd arrived for his date with Hannah.

I'd actually somehow managed to forget about their date during my walk, thus proving how persuasive my powers of denial truly are. But it was hard to deny that he was here now, especially when the driver's-side door opened and Emmett hopped out. He was wearing a navy blue polo shirt over tan cargo shorts, and I felt a wave of longing wash over me at the sight of him standing there, all beautiful and golden and Emmett-like.

"Hey, Bloom," Emmett said when he saw me.

*Ugh.* Bloom again.

Emmett stopped and waited for me to catch up, so I had no choice but to walk over to him, hoping I wouldn't do or say anything dumb in his presence. But as soon as I got closer to him, I felt almost dizzy with longing. Not only did Emmett look great, but he smelled fantastic, too. Like soap and sun-warmed skin.

"Hi," I said. My voice sounded oddly high. I hoped he didn't notice.

Emmett hesitated. He looked at me, and then at the door. "Um, should I ring the bell?" he asked.

I realized then that I'd been staring at him. I *had* to stop doing that.

"No, of course not. Just come in. I'll get Hannah for you," I offered. The words tasted like sand in my mouth, but Emmett didn't seem to notice.

"Great," he said, brightening. "Cool dog, by the way." He held out his hand for Willow to sniff, but she loyally ignored him.

"Thanks," I said.

I opened the front door, and Emmett followed me inside. I took off Willow's leash, freeing her to amble off to the laundry room where her water bowl was kept, and then led Emmett back to the kitchen. Hannah was there, using a small mirror to pluck her eyebrows. She was so busy trying to extract a hair, her face scrunched up in concentration, that she didn't notice us come in.

"Hannah," I said.

"What?" Hannah asked in the bored voice she reserved for me. She still didn't look up from her mirror.

"Emmett's here," I said flatly.

"Hi," Emmett said.

"What?" Hannah asked. She finally looked up. When Hannah saw Emmett standing behind me, she whipped the mirror and tweezers behind her back. "Oh! Hi! I didn't hear the doorbell," she explained. Hannah blushed prettily, so that the tip of her nose turned pink.

"I came in with Miranda," Emmett explained. He smiled his amazing smile, where the right corner of his mouth curled up higher than the left.

"Oh," Hannah said, laughing nervously. "I'm so embarassed."

"It's okay. I thought you looked cute," Emmett said.

He did?

"You did?" Hannah asked. Her mouth curved up into her sex-kitten smile. She looked lovely in her new skirt paired with a strappy pink tank top. I felt a stab of defeat. I would never look that pretty. Never.

Emmett nodded, still grinning, and I was suddenly acutely aware of how superfluous I was to the conversation.

"Ready to go?" he asked.

Hannah nodded. "All set," she said, picking up a pink cardigan from the kitchen counter and draping it over her bare shoulders.

"Okay. Um. Well. Have fun," I said, and then I practically ran away from the kitchen. If Emmett or Hannah replied—or even heard me—they didn't let on.

The only silver lining in this bleak, black storm cloud was that I managed to wait until I got back to my room with the door safely shut behind me before I burst into tears.

# Chapter 15

$$\int_a^b \varphi'(t)\,dt = \varphi(b) - \varphi(a)$$

*SOCIAL SUICIDE?*
*GEEKHIGH.COM has learned that Miranda Bloom has been*
*put in charge of planning this year's Snowflake Gala. The event*
*has sucked hard in years past. . . . Will this be the first Snow-*
*flake worth attending? Or will Bloom make it even worse, thus*
*turning herself into the most reviled student at Geek High? Stay*
*tuned . . .*

"Finn!" I shrieked, when I found him in the dining hall, eating chicken-salad sandwiches with Charlie.

As my voice carried across the room, several heads swiveled toward me.

"Hey, Miranda," Padma called out in a tone of voice that made me know with absolute certainty that she'd already seen the blog. She tilted her head sympathetically to one side. "Are you okay?"

"Hey, Padma. I'm fine," I said, my teeth gritted. I hurried over to Finn and Charlie's table and sat down.

"You read it?" Finn asked, looking offensively cheerful. "What'd you think?"

"What did I think?" I repeated loudly.

"Shhh," Charlie admonished me. "What if someone hears you?"

Charlie was tired today. Her face was pale and wan, and she was speaking slowly and deliberately, as though her head hurt.

"I don't care!" I said.

"If anyone finds out Finn's the one writing that stupid blog, he'll get kicked out of school," Charlie reminded me wearily.

"Fine by me. Shout as loud as you want, Miranda," Finn said.

"Did you see what he wrote about me? Did you?" I asked Charlie. Charlie pushed the platter of sandwiches toward me, and I took one without enthusiasm.

"Yes. And I've already reamed him out about it," Charlie said patiently. Today she was wearing a frilly-edged purple blouse that clashed with her pink hair over skinny jeans tucked into knee-high brown suede boots. The outfit would have looked ridiculous on me, but Charlie looked like a fashion model.

"Haven't I been a good friend to you? Didn't I go to that ridiculous computer gaming convention with you in West Palm last year?" I asked Finn in an anguished whisper.

"I did it for you," Finn said, as he popped a carrot stick in his mouth.

"And exactly how does your twisted little brain figure that?" I asked.

"The only way to convince people that you're not the one writing the blog was to target you in it. Tomorrow I'm going to post a blind item: 'Guess which Geek High art genius and fashion maverick is being crushed on by a certain bespectacled barista at Grounded? Right now, he's expressing his love with free lattes . . . while he works up the nerve to ask her out.' "

"Oh, please," Charlie said, although I could tell from the way she'd perked up that she was pleased.

"So let me get this straight: You predict everyone's going to hate me after the Snowflake is a flop, and then think it's supposed to make me feel better when you blog about Mitch being in love with Charlie?" I asked.

"He's not in love with me," Charlie said. She smiled and shrugged modestly. "He's just a little smitten."

"You're not helping," I said to her.

"And next week I'm going to blog: 'What studly computer whiz was recently seen kissing an unknown curvy blonde? Inquiring minds now want to know exactly who she is, but word on the street is that she's an older woman. Developing . . .' "

"So now you're just making stuff up?" Charlie asked him.

"Who said I was making it up?" Finn asked, winking at her before popping another carrot stick into his mouth.

"The only person you kissed last week was your mother," Charlie shot back.

"That just goes to show how much you know," Finn said smugly.

Charlie just snorted.

"Jealous much?" Finn teased her.

"Why would I be jealous of your imaginary friend?" Charlie retorted.

But I couldn't pay attention to their bickering. I was too busy feeling sorry for myself. First, I was being forced to plan the Snowflake, totally against my will. And now Finn had broadcast to the school that if the Snowflake sucked yet again, it would be all my fault. I knew he meant well, but still. I really didn't need the added pressure.

"I guess I'd better start planning the stupid Snowflake," I said bleakly. "Headmaster Hughes said I should get a committee together to work on it. I'll put a sign-up sheet on the announcement board after lunch. Not that anyone's going to volunteer."

"Don't worry," Charlie said. "Finn and I will sign up."

"Finn will not sign up," Finn said.

"Finn, you *will* be on the committee," Charlie said menacingly.

"Stop being so bossy," Finn complained. "You can't make me."

"Oh, yes, I can. Don't forget: I can still totally kick your butt," Charlie said. She always gets irritable when she's in one of her down moods.

"I'd like to see you try," Finn said.

I just sighed and pushed my uneaten chicken-salad sandwich aside.

Considering how badly my week—no, my *year*—was going, I shouldn't have been surprised when Emmett approached me the next day before mod lit class began.

"Hey, Bloom," he said, plopping down into Charlie's vacant chair. She'd ducked into the ladies' room before class began, and hadn't come out yet.

"Oh . . . hey," I said.

"I was wondering . . . has your sister talked to you about me?"

"She's not my sister," I said automatically.

"Oh, right. I knew that," Emmett said. "Hannah told me that you're stepsisters."

I suddenly wondered what else Hannah might have said to him about me. After all, she wasn't exactly my biggest fan.

"Why?" I asked again. "I mean . . . did she say anything else about me?"

"No, not really," he said vaguely. "Just . . . you know. The usual."

*Gah! The usual?* What did that mean? Knowing Hannah, she probably said something like, "Miranda is the biggest dork I've ever met. Have you noticed the size of her nose? It's freakishly large. And her hair is so frizzy, it looks like she stuck her finger in a socket."

Total. Nightmare.

"The usual?" I repeated. My voice sounded a bit squeaky.

"Oh, she didn't say anything bad," Emmett said quickly. Too quickly.

Which meant that she'd said lots of bad things.

"Right," I said. "Well . . . I think class is going to start in a minute. . . ." *And clearly I can never speak to you ever again, since every time you see me you'll be thinking, "There's Miranda with the big nose and frizzy hair."*

"It's just . . . I couldn't tell if she had fun the other night when we went out. I mean, *I* had fun. And I *thought* she did. But I couldn't tell. And I wanted to ask her out again . . . I mean, I'm *going* to ask her out again . . . I was just hoping to get some inside information," he said with an embarrassed chuckle.

Well, wasn't that just *great*. As if it wasn't bad enough that Emmett was going out with my horrible stepsister, now he was expecting me to give him dating tips on how best to woo her.

I shrugged. "Honestly, I don't know. I'm not the person to ask," I said truthfully.

"Okay. Well, thanks, anyway. And if she does say anything to you . . . ?" His voice trailed off in a question mark.

"I'll tell you," I promised, although I was thinking, *I will?*

"Thanks," he said.

Charlie came into the classroom then, and Emmett quickly stood to vacate her chair.

"See you later, Bloom," he said.

"Bye," I said.

Charlie slid into her seat and turned to look at me, her eyebrows raised.

"I'll tell you later," I said quietly.

The last thing I wanted to do was go into it now. Especially since when I'd said good-bye to Emmett, I'd noticed that Felicity Glen had been leaning so far forward in an attempt to overhear our conversation, she'd nearly toppled out of her chair.

Mrs. Gordon walked in the room just as the bell rang.

"I hope everyone read the first five chapters of *Brave New World* and came prepared to discuss them," she said brightly. "Can anyone tell me the difference between a utopian and a dystopian society?"

Finn immediately raised his hand—which startled me. Finn never volunteers in class. Mrs. Gordon looked surprised too, and she nodded at him.

"A utopian society would be ideal," he said. "While a dystopian would be the opposite. A bad place with a totalitarian government."

"And which would better characterize the society Aldous Huxley has created in *Brave New World*?" Mrs. Gordon asked.

"Utopian," Finn said promptly.

"You would consider a society where free will and individuality have been stamped out a utopia?" Mrs. Gordon asked.

"No," Finn admitted. "That part would clearly suck. But I have to say, I would dig the free love vibe they had going on."

Tate Metcalf and Padma Paswan both snickered at this, although Tabitha Stone—who clearly didn't believe in joking around when it came to literature—sniffed and cast a disapproving look at Finn.

"Are you going to tell me what Emmett said?" Charlie asked later, when she and I were camped out at our usual table at Grounded. Finn had a teleconference with executives from a gaming company, so he hadn't joined us. I was starting to think that Finn had been right about Mitch, the counter guy, having a crush on Charlie. Mitch had been smiling dopily at her ever since we'd gotten there, and he'd already given us two rounds of mocha lattes on the house.

Mitch was actually sort of cute, although he used an inadvisable amount of hair gel to get his dark hair to stand up like porcupine quills. But he had a nice enough face—open brown eyes, a snub nose, a square chin, only slightly marred by a patch of acne on his forehead.

I gave Charlie the quick and dirty recap of my conversation with Emmett.

"At least he's talking to me," I said, determined to look on the bright side.

"About Hannah. And this was after he'd spent an evening out with her, and wasn't repulsed. So he has no excuse," Charlie said.

"She isn't always awful," I said, remembering how nice Hannah had been to me on our shopping trip. Even though I suspected that it was just an attempt to suck up to me on Avery's behalf.

"Are we talking about the same Hannah who gets up two hours early to maximize her before-school mirror time? Who knows all of the magazine beauty editors by name? Whose deepest thought is to wonder if they'll ever create a lip gloss that's both long-wearing and shiny?" Charlie asked. She licked a spot of whipped cream off her upper lip.

"I know," I said with a defeated moan. "What could she and Emmett possibly have in common? What would they talk about?"

"Maybe he's deeply interested in what the spring hemlines are doing," Charlie said.

"Or maybe he'll create that long-wearing lip gloss for this year's science fair," I suggested, my lips twitching up in a smile.

"Wouldn't that be quite the coup," Charlie said, snickering. "Hey, I saw your sign-up sheet for the Snowflake committee on the announcement board."

"Did you also notice that no one's signed up yet?" I asked.

"I signed up. And I signed Finn up, although we're going to have to blackmail him into actually showing up. Which won't be easy, considering Finn has no shame," Charlie said with an exasperated eye roll.

I felt a rush of gratitude toward her. Charlie wasn't going to let me crash and burn all alone . . . she was going to go down with me. And if that isn't friendship, I don't know what is.

"I should get going," Charlie said, stretching like a cat. She yawned. I knew that once she got home she'd go right to bed and sleep for fourteen hours straight, and even then her mom would have a hard time waking her up for school. I glanced over at Mitch. He was practically drooling as he watched Charlie, although she seemed completely unaware of his presence.

"I don't know what I'm going to do for the short story Mrs. Gordon is making us write. I have zero ideas," Charlie continued. She ran a hand through her short pink hair, leaving it adorably tousled.

"It's going to be tough," I said, thinking back to the assignment Mrs. Gordon had given us that morning. We had to write a short story in the spare style that many of the great modern writers favored.

"Yeah, right," Charlie said with a snort. "It'll be a breeze for you. In fact, you probably already have one lying around somewhere you can turn in."

"No, I don't," I protested. "First of all, nothing that I write is good enough to use for a class assignment. And second, she said to write it in a modern style. I don't do that. I don't even know how to do that."

"Okay, whatever you say," Charlie said, sounding annoyingly superior.

"What?" I asked.

"Miranda, sometimes you are so clueless," Charlie said, shaking her head.

I love Charlie, and she's a good friend and all, but I hate it when she gets like this. It's so irritating.

# Chapter 16

$$\int_a^b \nabla\varphi \cdot d\alpha = \varphi\,(b) - \varphi(a)$$

"**M**iranda, stay after class for a minute, please," Mr. Gordon said when the bell rang at the end of the study hall that doubled as my math class. I'd already completed all of the mathematics coursework that Geek High offered, and so I was now enrolled in a special self-study course. This semester I was working on advanced multivariable calculus. Mr. Gordon had gotten my syllabus from the math department at Harvard. Which sounds impressive, I know, but trust me: *yawn*.

I once read a book about an autistic man who could calculate sums in his head, like me. But, unlike me, numbers soothed him. He saw numbers as colors, experienced them as emotions. And he viewed his extraordinary math talent as a gift.

It's the exact opposite for me. I don't love numbers, and I can't lose myself in them, like when I get absorbed in a good book. When presented with an equation, I can solve it easily. But that doesn't bring me any pleasure. All it does is remind me what an oddball I am.

"Sure," I said to Mr. Gordon. I shoved the heavy textbook into my already bulging knapsack.

Mr. Gordon waited until the other students had trooped out of the room, and then he leaned back against his desk and looked at me thoughtfully. He was tall and gangly and bald on top, with a fringe of hair around his ears, like Friar Tuck. He wore round tortoiseshell glasses and a revolving selection of argyle sweater-vests and bow ties. On cold days he always sported an ancient tweed jacket with worn leather pads on the elbows.

"We had our first meeting for the Mu Alpha Theta team yesterday afternoon, and I noticed you weren't there," Mr. Gordon said.

I'd known this conversation was coming, and I'd been dreading it. Because the thing is, I hate to let anyone down. And I knew that what I was about to say was going to disappoint Mr. Gordon, who was my second-favorite teacher, after his wife.

"Yeah, I know. I decided not to be on the team this year," I said.

"I see. Would you mind telling me why?" Mr. Gordon asked.

"I just thought I'd like to try a different extracurricular. I was thinking about signing up to work on the *Ampersand*." The *Ampersand* was the literary magazine that Geek High published four times a year, and it won all sorts of national awards. I knew I'd never get published in it, not as a sophomore, but I was hoping to get one of the grunt jobs and work my way up.

"I see. Well, we'll certainly miss you," Mr. Gordon said.

"Thanks," I said, smiling awkwardly at him.

"See you tomorrow," Mr. Gordon said.

"Bye." I headed out of the class feeling like a total heel. Mr. Gordon couldn't have been nicer about my defection from the team . . . yet somehow that made me feel even worse than if he'd tried to guilt me into staying on.

But right now I had bigger problems to worry about. The first meeting of the Snowflake Gala committee, of which I was chairperson, was to take place that afternoon after school. And the last time I'd looked at the sign-up list I'd posted on the school bulletin board two weeks earlier, Charlie was still the only one who had signed up. And since Finn had pointedly drawn a line through his name, it looked like we were going to be a committee of two.

• • •

"I don't think anyone else is going to show up," I said gloomily.

"Who cares? It'll be fun having just the three of us," Charlie declared. She gave Finn—whom she had practically dragged into Mr. Aburro's room, where I was holding the meeting—a meaningful look. "Right, Finn?"

Finn looked up from his laptop. He was online, playing a computer game.

"Don't distract me," he said, waving Charlie off. "I'm conquering Eurasia."

The door to the room suddenly banged open. I looked up hopefully. A late arrival to the committee, perhaps? But my hope quickly soured to stunned disbelief when I saw who had entered: Felicity Glen and Morgan Simpson.

"What do you want?" I asked ungraciously.

"We're here for the Snowflake meeting," Felicity said.

"Oh, ha, ha," Charlie said. "Very funny. Now why don't you two just scurry along. I'm sure the coven is missing you."

Felicity dumped her pink tote bag on a desk with a thud. She was wearing a sky blue twinset, and a matching headband pushed back her shiny dark hair. A silver Tiffany Beane necklace hung around her neck. (I knew that it was a Tiffany Beane necklace only because Felicity had one in gold that her dad got her the last time she visited him in Manhattan, and she wore it everywhere.)

"We're joining the committee," she said stubbornly. "And you can't stop us."

"But . . . *why*?" Charlie asked her.

I knew what Charlie was thinking. Felicity was no more fond of us than we were of her. Why would she go out of her way to sign up for a committee that would mean we'd all have to work together?

"Just because you were put in charge—which was totally unfair, by the way—doesn't mean that you should be able to run the Snowflake all on your own," Felicity said, sounding resentful.

"What? Do you mean . . . *you* wanted to be in charge of the Snow-flake?" I asked, utterly dumbfounded that this could possibly be true. Who would want this thankless task?

Felicity crossed her arms and glared at me. "You don't have to rub it in that you got picked, Miranda," she said.

Picked? *Picked?* I was just about to open my mouth to point out that I hadn't been *picked* so much as *forced* into heading up the Snowflake com-mittee, but before I could set the record straight, Morgan jumped in.

"And don't think you're going to stick us with all of the crap jobs, either," Morgan said. "We want to work on something fun. Like picking out the theme or auditioning bands."

"Huh?" I said. Theme? Bands? What were they talking about?

"Let's face it: The Snowflake has totally sucked in recent years," Fe-licity began.

None of us could argue with her on this point.

"What we need to do is make the Snowflake more like a prom . . . and less like a lecture. In fact, I think we should cut the speakers out altogether," Felicity continued.

"Actually," I said, "I was thinking along the same lines. Not the prom part . . . although actually that isn't a completely terrible idea."

"Gee, thanks," Felicity said sarcastically.

"The problem is that I don't know if Headmaster Hughes is going to go along with it. He thinks the speakers are the whole point of having the Snowflake," I continued.

"Well, it's your job to convince him otherwise," Felicity said. "Now, what's our budget? Because I know of a great band, but they won't show up for less than a grand."

"Last year, Headmaster Hughes got Mr. Sanchez to deejay for free," I said dryly. Mr. Sanchez, who taught Spanish, French, and German, had a music collection that consisted largely of Lionel Richie and Whitney Houston. "So something tells me he's not going to spring for a thousand dollars for your band."

"Well, my boyfriend's band might do it for free," Morgan said.

Charlie, Finn, and I looked at her in stunned disbelief.

"What?" she said defensively. "I have a boyfriend. So what?"

"Who is he?" Charlie asked.

"His name is Snake. He goes to Orange Cove High," Morgan said.

"Is his band any good?" I asked, managing to keep a straight face at the name *Snake*. I hoped for his sake that it was just a nickname, and not what his parents had actually named him.

"They're . . . not bad," Morgan said uncertainly.

The expression on Felicity's face suggested that she didn't agree with Morgan's lukewarm endorsement, but just didn't want to say so out loud. Which didn't bode well. Not at all.

"But they are free," Morgan pointed out. "Snake said they needed more gigs for the experience."

"Well," I hedged, "it's certainly an idea. But like I said, I don't know if Headmaster Hughes is going to go for the idea of a live band, even if they are free."

"I think we should plan as though he will. And you'll just have to find a way to persuade him," Felicity announced. And then, with what could only be described as an evil glint in her eyes, she continued. "Besides, what will people think if they find out you had a chance to actually do something cool for the Snowflake this year and didn't? Everyone will hate you."

Her threat was clear: If the Snowflake was the same old boring-speeches-and-bad-music it had been in recent years, Felicity would make sure everyone knew it was my fault. I wanted to tell her not to bother—Finn had already taken care of disseminating this tidbit to the entire student body, although he continued to insist that he did it to "protect" me.

"Felicity, why don't you take your prom idea and stick it up your—" Charlie began, but I cut her off before she could complete the thought. Like it or not, we'd need all the help we could get on the Snowflake committee. Even if that help was in the form of the Felimonster and her Toady.

"Charlie, it's okay. Look, I'll talk to Headmaster Hughes and see what I can do. But I'm not making any promises—he has the final say. Okay?" I said.

"Excellent," Felicity said with satisfaction. "Now, what should we do for our theme? Would it be too lame to do Under the Sea? Because another idea I had is the Enchanted Forest." Felicity made a game show hostess sweep of the hand in emphasis. "We could fill the entire auditorium with trees and twinkle lights. How does that sound?"

"Expensive," I said. "I think our budget is more along the lines of streamers and balloons."

But Felicity just waved at me. "Details, details," she said airily. "Don't worry about that yet. Let's just try to come up with a theme, and we'll worry about the specifics later."

# Chapter 17

$$\iint_Q f = \int_c^d \left[ \int_a^b f(x, y) \, dx \right] dy = \int_a^b \left[ \int_c^d f(x, y) \, dy \right] dx$$

After the Snowflake meeting, Charlie's mom dropped me off at the beach house. I had to swallow back a groan when I saw a familiar Jeep parked next to Avery's Jetta in the driveway. I sighed. Emmett was here. Again. He'd been over every day after school for two weeks straight. I was handling it the only way I knew how—avoiding the happy couple. Whenever Emmett was over, I made a point of staying in my room. Or the "guest room," as Peyton continued to refer to it.

I wasn't in denial any longer. It was pretty clear that Emmett and Hannah were an official item. But that didn't mean that I wanted to see them snuggled up together on the couch, his arm draped casually over her shoulders, either. I wasn't a masochist.

I let myself in the house as quietly as I could, and was about to head down the hallway toward my room when I heard someone calling my name from the direction of the living room.

"Miranda? Is that you?"

I recognized the voice. It was Avery. I could hardly suppress my groan. I'd been just as intent on avoiding Avery. Avery always had an angle. A few weeks earlier—the day after the shopping trip, as a matter of fact—she'd tried to cajole me into helping her with her book report on *Romeo and Juliet*. I'd agreed—unenthusiastically—only to find out that when she'd asked for help, what she'd really wanted was for me to write it for her. I refused, of course, but it hadn't dampened her enthusiasm for trying to enlist me into service as her own personal homework slave.

I was about to make a run for it, but Avery appeared in the hallway, an ingratiating smile stretched across her face.

"I'm so glad you're home. I totally need your help," she announced.

"Sorry, I can't. I'm crazy busy this afternoon," I said, although I really wasn't at all sorry. But it was true that I was busy. I had a ton of homework, including finishing up the short story Mrs. Gordon had assigned us to write for mod lit.

"Oh, this won't take that long," Avery said. "Come on." She grabbed my hand and pulled me after her.

I hesitated, but finally allowed myself to be led back to the living room. I knew at once that this was a mistake, and that I should have found an excuse to get out of there. The room was awash in couples. Emmett and Hannah were ensconced on the couch, wrapped around each other as usual. Hannah's cat, Madonna, was curled up next to them, her creepy yellow eyes open just a crack. The Wonder Twins, Britt and Tiffany (I still couldn't tell them apart), were there with their hulking and not very bright-looking football-player boyfriends. One twin was perched on her boyfriend's lap; the other was lying down on the floor resting her head on her boyfriend's leg while she watched E!. And off to one side, sitting on a modular cream leather chair, was Dex.

I hadn't seen Dex since the afternoon my dad and I had watched him parasurfing, and he smiled at me in that slightly mocking way he had. I could feel myself flushing red under his gaze, and looked quickly away . . . but not before I noticed that Avery's purple knapsack was resting just a few inches away from where Dex was sitting. It wasn't hard to figure out that the two of them had gotten together after all.

Not that I cared. Obviously. It wasn't any of my business who Dex dated.

"Hey, Miranda," one of the twins said with a lazy wave.

"Hi, Bloom," Emmett said. "Did you finish your short story for mod lit? It's due tomorrow."

I nodded. "I just have to spell-check it one last time, but it's mostly done. You?"

"Yeah, finally, but it was tough. What did you write about?"

This I didn't want to answer. Because my short story was about a girl whose boyfriend had been stolen away by her awful stepsister. And—other than the part where Emmett had never been my boyfriend, of course—I'd borrowed quite heavily from my own life to write it. At least, the emotions were all mine.

"Just, you know . . . a coming-of-age story," I lied, and gave a silent prayer that Mrs. Gordon wouldn't ask us to read our stories aloud.

"So, is there any way you could possibly look this over for me? Pleeeeease?" Avery asked, thrusting a piece of paper into my hand. I glanced down at it. It was a homework assignment. The directions instructed that the students were to graph out a series of geometric equations. The only part that Avery had filled out so far was her name at the top of the page.

"Check what? You haven't done it yet," I said.

Avery laughed. "I know! But aren't you supposed to be a math genius? Emmett said you're the best math student in your school."

I felt myself blush even darker. Emmett had said that about me?

"Well . . . I don't know about that. But I can't check an assignment you haven't done yet," I said.

"I thought maybe you could just do it for me," Avery said in a wheedling tone. "It would only take you a few minutes, right?"

Of course. Typical Avery.

"But don't you have to learn this? Aren't they going to test you on it eventually?" I asked.

Avery shrugged. "I'll worry about that later. Anyway, homework counts for forty percent of our grade."

I stared at her, disliking her more and more with each passing minute. If it wasn't bad enough that she was trying to get me to cheat for her, she was putting me on the spot in front of everyone. Inadvertently, I glanced over at Dex. He was watching us, and when our eyes met a thrill shot through me. It was that zing again, the same one I'd experienced the first time we met.

What was that? I wondered. And had he noticed it, too? Or was it a one-sided zing?

Dex raised his eyebrows and cocked his head slightly to one side, as if to say, *How are you going to handle this?* I felt my cheeks grow hot. *Great.* And now he was going to mock me.

Well. It didn't matter. Because either way my answer would be the same. Forcing myself to look away from Dex, I handed the paper back to Avery.

"I'm not doing your homework for you," I said firmly.

Avery's smile slipped off her face, and her lips extended into a bratty pout. "I guess you're not as smart as everyone thinks you are," she said pointedly.

I almost laughed at this. Did she really think I was going to fall for that?

"Miranda's amazing in math," Emmett said. I turned to stare at him, shocked that he was coming to my defense. Emmett was frowning at Avery. "She's the star of the Mu Alpha Theta team."

Okay, that wasn't so helpful. I really didn't want it broadcast to Dex . . . I mean, to everyone, not just Dex . . . that I had been in Mu Alpha Theta. I might as well have the word *dork* tattooed on my forehead.

Avery's nose crinkled up. "Mu Alpha what-a?" she repeated. "What's that? I've never heard of it."

"Isn't that, like, the *math* club?" Hannah asked, looking horror-struck.

Suddenly everyone was staring at me as though I were some sort of sideshow freak. I could feel the stain on my cheeks darken and spread down over my neck and chest.

"Yes," I said crisply. "It is. Excuse me, I have to go walk my dog," I said, and then I turned and stalked out of the room with as much dignity as I could muster.

Willow was sleeping on the flokati rug when I walked into my room. She didn't get up, although she opened one amber-colored eye to see who'd come in, and her tail went *thump-thump-thump* against the floor when she saw it was me.

"Lazybones," I said.

Willow yawned and stretched, arching her spine up like a cat.

"Come on. Let's go for a walk," I said, grabbing her leash off my bed. I leaned over and slipped the martingale collar over Willow's narrow head, and she finally deigned to stand up.

I decided to go out the front door and walk around the house to the beach, rather than head through the living room to the sliding glass back doors. I didn't want to have to have to see Hannah and her friends again. Besides, knowing my luck, I'd end up tripping over one of the twins sprawled out on the floor.

I tried to clear my thoughts and focus on how Emmett had called me Miranda—not Bloom!—for the first time, *and* he'd defended me when Avery was bullying me. That was progress. Of course, there was still the not-insignificant problem of Hannah, but surely Emmett would eventually—someday—figure out that my stepsister was a narcissist.

And yet . . . my thoughts wouldn't stay focused on Emmett. Instead, totally against my will, they kept flitting back to Dex, and those startling pale blue eyes, and that sardonic smile, and the zing that always hit me when I saw him. Which was really freaking annoying. Shouldn't I be able to decide which boy I was going to obsess about?

Willow and I had just started down the beach when I heard someone calling my name.

"Hey, Miranda! Wait up!"

I turned to see who was hailing me, and my mouth nearly dropped open. It was *Dex*. It was as though I'd been thinking about him so intently, I'd conjured him out of thin air.

"Hey," I said.

"Do you mind if I walk with you?" he asked.

"Well . . . sure. I mean, no, I don't mind," I said, although I was thinking: *What? What?* "But what about Avery?"

"What about her?"

"Won't she mind that you're with me? I mean, not *with me* with me, obviously—I didn't mean to imply that we were together in anything other than a proximity sort of way." *Gah.* "But . . . just that you're not, um, with her, I mean," I finished lamely.

"Why would she mind?" Dex asked. His brow puckered in confusion.

"Well . . . aren't you two going out?"

"You think I'm going out with Avery?" Dex repeated, and then he laughed and shook his head. He set off down the beach, and Willow and I had to trot a few steps to catch up with him.

"Why are you laughing? Avery's really pretty," I said. And it was true—Avery may not have been my favorite person, but there was no denying that she was attractive.

"For a shark," Dex said. "She'll make a great lawyer someday; that's for sure."

I smiled at this—I could see Avery striding around a courtroom, terrorizing her opposing counsel—but glanced over at him. "Does *she* know you're not dating?" I asked.

"Let's put it this way—she made it clear she was interested, and I made it equally clear I was not," Dex said. "But that's as much detail as I'm going to give you."

Which, of course, made me insanely curious to know all of the details. Had Avery thrown herself at Dex? Asked him out? But then another thought occurred to me.

"So why'd you come over today?" I asked. "I had the impression it was a couples thing in there."

"Yeah, well, I didn't know that before I got here. Geoff and Roy are friends of mine, and I came along with them," Dex said.

"Those guys are your friends?" I asked.

I assumed that Geoff and Roy were the two mouth-breathers that the twins had been draped over. If so, they looked like they had the combined intelligence of a sneaker, and probably enjoyed crumpling soda cans against their rocklike skulls in their free time. But why was I surprised? Dex was a jock, and they were clearly jocks, and it was common knowledge that jocks hung out together.

But on the other hand . . . Dex didn't strike me as the typical jock. I didn't know him very well, of course, but he just seemed . . . sharper than that. Like there was more to him than just muscles and testosterone.

"Yeah, we're friends. Why?" Dex asked.

"I don't know. They just seemed . . ." I stopped, searching for an adjective that wouldn't offend him, but also wouldn't make it sound like I was lusting after him. ". . . not like you," I finished.

"Maybe not. But then, you don't know me very well, do you?" Dex said, his lips curving up into a half smile. He leaned over to pick up a small pink shell off the sand, and threw it overhand into the surf.

"I guess not," I said.

"So what do you want to know?" he asked, winging another shell.

"About you?" I asked. I wasn't sure where we were going with this.

"About anything," Dex said. "Go ahead . . . ask me anything."

I tried to think of something interesting and witty, but I couldn't think of anything.

"What's your last name?" I finally asked.

Dex chuckled, and I flushed. Okay, it wasn't the most original question I could have asked him, but at least it was better than something really stupid, like, *If you were an animal what would you be?* (For the record, I'd be an elephant. They're really smart, and beautiful in a pachyderm sort of way, and they trample anyone who screws with them, which is a definite bonus.)

"McConnell," he said.

"Is that Irish?" I asked.

"Can't you tell?" he asked, pointing to his red hair.

"Hey, L'Oréal has some pretty convincing shades," I said. Willow stopped to examine a piece of seaweed, sniffing it from all sides, and I had to give her leash a gentle tug to get her moving again as we continued our walk down the beach.

"You think I'm the kind of guy who dyes his hair?" Dex asked with mock horror.

I shrugged. "Hard to say. As you yourself pointed out, I don't really know you," I said, shooting him a sideways smile.

Dex laughed. "You're right; I did."

"Besides, you're wrong. I know all about you," I continued.

"Oh, really?"

"Yup. You're the star lacrosse player at Orange Cove High. You like to take chances, hence the parasurfing. You're friends with jocks. And you have pretty girls throwing themselves at you. Doesn't that say it all?" I said lightly.

Dex stopped suddenly. I came to a halt, too, and turned to look at him. He had a curious expression on his face.

"Is that what you think? That I can be summed up by those four things?" he asked.

And suddenly I had the feeling that I'd offended him. For the first time since I'd met Dex, his expression was serious. Grave, even. All traces of the mocking light had disappeared from his light blue eyes.

"I'm sorry. I was just kidding," I said quickly.

"Were you?" he asked.

"Well . . . sort of," I said. I had to look away from the intensity of his gaze. "But is it so wrong to draw conclusions about someone based on their hobbies and friends? They say a lot about who we are," I pointed out.

"Do they?" he said softly. I looked back at him, then, and as our eyes met I felt a jolt that seemed to start in my heart before zipping out to the tips of my fingers and toes. It was a super-zing, a zing on steroids.

"I'd better get back," Dex suddenly said. "That Emmett guy said he'd give me a ride home. See you later, Miranda."

And then, without waiting for me to respond, Dex turned and walked back up the beach toward the house. As I watched him stride away, his shoulders squared and his gait relaxed and unhurried, an uncomfortable knot twisted in my stomach. Had I hurt his feelings? And if so, how? Surely, a good-looking, popular jock was used to people seeing him as a good-looking, popular jock, right?

But clearly I had offended him. And suddenly I had the distinct impression that perhaps I was guilty of judging Dex in much the same way that people judged me when they heard where I went to school and how I was gifted in math, and immediately concluded I was a geek.

*I'd better go apologize,* I thought. *For real, this time.*

I turned decisively and hurried back, Willow beside me, following Dex's footprints in the sand. But by the time I got to the beach house and went around the front to the driveway, Emmett's Jeep—along with Emmett and Dex—was gone.

# Chapter 18

$$\iint\limits_{R} \left( \frac{\partial Q}{\partial x} - \frac{\partial P}{\partial y} \right) dx\, dy = \oint_{C} P\, dx + Q\, dy$$

**M**rs. Boxer was at her desk when I arrived at Headmaster Hughes's office for our scheduled meeting.

"Is he in?" I asked.

Mrs. Boxer was stuffing and licking a stack of envelopes emblazoned with the Geek High emblem on the upper left-hand corner. I was secretly hoping that Headmaster Hughes had forgotten all about our appointment, that he had, in fact, forgotten about assigning me to head up the Snowflake altogether . . . but I knew this was unlikely. It would solve everything, though. I'd be off the hook, and Felicity could take over—as I knew she was itching to do—and everyone would be happy.

"Yes, indeedy!" Mrs. Boxer chirped in her girlie voice. "He said to send you right in the instant you got here."

"Great," I said without enthusiasm.

"Would you like a cupcake?" Mrs. Boxer asked. She twirled around on her task chair and whipped a shirt box off of her credenza. She turned back, popped the lid off the box, and offered it up to me. I peered inside. There were three rows of five cupcakes lined up inside, each topped with a mound of pink frosting.

"Oh, thanks, but I'm not hungry," I demurred.

"Go ahead . . . take one!" she insisted.

So I reached in the box and took a cupcake. It was wrapped in a silver-foil cupcake liner, which I peeled off before taking a bite. It tasted terrible, probably the worst cupcake I'd ever had in my life. I don't know anything about baking, but I suspected that Mrs. Boxer had added about four times the amount of sugar the recipe called for.

I forced myself to swallow the bite I'd taken, and then said, "Thanks. It's really good."

My mouth was so puckered up from sugar shock, it was hard to get the words out.

Mrs. Boxer beamed. "Baking is a hobby of mine," she confided. "People are always telling me I should write a cookbook."

"Oh, yeah, you totally should," I lied. What would she call her cookbook? *Baking Your Way to Diabetes*?

"Maybe someday," Mrs. Boxer trilled happily. "You'd better hurry along. The headmaster is waiting for you."

I smiled at her, and, still clutching the rest of my cupcake (I'd have to hold on to it until I could find somewhere to throw it out), I pulled open the door to Headmaster Hughes's office and walked in.

Headmaster Hughes was again sitting behind his enormous desk, the telephone tucked under one ear. I hesitated at the door, not wanting to interrupt, but he gestured for me to come in and sit down.

"Yes, that's right.... No, I quite agree.... Yes ... No ... No ... Yes ... I see ... How about that," he was saying into the phone. "Thank you for bringing this to my attention. I'll definitely look into it. Although I don't know if a campus-wide ban on pencils would necessarily be the *best* course of action to take. Perhaps we could first try incorporating classroom instruction on how best to use—or not use—the pencil sharpener." He paused and held up a finger, signaling to me that he'd be off in one minute. "Thank you for calling, Mrs. Brown ... Yes ... You have a good day too. And I hope Aidan's finger heals soon ... Yes ... No ... Yes ... All right ... Good-bye."

Headmaster Hughes hung up the phone, looking remarkably unflustered. Apparently he was used to dealing with ridiculous requests from parents. If I were headmaster of a school—a school for gifted children, no less—and a parent called me up insisting that the school ban all pencils because her son had self-inflicted an injury while goofing around with the pencil sharpener, I'd probably get a little snippy. But not Headmaster Hughes. He looked utterly calm as he gazed unblinkingly at me.

"Miranda," he said meaningfully.

I had the feeling I was supposed to answer, so I said, "Yes, sir?"

"How *are* you?" he asked.

"Fine, thanks. Um. And you?" I always feel ridiculous making small talk with grown-ups. It probably stems from a childhood where nearly every grown-up I came into contact with immediately began quizzing me. *What's 57 times 322? What's 5946 divided by 576?* It always made me feel like such a freak, I got used to looking down at my feet, muttering the answer, and then fleeing the scene.

"I'm in excellent health, thank you for asking," the headmaster said gravely. "What can I do for you today, Miranda?"

A flicker of hope. Had he forgotten about Snowflake?

"You wanted to see me," I reminded him cautiously.

"So I did. Mr. Gordon has informed me that you're not participating in Mu Alpha Theta this year," Headmaster Hughes said.

This threw me for a loop. It was the last thing I'd expected we'd be discussing during our meeting. And wait . . . why had Mr. Gordon told the headmaster I wasn't going to be on the Mu Alpha Theta team? First Sadie, now Mr. Gordon . . . Why was everyone suddenly so keen on talking to Headmaster Hughes about me?

"That's right," I said.

He steepled his hands together so that the index fingers pointed straight up and pressed against each other, and continued to stare at me.

"And why," he asked, "did you make that choice?"

"Not to join Mu Alpha Theta?" I asked. He nodded. "I just wanted to try something different. I'm going to work on the *Ampersand* instead."

"I see," Headmaster Hughes said, sounding like he didn't see at all. "Well. That puts us in a very difficult position."

What was he talking about? And why did I suddenly feel like a bug flying too close to a spider's web?

"A difficult position?" I repeated.

Headmaster Hughes sighed portentously. "The Mu Alpha Theta team doesn't have what you might call a deep bench. As you know, Barry Sonnegard graduated last year, which has left a hole on the team. But that's nothing compared to losing you. . . ." He shook his head sadly. "Without you, the team doesn't have a hope of beating St. Pius at the first matchup in January, much less of winning state."

"That's not necessarily true," I said. "Leila Chang did really well last year. And Sanjiv Gupta could be a strong player, if he gets over his performance anxiety. I think his parents put a lot of pressure on him. He always did better at competitions when his dad wasn't there."

"But St. Pius has Austin Strong," Headmaster Hughes said.

Austin Strong. Just the name set my teeth on edge. Austin's almost as good at math as I am. *Almost*. He's also an egotistical pain in the butt. He'd probably go to Geek High if he didn't live all the way down in Fort Lauderdale, where he's by far the smartest kid at his school. It's totally gone to his head. On his MySpace Web page, he even claims that *his* nickname is the Human Calculator. Which shouldn't annoy me—after all, it's not like I was ever fond of being called that—but for some reason, it rubbed me the wrong way. And if St. Pius was able to actually beat Geek High at a Mu Alpha Theta competition for the first time in history, Austin Strong would be unbearable.

Well. It wasn't my problem. I was off the team. The Geek High Mu Alpha Theta team would have to go on and do their best without me.

But Headmaster Hughes seemed to be sensing my ambivalence.

"Is there any way I can talk you into rejoining the team?" he asked.

I shook my head. "No. I'd really rather be on the *Ampersand* staff," I said. The headmaster looked at me skeptically, so I took in a deep breath and told him the truth. "I made a promise to myself that this year I'd find my passion. Figure out what I love to do. I know it isn't math . . . but it's possible it might be writing. So I want to explore that."

Headmaster Hughes sighed. "Well, if your mind is made up, I suppose there's nothing I can do to change it," he said. He sounded disappointed but resigned.

Which actually sort of startled me. Headmaster Hughes wasn't the type of guy to give up easily. I'd been bracing myself for at least another ten to fifteen minutes of guilt trips and bullying.

"So, why don't we turn our attention to other matters? How are your plans for the Snowflake Gala progressing?" the headmaster asked. He laced his hands and tapped his two index fingers together.

*Rats.* He hadn't forgotten.

"Well. We had our first committee meeting a few weeks ago," I began. I'd been trying to think of a way to broach our proposal to overhaul the Snowflake, and finally decided that a direct approach would be best. "And I think—the whole committee thinks—that the single most effective thing we could do to increase student body interest in the Snowflake would be to . . . well, change things a bit."

I didn't chicken out. Not exactly. But Headmaster Hughes was looking so stern—in fact, more stern with each passing moment—and I thought he might respond better to a subtler approach.

"Change things," he repeated slowly. "And what exactly are you proposing to change?"

I drew a deep breath and plunged in. "Well. First of all, the sit-down dinner isn't very popular. So I thought that maybe we should start by cutting that."

The headmaster's brow furrowed. "No dinner? But then when will the speakers address the students?" he asked.

"They wouldn't," I said. "I thought—that is, the whole committee thought—that the Snowflake would be a lot more popular if we didn't have speakers."

And there it was. Headmaster Hughes stared at me. I seemed to have stunned him into silence, which was ... well, it was a bit intimidating. Although I did learn that when his office was that quiet, I could actually hear the rhythmic *tick-tick-tick* of his gold-domed desk clock.

"No speakers?" he finally asked, carefully enunciating the words, as though to make sure that there was to be no confusion.

"Yes. The thing is, if you really want to make the Snowflake more popular with the students, then you have to make it into the sort of event that they'll actually want to go to. And what teenager wants to spend a Saturday night listening to some boring speaker drone on and on about integrating programs for the gifted and talented into regular school curricula?" I said.

"Dr. Keith is one of the preeminent authorities on academically gifted teenagers in the country. I would have thought the students would be eager to hear what he had to say on the subject. In fact, I've always taken great care to choose speakers of interest to the students," Headmaster Hughes said, sounding rather stiff.

*Gah.* I'd offended him, which I really hadn't wanted to do. Not because what I was saying wasn't true—Dr. Keith, the speaker last year, had been so boring, kids were actually face-planting right into their plates of chicken parmigiana—but because I was worried that if Headmaster Hughes got defensive, he might be less open to making the changes I was proposing.

"They *were* of interest." A lie, but it was for a good cause. "It's just..." I struggled to find the right words. "If your goal is to make the Snowflake more *popular*"—I emphasized the word, hoping that I could make my point without having to mention that every year, a full third of the student body simultaneously came down with the flu on the night of the Snowflake—"I think cutting the dinner-and-speeches part of the night would really help with that."

More silence. More clock ticking.

"Did you have any ideas other than cutting the dinner and speeches?" Headmaster Hughes finally asked.

"Actually, yes," I said brightly. "We thought that we could get a band to play. And decorate the gym in a theme. Like Under the Sea or Enchanted Forest. And everyone would get dressed up in black-tie."

"So you're suggesting that we turn the Snowflake into a *prom*," Headmaster Hughes said, his voice dripping with scorn.

Apparently the headmaster was not a fan of proms.

I did one of those nod-and-a-shrug moves. "I think it would be fun. And, after all, Geek High doesn't have a regular prom," I said.

"Notting Hill Independent School for Gifted Children," Headmaster Hughes automatically corrected me.

And apparently he wasn't a fan of the Geek High nickname, either.

He drew in a loud, deep breath, and then took a long time blowing it back out. Then he bridged his hands together again and stared down at them for what felt like a very long time.

"It would seem that we have a dilemma," he finally said.

"We do?" I asked. I was getting that bug-near-a-web feeling again.

"We both want something that we can't have unless the other agrees. And in both cases, the other isn't agreeing," he said.

"I'm sorry, sir . . . I don't think I really understand what you're saying," I said.

"First, you want to turn the Snowflake Gala into a prom, while I want the basic format to remain unchanged. And unless I agree, you can't make your proposed changes," he said.

I suddenly had the feeling that I didn't want to hear the second part.

"And second, I want you to be on the Mu Alpha Theta team, and you've decided you don't wish to participate. Since extracurricular activities are elective, I can't force you to be on the team," he said.

"No, sir," I said firmly. "You can't."

"So I'd say this is quite a pickle we have," the headmaster continued, ignoring my comment.

Silly me for thinking we'd gotten past the whole Mu Alpha Theta issue. I should have known that Headmaster Hughes wouldn't have given up on it so easily. It wasn't his style. The man was like a pit bull. A *bald* pit bull.

"I guess," I said cautiously.

"Do you have any ideas on how we could solve our problem?" Headmaster Hughes asked. He looked a little . . . well, gleeful, actually. He was frown-smiling wider than I'd ever seen before. I'll be honest: It freaked me out.

"No," I said. "Do you?"

"Why, yes, I do," Headmaster Hughes said. His frown-smile grew even wider, and he quirked one eyebrow. "I think you and I should make a deal. I'll agree to let you make the proposed changes to the Snowflake." I felt a whoosh of relief, and was just starting to smile my thanks when he lifted a finger before I could say anything. "On one condition," he continued.

I felt a chill run down my back, and waited.

"You have to agree to rejoin the Mu Alpha Theta team," he said.

My mouth dropped open. Literally. "You're *blackmailing* me?" I gasped.

The frown-smile turned into a genuine frown. "Blackmail? I hardly think there's cause to make a charge like that," Headmaster Hughes said coldly. "I'm simply offering a solution to our problems. This way we're both compromising. We both get something we want, while each giving up something."

As my shock wore off, I could feel my temper bubbling up. "Something I want? I didn't *want* to organize the Snowflake in the first place! You made me do it!" I said, louder than I meant to.

"There's no cause to shout," Headmaster Hughes said, his voice frosty.

"I'm sorry," I said immediately. I hadn't meant to shout. "It's just . . . this is really unfair. You know I didn't have anything to do with the Geek High Web site, and yet you punished me for not telling you who is writing it by putting me in charge of turning the Snowflake into a more popular event. And so fine, I'm planning it, even though I really, really don't want to. And now that I've brought you my ideas for making the Snowflake more popular, you're telling me you won't act on them unless I join Mu Alpha Theta, which is something else I really, really don't want to do."

Headmaster Hughes took a minute to resteeple his hands, and tapped his index fingers together.

"Miranda, sometimes grown-ups do things that you won't agree with. And even though you might not understand their motivations, sometimes you have to take a leap of faith and trust that they're acting in your best interest," he said.

Why did he keep talking to me like I was five years old? I gritted my teeth.

"Sir, do you really think it's in my best interest to organize the Snowflake?" I asked.

"Yes, I do. But I wasn't talking about the Snowflake just now. Or the Mu Alpha Theta team, for that matter," the headmaster said.

I was confused again. Was he going to start talking in riddles now? Or, even worse, would he force me to *solve* the riddles before allowing me to leave his office? Like a bald headmaster version of the half-woman/half-lion sphinxes that always pop up in fictional mazes, and force the hero to solve riddles before being allowed to pass?

My confusion must have been reflected on my face, because the headmaster decided to give me a hint. "Have you talked to your mother recently?" he asked.

I stiffened. "No," I said. I knew my dad had talked to her a few times, giving her progress reports on me ("She and Hannah are becoming the best of friends! They even went to the mall together!"), but I still hadn't returned any of Sadie's phone messages or e-mails, even though she was getting seriously mopey. She'd sounded like Eeyore from *Winnie-the-Pooh* in her last e-mail to me.

"I think you should give *her* the benefit of the doubt," Headmaster Hughes said.

And to this, I had no reply. I glanced at my watch. "I really have to go. I'm already late for Latin class," I said. I was still holding the cupcake, and it was crumbling in my hand.

"And as for the Snowflake? And Mu Alpha Theta?" he asked, crooking one furry eyebrow up again. Sunlight streamed in from the windows behind his desk, bouncing off his baldpate. If he wore an earring, the headmaster would look a lot like Mr. Clean, I thought.

I considered his proposal. If I made the changes to the Snowflake, then maybe—*maybe*—I'd get through the school year without everyone in the school hating me. In fact, maybe my fellow students would even appreciate me for saving them from having to sit through a marathon of the world's most boring speeches. And as much as I didn't want to rejoin Mu Alpha Theta, it wasn't like being on the team was all that bad. The actual work was pretty easy for me. I'd have to go to practice once a week, and the competitions, of course. But maybe if I studied extra hard, I could find a way to fit in the *Ampersand*, as well.

So, in the end, I gave in.

"Okay," I said dully. "It's a deal."

Headmaster Hughes's face lit up like Christmas.

"That," he said happily, "is excellent news."

*We'll just have to agree to disagree on that point*, I thought grimly, and I stood to leave.

# Chapter 19

$$\iint_S f(x, y)\, dx\, dy = \iint_T f[X(u, v), Y(u, v)] \mid \mathcal{J}(u, v) \mid du\, dv$$

*DEVIOUS DEEDS*
*Which Geek High math brainiac was recently blackmailed*
*into rejoining the Mu Alpha Theta team by Headmaster C.*
*Philip Hughes? And just how exactly did he blackmail her?*
*GEEKHIGH.COM plans to get to the bottom of this shocking*
*allegation. . . .*

"We're going to have a prom!" Felicity screamed at a truly surprising decibel level, after I told her the news the next morning just before mod lit class began. She even began shimmying around in a victory dance, and looked unfairly adorable doing so.

Morgan, as usual, began to ape Felicity, even getting up from her chair so that she could dance, too, although she looked ridiculous bumping and grinding around her desk.

"All right, well . . . just thought you should know," I said, turning away before anyone would further associate me with the pair of them. I quickly crossed the room and sat down in my regular seat next to Charlie and Finn, who were in the middle of debating whether late-seventies disco was bad in a good, retro-kitsch way or just plain bad.

"How can you say ABBA is overrated?" Charlie argued. "Their music was brilliant!"

"Um, because it sucks?" Finn suggested.

"ABBA," Charlie said severely, "does *not* suck. Besides, I don't know why I'm even talking to you about this. You think Beck is the epitome of modern music."

"You don't like Beck? I don't think I can be friends with someone who doesn't like Beck. The man is a genius," Finn exclaimed.

Charlie shrugged. "He's okay. But he's no ABBA."

Finn made a choking sound.

I've found that it's best to ignore Charlie and Finn when they start going at it like this, so I dug my laptop and copy of *The Sun Also Rises* out of my backpack, and tried not to look at Emmett as he walked in the room and dropped into his seat. I was doing much better at not staring at him. I only stole the occasional peep in his direction, and even then, I limited myself to three peeps per class period. And, oddly enough, the less I looked at him, the less I wanted to. Which caused me to feel conflicted. If Emmett was losing his hold over me, that should be a good thing, right? Especially since he was dating my odious stepsister. But it also made me sort of sad. My crush on Emmett had kept me company for two years.

"How do you explain 'Dancing Queen'?" Finn asked, his voice dripping with disdain. "It's not a song; it's a *jingle*. It's toothpaste-commercial music."

" 'Dancing Queen' is a classic!" Charlie sputtered. "You have no taste!"

"I'm all taste, baby," Finn said.

"Will you two please stop? You're giving me a headache," I muttered.

"Cranky much?" Finn asked me.

"How can you even ask her that? It's basically your fault she's back on the Mu Alpha Theta team," Charlie admonished him.

"Not even I could have predicted that Headmaster Hughes would be so devious as to blackmail her into that," Finn said. He grew thoughtful. "It almost makes me respect the man."

"First of all, I'm not talking to you," I said.

"Why not?" Finn asked.

I shot him my dirtiest look. "I can't believe you blogged about me *again* on that stupid Web site."

"I had to," Finn insisted. "It was a great piece, and I owed it to my readers. It has it all—the struggle between good and evil, a contest of wills, life hanging in the balance. . . ."

"Whose life is hanging in the balance?" Charlie asked.

"Stop nitpicking," Finn said.

"And second of all," I continued, ignoring them, "I don't want to talk about it."

"You know, if you wanted to get back at him, you could say you're going to compete in Mu Alpha Theta, and then not follow through. The first competition isn't until January, right? So that's after the Snowflake," Finn said.

"I *said* I don't want to talk about it," I repeated through clenched teeth.

"And besides, she'd still have to go to practice every week in the meantime," Charlie said.

"That's true," Finn said. "But if the point is to screw with the headmaster, then—"

"You guys!" I exploded. "I. Don't. Want. To. Talk. About. It."

Charlie and Finn exchanged a significant look, which just irritated me even more. I cracked my paperback open, and tried to lose myself in Hemingway's spare prose. I'd looked at the online reader's guide the night before, and apparently the narrator, Jake Barnes, was impotent (hence all the wounded-bull imagery). But I'd read the novel all the way through, and hadn't caught a single reference to impotence. This was what bugged me about literary fiction—you had to interpret everything. Why couldn't a story just be a story? If the man is impotent, just *say* he's impotent. Maybe Sadie's books wouldn't win any literary awards, but at least they're good stories *and* they spare the reader from having to slog through page after page looking for hidden symbolism just to figure out what's going on.

"Good morning, all," Mrs. Gordon said cheerily as she entered the room. She was holding a stack of papers in her arms. "I have your short stories graded."

Mrs. Gordon began handing the stories back, turning them face-down on our desks, as was the policy of Geek High. (A few years back, some kid came close to having a nervous breakdown when a classmate saw that he'd gotten a C-plus on a geology exam. Shortly thereafter, the school enacted the facedown-hand-back rule.) Mrs. Gordon set my story down on my desk. I drew in a deep breath for luck before flipping it over . . . and once I did, all I could do was stare down at my story in horror. There was a big red B-minus scrawled on the top right corner of my story. Below the grade was a note, also written in red pen: *Miranda, see me after class.*

I felt numb all over, except for my cheeks, which were unbearably hot. A *B-minus?* I'd never gotten a B-minus before. Up until now, the lowest grade I'd ever gotten was a B, and that was in the eighth grade when I had strep throat, but insisted on taking my earth science midterm anyway. And I'd certainly never gotten such a low grade in English before. I normally rock English. It's always been my biggest academic strength after math. I pressed my hands to my cheeks, hoping to cool them down, but instead I just warmed up my hands.

"How'd you do?" Tate Metcalf asked Tabitha Stone.

"An A," she said smugly.

"Cool," Tate said. "I got an A-minus."

"Oh, my God, I can't believe it; I pulled off a B-plus!" Charlie whispered excitedly. "I thought for sure I was going to fail. I pulled an all-nighter the night before the story was due, and by the end I didn't even know what I was writing."

Charlie had done better than I had on an English assignment? I could feel the jealousy winding snakelike through me. I always got better grades than she did in English. *Always.* Of course, she kicked serious butt in art and science, so it all balanced out, but *still.* How had she done better than me? I'd worked on my short story for weeks.

But I couldn't say any of that to her. So I just swallowed back my disappointment and tucked my story into my backpack before Charlie could see the big red B-minus at the top of my paper.

"Great," I said dully.

"You okay?" Charlie asked, her brow furrowing with concern.

I nodded, smiled briefly, and then pretended to turn my attention to the class discussion of *The Sun Also Rises.*

At the end of the period, I waited for everyone to leave before approaching Mrs. Gordon. Charlie and Finn took forever to pack up their books, distracted as they were by the recommencement of their "does disco suck?" argument.

"I don't know why I even bother to talk to you," Charlie said, exasperated after Finn made a crack about Gloria Gaynor.

"It's my dark good looks and my witty personality," Finn said. "The chicks can never leave me alone."

Charlie whacked him on the arm, and Finn yelped.

"Damn, woman," he said, rubbing his arm. "Been lifting weights?"

"Wuss," Charlie said to him. She turned toward me. "Are you coming?"

"I'll catch up in a minute. I have to talk to Mrs. Gordon about something," I said.

Curiosity flickered in Charlie's face, but she didn't press me. "Okay. I'll see you later," she said.

After Charlie and Finn left, I approached Mrs. Gordon, who was sitting behind her desk, typing on her laptop. When she saw me standing there, she smiled kindly up at me.

"You wanted to see me?" I asked, hoping I didn't look as forlorn as I felt. I'd been fighting back tears all period.

"I wanted to talk to you about your short story," Mrs. Gordon said.

"I guess you didn't like it," I said with a hollow laugh.

"On the contrary, I loved it," Mrs. Gordon said.

I blinked. "You did?" I asked.

She nodded. "It was wonderful—witty, warm, insightful. And the writing was superb."

"But . . . but . . . but then why did you give me such a low grade?" I blurted out.

Mrs. Gordon sighed and took her glasses off. They hung around her neck on a black nylon cord. "To be honest, Miranda, I gave you a higher grade than I should have. You ignored the assignment. You were supposed to write your short story in the style of one of the writers we've studied this term in class. Your story read more like a Jane Austen novel of manners," she said. "It was an updated fairy tale, not a modernist piece."

"But I worked so hard on it," I said, and yet again I found myself fighting back tears.

"And it shows. It's a wonderful story. . . . It's just not what I assigned you to write," Mrs. Gordon said.

I knew that there was no point in lobbying her for a grade change. Mrs. Gordon was fair, but tough.

"Okay," I said, turning to leave. "Thanks for telling me."

"Wait, Miranda. I didn't ask you to stay because of your grade," Mrs. Gordon said.

"You didn't?" I stopped and pivoted back around to face her.

"No. As I said, I thought your story was wonderful. In fact, I think you should submit it to a short-story competition." Mrs. Gordon pulled out an orange flyer and handed it to me. The heading on the flyer read: ALFRED Q. WINSTON CREATIVE WRITING CONTEST. "This is a national writing competition for high school students."

I stared down at the flyer. "Really? Do you think I have any chance of winning?" I asked, doubtful that a story that had earned only a B-minus would be a contender in a national writing contest.

"I do. The competition will be stiff. This is the preeminent national writing competition for high school students, after all. But it would be a wonderful experience for you, and a real feather in your cap if you made it to the finals," Mrs. Gordon said.

"Finals?" I repeated.

Mrs. Gordon nodded. "They're held every spring in Washington, D.C.," she said. "So are you interested? I'll have to enter it for you. Each student has to be sponsored by a teacher."

I could feel a nervous tightening in my stomach. A writing competition? Me? The idea that a bunch of strangers would be reading my story—and comparing it to other, probably better stories—made my toes curl with horror.

But at the same time . . . wasn't this what I'd wanted? To find out if I was good at something other than math? And if that turned out to be writing . . . well, that would be amazing.

So I nodded, and swallowed. "I'd like that," I finally managed to say.

Mrs. Gordon beamed at me. "I'm so glad. Why don't you give me your story back, and I'll send it in."

I hesitated. "You're not going to use the copy you graded, are you?" I asked.

"Well . . . yes, I was. Why?" she asked.

"Because this one has an enormous B-minus written across the top," I said. I pulled it out of my backpack and held it up to show her. "Don't you think that might work against me?"

Mrs. Gordon laughed. "I see your point."

"I'll go print out a fresh copy for you in the computer lab," I said, tucking the graded copy back into my bag. I grinned at her. "Thanks, Mrs. Gordon."

"It's my pleasure, Miranda."

My good mood over the writing contest kept me elated through the rest of the day . . . right up until the final bell rang, and it was time for my first Mu Alpha Theta practice. I dropped my books off in my locker, and closed the door with a resigned metallic slam. Charlie loved to paint, and Finn could—and frequently did—spend all day and night parked in front of his computer. Why was it that the one subject I was gifted in bored me to tears?

The rest of the Mu Alpha Theta team was already assembled in Mr. Gordon's classroom when I arrived. Sanjiv Gupta—a gangly kid with enormous brown eyes and a prominent Adam's apple—was writing out equations on the dry-erase board with a black marker. Mr. Gordon, Leila Chang, Kyle Carpenter, and Nicholas Pruitt were all sitting at desks facing the board.

Mr. Gordon brightened when he saw me. "Hello, Miranda," he said, so warmly I immediately knew that he'd had nothing to do with Headmaster Hughes's blackmail plot. "I'm so glad you changed your mind about being on the team."

"Thanks," I said. I slid my knapsack off my shoulder and sat down at a desk. Sanjiv continued to write out equations with a fierce concentration.

"Sanjiv came across a series of math theorems on a Mu Alpha Theta Web site that he thought would be good for us to practice on," Mr. Gordon explained to me.

"And don't give away the answers before we get a chance to solve them, Miranda," Sanjiv said, pushing his thick glasses up his nose as he turned around. He capped the marker.

"I don't do that," I protested.

Kyle snorted. "Are you kidding?" he asked.

Kyle was a squat, heavy boy with a hairline that started a half inch over his eyebrows that made him look like the Wolfman. He wasn't a math whiz—his biggest academic strength was chemistry—so he always had to work hard on the Mu Alpha Theta drills. I'd gotten the definite feeling that he resented how easily math came to me.

"You do sort of jump on the answer quickly," Leila said in a much less friendly tone than usual.

I looked around at my teammates, getting the distinct impression that none of them appreciated my return to the team. In fact, the only one of the group who wasn't eyeing me with barely concealed antagonism was Nicholas, a freshman who hadn't been on Mu Alpha Theta last year. He was a short, thin kid with dark curly hair cut close to his head. I smiled warmly at him, and he turned bright red and dropped his pencil. Puzzled, I watched him for a moment, but he suddenly seemed fascinated in his notebook . . . which, from where I was sitting, looked blank.

"Why all the hostility?" I asked.

Kyle and Leila exchanged a look.

"What?" I asked.

"You bailed on us," Kyle said bluntly.

"We saw the Geek High blog, Miranda. We know you didn't want to be on the team," Leila said.

"And that Headmaster Hughes made you rejoin," Kyle said.

"No, he didn't." Yes, this was a lie, but telling them the truth would just make them even angrier. "But before, when I didn't join right away . . . that wasn't because of you guys," I protested. "I just wanted to try something else."

Kyle and Leila looked at me. Clearly, they saw my defection as a personal insult.

"Look, I'm sorry," I mumbled, thinking that when I next saw Finn, I'd wring his scrawny neck.

"All right, people, let's get to work and solve these theorems," Sanjiv said, clapping his hands and saving me from having to explain myself further to my teammates. I never thought I'd actually be grateful for one of Sanjiv's officious interruptions, which just goes to show that life is always full of surprises.

I glanced at the theorems on the board, and jotted down my solutions. Everyone else was still working, so I pulled out my planning book for the Snowflake and started to go over my to-do list again. We still had to find a band. Morgan continued to push for Snake's garage band, but

I wasn't committing until I at least heard their demo. We had to figure out a budget for decorations and snacks, and start working on posters to hang around school announcing the new Snowflake.

One task we had completed was to come up with a theme: the Black-and-White Ball. It was based on Truman Capote's famous ball of the same name that he hosted at the Plaza in New York City.

It was my idea, and I had to admit I was pretty proud of it. Even Felicity had loved it. Everyone would wear black or white, and we'd fill the school auditorium with black and white balloons. And Charlie had the great idea of blowing up black-and-white photographs of old movie stars and hanging them on the walls. It would be drop-dead elegant, and totally romantic.

"Miranda?"

I looked up, and the rest of the team was looking at me.

"What?" I asked.

"Did you finish the theorems?" Sanjiv asked.

"Yeah. Do you want the answers?" I asked.

"No," Sanjiv said, exasperated. "I just wanted your attention so we could go over the solutions *together*. As a group."

"I have a question," I said. "Why exactly are we practicing with written theorems?"

"It's practice. *Obviously*," Kyle said. Sanjiv could be annoying, but Kyle was even worse. He was so argumentative, I wanted to bop him over the head with my spiral notebook.

"What I meant," I said slowly for Kyle's benefit, "was: What's the point? In the competitions, all of the problems are given verbally. Shouldn't we be practicing the same way?"

"Just because you can do these in your head, Miranda, doesn't mean the rest of us can," Leila said.

"Or, even if we can," Sanjiv quickly interjected, "it's still good practice."

I knew I was the thorn of Sanjiv's life. He loved math. In fact, his dream was to be hired as a code breaker for the NSA. And were it not for me, he'd be the math star of Geek High.

"I think Miranda's right," Nicholas said. "If the competitions are all oral, that's how we should practice."

He shot me a quick, shy glance, and I smiled at him again, glad that at least someone on the team was on my side. His eyes—which were the color of root beer—widened, and he quickly looked back down at his notebook, hunching his shoulders up to his ears. I frowned. Why was he acting so frightened of me? I wasn't a scary person. *Miranda Bloom, friend to all*, that's my motto. Well. Except for Hannah. And Avery. And Felicity and Morgan. Okay, new motto: *Miranda Bloom, friend to all who deserve it*.

I turned my attention back to Sanjiv and his theorems. "All I'm saying is that what wins competitions is the ability to solve the problems in your head. Sure, you could take the time to write it out and solve it on paper, but unless the other side is doing the same thing, you'll lose too much time. If you want to win, you have to wean yourself off of using a pen and paper," I explained. "And I guarantee that if we actually do make it to the state finals, none of the other teams will be writing down the problems."

"She has a point," Leila said. "I read on Austin Strong's MySpace page that he's trained himself to solve all of the problems in his head."

"Really?" Sanjiv asked, looking impressed.

"Austin Strong is going to be tough to beat," Kyle said.

Which, I had to admit, annoyed me. When I suggest it, they all roll their eyes, but if Austin Strong recommends it, they think it's a great idea? It was as though they were all forgetting that we'd *beaten* Austin Strong and his St. Pius team last year. So I decided to remind them.

"Don't worry about Austin. We beat him last year, and we're going to beat him this year," I said, trying to rally the troops.

"We only beat St. Pius last year because the rest of their team stank. But on Austin's Web site, he said they have a great team this year.

They even have a Chinese exchange student," Kyle said, and the others groaned.

"You guys! You shouldn't assume that just because someone's Chinese that they're good at math," I said, outraged at the assumptions they were leaping to. "You can't make stereotypes just on someone's ethnicity or country of origin!"

"But Austin said the guy was a math champion at home. He even went to an accelerated Chinese school for it. And now that he's in the U.S., he's studying math at the college level," Leila said.

The others groaned. Sanjiv looked like he might throw up right there on his desk.

"So what? Some of us are studying at the college level, too," I said. Okay, just me, but they were already touchy enough as it was.

"I think that maybe we should focus on our own practice, rather than on what St. Pius is doing," Mr. Gordon suggested.

"I agree," I said.

"Me, too," Nicholas said, and his dark eyes darted over toward me. He was reminding me of someone . . . but I wasn't sure who.

But then suddenly it came to me . . . and I knew *exactly* who he reminded me of. *Me*. Those were the exact same sort of looks I'd been darting at Emmett for the past two years.

*Oh, no,* I thought with a start, as I turned away from Nicholas, staring down hard at my desk. *Oh, no no no no no no no.* This wasn't good . . . not at all.

# Chapter 20

$$\iint_S f(x, y)\, dx\, dy = \iint_T f[r \cos \theta, r \sin \theta)\, r\, dr\, d\theta$$

"My white short-sleeved TSE cashmere sweater is missing," Peyton announced over dinner.

We were having pizza, which Dad had picked up on his way home from work. Despite the house's enormous kitchen outfitted with professional-grade appliances, no one in residence house ever cooked. It almost made me miss Sadie's bizarre concoctions, even the disasters, like her microwaved baked Alaska or her grape-jelly-coated Crock-Pot shrimp (which was so disgusting, I haven't been able to stomach the smell of grape jelly ever since).

"Maybe it's at the dry cleaners'," Dad suggested.

"It's not," Peyton insisted. "I even called the cleaner's and double-checked. But I knew it wasn't there. I specifically remember taking it out of the cleaner bag and setting it in the right-hand drawer in my closet."

"Well, I'm sure it's in there somewhere," Dad said, sounding unconcerned. I didn't blame him. Peyton's closet is enormous, nearly the same size as their master bedroom. It would be easy for a little scrap of cashmere to get lost in one of the dozens of built-in drawers and cabinets.

Peyton dropped the fork that she'd been using to push her pizza around on her plate, and stared at my father with ill-concealed irritation.

"No," she said, overpronouncing her words, "it's *not*. I just told you, I looked. And my sweater isn't there."

My dad raised his eyebrows. "Well, Peyton, I doubt that it sprouted legs and walked out of the closet on its own," he said. His voice was testy, which wasn't at all like him. Normally he was Mr. Jolly around Peyton.

"I agree. I think it's much more likely that *someone* took it," Peyton said.

"It wasn't me; I swear," Hannah said quickly.

"I know, sweetheart. I'm not blaming *you*," Peyton said.

At that moment I was bending over to take a sip of Coke, and was trying to decide whether Peyton's head was freakishly large, or if it was just that her neck was so spindly that the head looked big in comparison, when it hit me that everything had suddenly gotten weirdly quiet. My dad crossed his arms and frowned, Hannah shifted uncomfortably in her chair, and Peyton was staring hard at me. I looked up, my lips still puckered around the straw.

"What?" I said. And then I understood exactly what Peyton was implying. "Wait . . . you think *I* took it?" I asked, too stunned to be indignant.

And, weirdly, even though I *hadn't* taken her sweater, I suddenly felt uneasy. Guilty even. It was as though the accusation itself tainted me. But what did I have to feel guilty over? It wasn't my fault the sweater had gone missing.

"Did you?" Peyton asked icily.

"Miranda, you don't have to answer that. Peyton, you're out of line," Dad snapped.

"I never had clothes go missing before Miranda moved in," Peyton said. "So doesn't that make her the most likely culprit?"

"First of all, you don't know that the sweater is actually missing. It's just not where you think you put it," Dad said. "And second, even if it is missing, it's unfair to blame Miranda without any proof."

"I haven't heard her deny it," Peyton said, pursing her lips.

"I didn't take it!" I exclaimed. "I wouldn't do that!"

*And I'm not the one in the house who's obsessed with designer clothes*, I added silently, stealing a look at Hannah. She was staring down at her plate, a troubled look on her face. Was it guilt? Or concern about the number of fat grams in a slice of pizza? With Hannah, one could never be sure.

"There. Now you have your answer," Dad said. He picked up his napkin, dabbed away a spot of tomato sauce from the corner of his mouth, and then abruptly stood. "Now, if you'll excuse me, I have some work to finish up in my office." And with that, he turned and walked out of the room.

Peyton's face pinched with anger as she watched my dad leave. *Uh-oh*, I thought. The Demon was angry. She flung a filthy look at me, and then stood and stalked off. I could hear her stilettos clicking angrily down the marble hall toward the master bedroom. Hannah and I sat in silence for a moment, neither of us eating. I'd been starving before dinner, but Peyton's accusation had soured my appetite.

I glanced up at Hannah. She was still sitting with her head bowed, her face clouded. Waves of guilt seemed to rise up from her. *She knows something*, I thought, and the realization was like a slap across the face. But why would she lie? Peyton wouldn't care if Hannah had borrowed her sweater.

"Do you know anything about this missing sweater?" I asked her.

She shook her head once, but a hand flickered up to her cheek. *Got you*, I thought. People always touch their face when they lie. It's called a "tell." Finn read about it in the sociology class he took as an elective last year. Finn, being Finn, used the knowledge to mask his own tells, so he could lie more effectively when Headmaster Hughes questioned him about his latest prank.

"I don't believe you," I said.

Hannah looked up sharply. "I didn't take it," she insisted.

"Well, I didn't take it," I said. "And it's not like there's anyone else. . . . Wait a second." I stopped, suddenly remembering. Avery had been over yesterday. And I could have sworn I heard her and Hannah going into the master bedroom. I thought they were just trying on Peyton's Chanel lipsticks . . . but had they been going through her closet, too?

"Did Avery happen to try on a certain cashmere TSE sweater yesterday?" I asked quietly.

Hannah looked stricken. She'd make a terrible spy. Now there was a truly scary thought: Hannah as a secret agent. Just wave a Sephora bag in front of her, and she'd pour out every state secret she knew.

"Yes, but . . . Avery wouldn't have taken it," Hannah said. "She just wouldn't do that."

"Are we talking about the same Avery who borrowed your new bracelet without asking, and still hasn't given it back? I saw her wearing it just yesterday," I pointed out.

"This is different," Avery insisted.

"At some point borrowing becomes stealing if you don't return what you borrowed," I said.

But Hannah resisted this stellar bit of logic. She shook her head obstinately. "I'm telling you, Avery wouldn't have taken it," she said. But I could tell from the quaver in her voice that she wasn't really so sure.

"Are you going to tell Peyton that Avery was trying on her sweater?" I asked quietly.

"I can't! Mom would freak out. She has this weird obsessive-compulsive thing about her closet. She wigs if anything's ever out of place. And besides, I don't have any proof that Avery was the one who took it," Hannah bleated.

"Lack of proof didn't stop Peyton from blaming me," I said, sounding as bitter as I felt.

"Just don't say anything. *Please.* I'll think of something. Maybe Avery just put the sweater back in the wrong drawer. I'll ask her," Hannah said.

"Well. Okay. Ask her. But if the sweater doesn't turn up, you're going to have to tell Peyton the truth," I said.

It wasn't that I'd developed any loyalty toward Peyton, and I certainly didn't care one way or other about the sweater. Peyton had a closet full of clothes, all of them expensive. But I didn't like being thought of as a thief and a sneak. And even if it didn't matter what Peyton thought of me . . . well, I just didn't want my dad to ever think that I'd do anything so dishonest.

I still hadn't talked to my mom, even though more than two months had passed since she'd left for England. I had, however, finally started responding to her e-mails. First, I'd kept my replies brief, to make it clear that I was still angry at her. But as the weeks crawled along, I'd been slowly defrosting. And if there was anyone who would appreciate just how horrible the Demon was to accuse me of thievery, it would be Sadie.

As soon as I got back to the guest room, I pulled out my laptop, opened my e-mail program, and began writing. I detailed the Saga of the Missing TSE Sweater, and how Peyton had accused me of taking it while I thought Avery was the culprit, and how Dad had stood up for me. I read over the e-mail, and when I was satisfied, I hit the send button. I knew I wouldn't get a response from Sadie that night—it was two in the morning in London—but I had to admit, I felt better. I missed Sadie . . . more than I'd thought I had.

I spent the next hour working on a new short story that I was hoping to submit to the *Ampersand*. I normally wouldn't have had the guts to do it, since most of the articles published in the school magazine are written by upperclassmen, but Mrs. Gordon's response to the short story I'd written for mod lit had bolstered my confidence. Plus, the editorial staff of the *Ampersand* would be picking which sophomores would be invited to join the journal staff soon, and I was hoping that my story would make a good enough impression that they'd pick me.

The story was about a teenage girl who had the ability to read other people's minds—which sounds like a gift, but was actually slowly ruining her life, especially once the evil headmaster of her private school set about exploiting her superpowers for his own gain. I figured that after this year I had a special insight into manipulative headmasters.

And just as I was starting to yawn and my hand was cramping up, my computer gave a little electronic bleep, signaling that I had a new e-mail. I pulled my laptop closer, and maximized the window the e-mail was running in. It was from Sadie! But it was three in the morning her time. What was she still doing up?

I opened the e-mail:

TO:      mirandajbloom@gmail.com
FROM:   Della@DellaDeLaCourte.com
RE:      Saga of the Missing TSE Sweater

Miranda, darling,

First of all, congratulations on having your short story entered in the writing contest! Clearly your English teacher has excellent taste. Although, just so you know, the life of a writer isn't all glamorous parties, darling. I'm up pulling an all-nighter, trying to finish the first draft of *A Victorian Widow*. I'm far too old to be missing out on my beauty sleep—I don't want to even think about what this is doing to my skin. If you get a chance, do ask Peyton how she likes those Botox treatments she's so fond of (and don't believe her if she denies it—no one's face is naturally that frozen).

And speaking of Peyton ... how *dare* she accuse you? You, who are the most honest person I know. I still remember the time when you were five, and I opened that box of cookies at the grocery store before buying them and tried to get you to eat one because your blood sugar was so low. You refused, and said that they weren't ours until we paid for them. *And* you told the cashier on me. That's character, darling, *character*.

I'm glad your father stood up for you. It's about time. But if you don't get things sorted out, please let me know. I'd be more than happy to call Peyton and tell her what's what.

Now. Why don't you come visit me over your Christmas break? I thought you could fly out the day after the Snowflake (bravo on the black-and-white theme—Truman would definitely approve), and stay until classes start back up. What do you think?

Love you, XXXXOOOO, Sadie

P.S. I've already bought your ticket!!!

I let out a little shriek of happiness. I was going to London for Christmas! London! The city of Sherlock Holmes and Paddington Bear! Of the Tower of London and the London Eye! The home of the queen and Madonna! And I was going to see it all!

# Chapter 21

$$\iiint\limits_{S} f(x, y, z)\, dx\, dy\, dz = \iint\limits_{Q} [\int_{\varphi_1(x,v)}^{\varphi_2(x,v)} f(x, y, z)\, dz]\, dx\, dy$$

As the October heat melted away, and we found ourselves in the cooler November temperatures, preparations for the Snowflake were well under way. I could hardly believe it, but the dance was only six short weeks away . . . and there was still so much to do. Who would have thought that planning a simple dance would be so much work? But there was the food to arrange, and the decorations, and the chaperones (something Headmaster Hughes had insisted on, although I'd bargained him down to having only five). And then there was the biggest problem: We still didn't have a band.

Morgan continued to lobby us to hire her boyfriend's band, but Felicity—the only one on the Snowflake committee who'd actually ever heard them play—had been the one to finally nix the idea.

"No, Morgan," she finally said one afternoon, while we were painting posters advertising the Snowflake that would hang in the Geek High corridors. "No way. We didn't go to all of this work to finally have a real prom, just to have a bunch of pothead losers who aren't even organized enough to be a real band ruin it."

"Snake is not a loser," Morgan insisted, her voice growing shrill. "He's an artist."

I could have sworn that Felicity snorted at this, but when she spoke, she tried a more tactful approach. "Look, I'm sure Snake's talented . . . in his own way. But you have to admit, his music isn't really . . . well, suited to a dance," Felicity said.

"Well, maybe you're right," Morgan said grudgingly. She went back to painting a big purple S on a piece of orange poster board.

Felicity smiled happily. "Good," she said. "Now that that's decided, we have to find a band."

"That may not be so easy. A lot of companies will be having their holiday parties that weekend. 'Tis the season and all of that," Charlie pointed out. Her poster was, unsurprisingly, the most artistic. She flicked her paintbrush to splatter blue acrylic paint all around a curlicued red SNOWFLAKE GALA. A few spots of the blue paint had also landed in Felicity's hair, and I wasn't at all sure it had been an accident.

"Right," I said. "Well. That's the assignment for next week's meeting. Everyone has to come back with at least one band recommendation, and a demo tape. We'll listen to the demo tapes and take a vote."

But Charlie was right: It wasn't easy. The Christmas party season had put a serious crimp on the availability of local bands. I called every listing under the "Musicians and Bands" heading in the Yellow Pages, and the only acts that were still available were clearly the dregs of the local music scene. One guy I spoke to could barely speak without wheezing, and told me that he liked to think of himself as "Willie Nelson crossed with Eminem." I told him I'd think about it and get back to him, but as soon as I hung up, I crossed out the listing with my black Sharpie marker.

Charlie hadn't had any more luck than me. "Don't worry; I'll think of something," she said when I called her later that evening.

"How about Finn? Did he find anyone?" I asked.

"I don't think he's even looked yet," Charlie said, sounding annoyed. Finn hadn't shown up to paint posters, either. "Although considering Finn's taste in music, that's probably just as well."

"We always have Snake as a fallback," I said, only half joking.

"Don't worry. We'll find someone," Charlie said.

"I hope so. Or else I'll be plugging my iPod into a set of speakers, and hoping that everyone likes old Blondie songs as much as I do."

"Who wouldn't?" Charlie said. "So . . . who do you think you're going to go to the Snowflake with? As a date, I mean."

"A date?" I repeated. Her question had taken me completely by surprise. Because somehow, even though thoughts of the Snowflake had been consuming a ridiculous number of my waking hours, I'd completely forgotten that we were expected to show up to the dance with a date. I felt a pang of discomfort. Why *hadn't* I thought about whom my date would be? Wouldn't that have been the normal thing to do? Or was it just more evidence that Peyton had been right about me when I overheard her telling my dad that I was odd?

"Yes, you know: a date. A guy in a rented tux who shows up at your house with a corsage in a plastic box?" Charlie said.

The thought caused my stomach to feel like it had been invaded by a pack of butterflies.

"Yes, thank you, I know what a date is," I said testily. "I just forgot that I needed one. Who are you going with?"

Charlie shrugged. "No one's asked me. I have a few ideas of guys I could ask, but I haven't narrowed the field down yet. There's still time."

"What about Finn?" I asked.

There was a weird pause. "What about him?" Charlie finally said.

"Does he have a date?" I asked.

"Not that I know of."

"One of us could go with him," I said. It would be the easy way out—bringing a friend as a date. And Finn was always good for a few laughs.

But there was just another weird pause. "You want to go with Finn?" Charlie asked slowly.

It took me a moment to realize what she was implying. "No!" I hurried to say. "Not as a real *date* date. Just as a friend. But you can ask him if you want."

"Why do you think I'd want to ask him?" Now she sounded angry.

"Why are you so upset?" I asked, confused.

"I'm not! Look . . . I just . . . Never mind," Charlie said with a sigh. "I have to go."

"Charlie, wait," I said. But it was too late—she'd already hung up.

I sighed and slumped back on the pillows I'd propped behind me on the bed. Willow looked up at me, and then dropped her head back on her fluffy dog bed with a self-satisfied groan.

"You know, Willow, sometimes I envy you," I said. "It must be nice to be a dog. You don't have to go to school, or worry about getting into a good college, and when you meet another dog, all you have to do is sniff each other's butts to know where you stand. I wish it were that easy for humans."

That night, as I was trying to fall asleep, the nervous butterflies invaded again. I had to have a date. What if no one asked me? I'd have to go to the Snowflake no matter what, since I was in charge of the stupid event . . . and I certainly didn't want to be the only one there without a date. I might as well have the word *loser* tattooed on my forehead. But who could I go with? I didn't have a boyfriend, didn't even have the potential for one. I'd spent the past two years obsessing about Emmett Dutch, and he obviously wasn't going to ask me. He'd bring Hannah. Well, that was just great. Hannah would have a date to the Snowflake, and she didn't even go to our school.

But, oddly enough, it wasn't Emmett's golden-tanned face that kept popping into my thoughts as I drifted to sleep. Instead, the face I was thinking of was freckled, with pale blue eyes, and topped with russet-hued curls that glinted in the sun.

Dex, I thought with surprise. And suddenly I was wide-awake, staring up into the darkness, while the butterflies flapped their wings faster than ever.

# Chapter 22

"**B**ye! Have fun!" Hannah said as Peyton, who was wearing a white pantsuit and teetering on tan high-heeled sandals, leaned over to hug her.

"We will. Now, you'll be okay here on your own?" Peyton asked. I'm sure her brow would have wrinkled in concern, had it not been frozen by Botox.

"They'll be fine," Dad said. He was holding two Louis Vuitton overnight bags, and had a matching garment bag slung over one arm. "After all, the girls have each other."

Hannah and I both cringed at this. Despite my dad's many efforts, Hannah and I were not—nor would we ever be—BFFs. And now that he and Peyton were heading off for a romantic weekend in South Beach, I think he actually thought Hannah and I would spend our Saturday night bonding over ice cream and face masks. That was *so* not going to happen. I had my thrilling night all planned out—I had to finish reading *The Great Gatsby* for mod lit, and then I was going to start studying for my astronomy final. And even though Hannah hadn't divulged her plans to me, I suspected that they probably involved Emmett and seeing how long they could kiss without coming up for air.

"That's right; we'll be fine," Hannah said, echoing my dad. "Now go on and have fun, and don't worry about us."

"All right. Well. We're off," Peyton said, smiling at Hannah. And then, as her eyes moved to me, the smile disappeared. "And stay *out* of my closet," she said coldly.

"Peyton," my dad said reproachfully.

The TSE sweater had still not turned up, and it remained a sore subject in the house. Peyton still thought I'd taken it. I think she even went through my room one day looking for it while I was at school. When I came home, my drawers looked as though they'd been tossed and then hastily straightened. I still thought Avery had pinched the sweater, although Hannah continued to insist that her friend wouldn't do that. My dad continued to stick up for me, and Peyton had—for the most part—finally dropped the subject. But she couldn't help getting a dig in here and there. I guess that's what comes of having a soul that's ten percent Botox and ninety percent pure evil.

I crossed my arms and glared at her. "Don't worry," I said, my voice just as icy.

My father looked concerned, his eyes darting from Peyton to me and back to Peyton again.

"We should go," Dad said.

After a final round of good-byes, Dad and Peyton finally left. Hannah stood at the open door waving as Dad and Peyton drove off. Once they were gone, she closed the door with a thud and turned to face me.

"Just so you know, I'm having a few people over tonight," Hannah said.

"You're having a party?" I asked, wondering why this surprised me. It was *exactly* what I'd have expected her to do, if I'd had thought about it.

"Not a party, exactly," Hannah hedged. "More like . . . a get-together."

"And you don't want me around," I said flatly. "Right?"

Hannah shrugged. "I don't care. Stay if you want. I was just giving you a heads-up," she said. And then she tossed her pale blond hair over her shoulders and walked off in the direction of the kitchen, leaving me to decide whether I should clear out for the evening.

If Hannah was throwing a party, I certainly didn't want to stick around for it. A houseful of her drunk friends lurching around and puking in closets was not my idea of a good time. Property damage was inevitable. I didn't want to get the blame when the five-thousand-dollar flat-panel television ended up crashing to the ground.

But a get-together . . . that sounded relatively harmless. No doubt there would be drinking, and where there was drinking, there was usually puking . . . but what were the chances that I'd even hear them in a house this size?

As it turned out, Hannah and I had very different ideas of what a "get-together" meant. To me, a get-together is five or six people hanging out, and maybe playing some music or watching a movie. A hundred kids and a keg? That's a party. And that party had taken over the beach house.

I was in my room reading *The Great Gatsby* when the doorbell began to ring. At first I just ignored it, sure that it was Emmett, Avery, the Wonder Twins, and a few other of Hannah's assorted friends. But then the noise began to get louder . . . and louder . . . and louder. Someone turned on music and cranked it up until it was so thunderous, my teeth started to vibrate. When I heard the crashing sound of metal against marble—it sounded very much like a keg being dropped in the front hall—followed by shrieks of laughter and applause, I put down *The Great Gatsby* and tried to decide what to do.

I called Charlie for advice.

"Hey," she said, talking very quickly and sounding distracted. "I'm just finishing up the sketches for a new installation piece. I'm thinking *big*. Like, *really* big. Three stories of nothing but undulating waves of black and purple."

I never have any idea what Charlie's talking about when she gets like this.

"Cool. So guess what? Dad and the Demon are out of town for the night, and the Demon Spawn is having a party," I said.

"Of course she is. Could she be any more of a cliché?" Charlie asked.

"Listen to this," I said, and I held out the phone toward the ruckus for a moment before returning it to my ear. "Pretty bad, huh?"

"Do you want to come over here? I'm going to be up all night painting. You can crash in my bed."

I thought about it for a moment. "Let me go out there and see how bad it is. Maybe it's not as crazy as it sounds," I said.

"I seriously doubt that. Call me back," Charlie said, and we hung up.

Willow was sleeping on her bed, happily oblivious to the comings and goings in the house. (She's the world's worst guard dog. She doesn't even bark when the doorbell rings.) I left her in my room and went down the hall on my recon mission to find out just how bad this party was.

The answer: pretty freaking bad.

There were people *everywhere*. In the kitchen, the living room, out on the back deck circled around the dented keg that had been set up there. The music blared, and everyone was drinking beer out of red plastic cups. A lot of Hannah's friends looked like they were already drunk—faces were red and sweaty, hair was starting to depouf, voices were getting louder. I saw the Wonder Twins dancing in the living room. Avery was in the corner wrapped around a guy I didn't recognize. He appeared to be eating her face. And where was Hannah? I looked around for her, finally spotting her ensconced on the couch, perched prettily on Emmett's lap.

I wondered if Dex was at the party. I hadn't seen him in weeks, not since the day that he'd walked with me on the beach. He hadn't been over since. I'd overheard Hannah and Avery talking one afternoon, and Avery had mentioned that Dex had joined the cross-country running team in order to stay in shape for lacrosse season. I had to admit, I was a little disappointed I hadn't bumped into him. While I knew that there was no way a guy who used to date a model would be interested in someone like me . . . still. There had been that zing.

But zing or no zing, Dex didn't appear to be at the party. I tried to ignore the resulting thud of disappointment, and decided I had to get out of the house before the party got even crazier. It was already way too big, and—as the door opened and more kids streamed in—getting bigger by the moment.

Someone tapped my shoulder, and I spun around. A guy I didn't recognize was standing there, grinning blearily down at me. He had a chubby baby face and hair so blond, it was nearly white. His brown eyes were bloodshot and unfocused.

He said something, but I couldn't hear him over the music.

"What?" I asked.

He leaned forward, so that his lips were about two inches from my ear. "I said, you look way too sober! You should definitely drink more! Want a beer?" he shouted. The explosion of noise actually hurt my eardrum. Plus, he stank of stale beer and sweat. *Gross*. I stepped back and shook my head.

But Sweaty Drunk Guy wasn't so easily put off. He grabbed my hand and tottered toward me. His palm was sweaty and hot, and he was suddenly standing so close to me I felt claustrophobic.

"Come on, dance with me!" he yelled over the music.

And then before I could stop him, he suddenly pulled me forward and began grinding against me. I suppose he thought we were dancing, but I just felt like I was getting mugged.

*That's it,* I thought. *I'm out of here.*

I pushed Sweaty Drunk Guy away, sending him careening off into the crowd, and turned to leave. I just needed to fight my way back up to my room, and once there I'd call Charlie. Maybe her mom would come pick me up.

A hand tapped my shoulder. I closed my eyes and felt my temper bubble up. *Great.* Sweaty Drunk Guy wouldn't take the hint.

"Look, I don't want to dance, okay!" I said furiously, spinning around so that I could tell him off face-to-face.

But it wasn't Sweaty Drunk Guy I was yelling at. . . . It was Dex.

*Zing!*

"Oh! It's you!" I said.

"It's me," Dex said. "And now I know better than to ask you to dance."

"Sorry. I didn't mean to yell at you. I thought you were someone else," I said. I felt my cheeks and the tip of my nose flush red with embarrassment.

"Hey, why'd you run off?" Sweaty Drunk Guy had reappeared next to me. He grabbed at my hand again, but I was too quick—and too sober—for him. I held up my hands, warding him off, even as he swayed drunkenly toward me.

"I. Do not. Want. To dance," I insisted, raising my voice so he could hear me over the blaring music.

"Ah, don't be like that," Sweaty Drunk Guy said, leering down at me with what he probably thought was a charming smile. It was not. His lips were thick and rubbery, and he had little piggy eyes.

But before I could reply, Dex suddenly stepped forward, so that he was standing between me and Sweaty Drunk Guy.

"She doesn't want to dance, Phil," Dex said. His voice was friendly, but firm.

"Dex!" Phil cried happily, and he leaned forward and hugged Dex, as though they were long-lost brothers. Dex patted him briefly on the back, and then tactfully extricated himself from the embrace.

"Have you met my new friend?" Phil continued, his voice slurring. "This is . . . hey, what's your name?" he asked me.

I just crossed my arms and stared him down.

"Phil, I just ran into Giovanna. I think she was looking for you," Dex said.

Phil's face lit up. "Giovanna's here?" he asked happily. "Later, man."

Phil lurched off in the opposite direction, and Dex turned around to face me. A smile was quirking his lips.

"My hero," I joked.

He blew on his knuckles. "All in a day's work," he said.

"Only now you've set Phil on the path of some other poor girl," I remarked.

Dex snorted. "Giovanna? Trust me; she can handle herself," he said. And then he nodded toward a tall, striking girl with jet-black hair and gorgeous olive-toned skin who was easily brushing Phil off, while he jumped and panted around her like a puppy. Dex was right; she did seem to be handling Phil just fine.

"I haven't seen you in a while," Dex said, turning back to face me. He leaned forward, so that he was speaking right into my ear to be heard over the music. This didn't hurt the way it had when Phil shouted into it. Instead, Dex's breath tickled. I shivered, and my skin erupted into goose bumps.

"I've been looking for you when I'm at the beach. I know you walk your dog there sometimes," he continued.

"Really?" I asked, my breath catching in my chest. He'd been looking for me? Hoping to see me?

The truth was, I'd looked for him, too. Every time I saw a parasurfer out on the water, I'd feel a bubble of hope swell in my chest . . . and was always disappointed when I saw it wasn't Dex's blue-and-yellow parasail. I'd wanted to see him. Partly to see if I'd been imagining the zing, and partly because I still felt bad over how our last conversation had ended. I'd had the distinct impression that I'd offended him, and I wanted to apologize for that.

"Look, I've been wanting to apologize to you," I began. But before I could finish, I heard someone shout over the music, "Man, that dog is fast!"

I turned to see Willow streaking through the living room in a blur of panicked brindle. She weaved her way through the crowd, her long, thin body easily dodging most of the partygoers . . . although one of the Wonder Twins danced into Willow's path at just the wrong moment, and Willow sent her flying back with a startled squeak into the solid wall of muscle that was the Wonder Twin's boyfriend.

"Oh, a puppy!" a girl cooed.

"Wow, man, look at that weird dog," a guy called out.

One or two of the more dramatic girls actually screamed—as though Willow had blood dripping from her fangs—and several others tried to pet her as she passed. But Willow was not interested in affection—her sole goal at the moment was to get as far away from the noisy crowd as possible. And I saw just where she was heading.

"Close the back door!" I yelled, rushing to head Willow off before she could get out. I should have known better. There's a reason why they race greyhounds, and not beagles or cocker spaniels.

"Don't let the dog out!" Dex shouted from behind me.

But it was too late. Willow streaked out the back door, down the steps toward the beach, and into the darkness. I had that awful sinking sensation in my stomach, the one I always get when I fall asleep in a car and then wake up feeling like I'm falling off a cliff. I pushed my way through the crowd and flew out the back door and down the stairs after Willow.

As soon as my feet hit the sand, I began turning around, looking for some sign of my beautiful brindle greyhound . . . but she was nowhere in sight.

"Willow!" I called. "Willow!"

Luckily, even though it was dark out, the beach was lit by a full, round yellow moon hanging low in the sky, as well by the lights that shone from the big houses that lined the shore. It was still too dark to see Willow's paw prints in the sand, so I ran in the direction that we normally took on our walks, hoping Willow would have done the same.

"Willow!" I called again, wondering if she'd be able to hear me over the loud thrum of the ocean.

"Miranda, wait up!" I turned and saw that Dex had followed me down to the beach.

"I have to find Willow," I said, fighting back tears.

"I know. I'll help you," Dex said simply.

"Thanks," I said, in a choked voice.

Dex reached out and took my hand in his. Any other time, this would have thrilled me. After all, *Dex was holding my hand.* No one had ever held my hand before. Well. Not like this. And Dex's fingers felt warm and reassuring wrapped around mine. But I was too upset about Willow's running off to think too much about the hand-holding, other than to register that it was happening.

"Don't worry. We'll find her," Dex said confidently. We started walking down the beach, the sand shifting under our feet, looking for Willow. It was low tide, and the waves lapped gently up onto the beach.

"The problem is, she's never off lead. I don't think she'd even know how to get back to the beach house on her own," I said.

"Dogs are smarter than you think," Dex said. "She knows where home is."

"That's just it; this *isn't* her home. I mean, it's not her real home. It's just a place where we're staying temporarily," I explained. "Normally, we live with my mom."

"Maybe she'd go there. To your mom's house," he said.

I shrugged, and felt the tears welling in my eyes. "I don't know. I don't even know how she got out," I said. "She was closed up in my room."

"Someone was probably looking for a free bedroom, and let her out by mistake," Dex said.

"Why would they be looking for a bedroom?" I asked. Then suddenly I got it. *Duh.* Obviously. I was thankful it was dark out, so Dex wouldn't be able to see how red my face was. *"Oh,"* I said, and tried not to think about just who was in my room . . . or what they were doing there.

"People always get stupid at these parties," Dex explained.

"I've never been to one before. I didn't even really go to this one. It just sort of happened around me," I said.

"Well, this is pretty typical. Everyone drinks too much, and then they act like idiots. It's why I stopped going to them," Dex said.

"Why did you come tonight?" I asked.

Dex didn't answer, and when I glanced over at him, I saw that he was looking down at me. For a moment his eyes were steady on mine. *Zing!* My heart gave an excited thump.

Did he mean . . . Was he saying . . . Had he come to the party . . . because of *me*?

Dex stopped suddenly. And even though his face was lit by the pale moonlight streaming down over the beach, I couldn't tell what he was thinking. Was it possible that he liked me? *Really* liked me? I wondered if he was going to say something amazing about how he couldn't stop thinking about me. Or maybe . . . maybe he'd *kiss* me. My breath caught in my throat, and I knew with certainty that if he did kiss me, my entire body would melt into a puddle right there on the sand. He'd kiss me . . . and then I could ask him to go to the Snowflake with me. My heart began leaping around in my chest at the thought.

"There she is," Dex said.

"What?" I asked, confused.

But then I realized that he was pointing over my shoulder, up toward the lifeguard stand at the back of the beach. I spun around and saw Willow, flopped down on the sand, her muzzle resting on her paws, her chest heaving. It looked like she was taking a nap.

"Willow!" I cried out, and ran toward her. Once I reached her, I knelt down beside her and stroked her neck. Willow opened one eye and looked at me. Her long pink tongue came out, slurped my hand, and then she closed her eyes again. I wondered if it was possible for dogs to be narcoleptic.

"Is she okay?" Dex asked. He'd followed me, and was now hovering behind me, looking concerned.

"She's fine. She's just tired from her big adventure," I said. "Come on, girl."

I tugged gently at Willow's collar, and she gradually, grudgingly stood up beside me. I didn't have a leash for her, so I just hooked my fingers under her collar and started to lead her back up the beach. Dex walked silently along beside me. I wondered if he'd take my free hand in his again. He didn't.

Suddenly I felt awkward with Dex. *He probably thinks I'm a freak, too,* I thought gloomily. *The sort of girl who completely loses it over something as minor as her dog getting out (and then only running a half mile down the beach before falling asleep under a lifeguard shack). And here I am, practically in tears, as though I'd never see her again,* I thought, my face burning. Total overreaction.

I was just glad I hadn't done anything really stupid. Like closing my eyes and puckering up my lips for a kiss that obviously wasn't coming. Now, *that* would have been truly mortifying.

"Thanks for helping me look for Willow. It was really nice of you," I gabbled nervously as we approached the house. "I don't know if I would have thought to look for her there. Under the lifeguard tower, I mean. I might have ended up walking ten miles down the beach without ever seeing her."

"I'm sure you would have found her eventually," Dex said.

We reached the wooden stairs that led up to the back deck of the beach house. I was just about to start up the steps when Dex spoke.

"Miranda," Dex said.

I turned around to look at him, and found myself standing eye-to-eye with him, now that I was up on the step. And suddenly I was *sure* he was going to kiss me. Sure of it. He stepped closer to me, so close that I could smell the clean scent of his shampoo. And then Dex reached out toward me, and I actually shivered . . . and it had nothing to do with the cool breeze blowing gently off the ocean.

*Is he going to rest his hand on my cheek when he kisses me?* I wondered. I've always loved that. Well. Not that I'd ever kissed anyone. But when I've imagined being kissed, the guy always rests his hand on my cheek just as he lowers his lips to mine. And then, as the kiss intensifies, he slides his hand back, until it's resting on my neck. . . .

But Dex didn't cup his hand against my cheek. Nor did he lean forward to kiss me. Instead, he brushed the tips of his fingers against my hair, while I stared mutely at him.

"You had a leaf in your hair," he explained.

"Yo, Dex!"

We both looked up. Some guy I didn't recognize was at the top of the stairs, a red plastic beer cup in his hand.

"Hey, Bruner," Dex said. He took a step back from me. "What's up?"

"Come on, dude; we gotta go. One of the neighbors just came over and said that if we don't take off, he's going to call the cops," Bruner said.

The news that the police might be showing up at any minute should have taken my mind off of the kiss that may or may not be coming . . . but it didn't. I stood there, rooted in place, still gazing hopefully at Dex. Unfortunately, Bruner didn't move either. He just guzzled down the last of his beer as he waited for Dex.

"I guess I have to go," Dex said.

"Tell me he's not your ride," I said, glancing back up at Bruner. He could barely stand up straight, and was clearly in no shape to drive.

"No. I'm his ride," Dex said. "I don't drink, so I'm always the designated driver. I guess I'd better get him out of here before he does something really dumb, like puke in your living room."

I nodded, swallowing back my disappointment.

But Dex hesitated. "What were you going to say?" he asked.

"What?" I asked.

"Earlier when we were inside. You said you wanted to apologize to me. What about?" he asked.

"Oh! I just . . . that day we were walking on the beach. I got the feeling that I offended you by calling you a jock," I said.

Dex shook his head and smiled faintly. "You didn't offend me," he said.

"Good. I thought . . . well, I thought I had. And I just wanted you to know . . . that's not how I see you. Just as a jock," I explained.

Dex's smile grew wider, the corners of his lips quirking up in that sardonic way.

"Good to know," he said.

I turned quickly so he wouldn't see that my face had turned the color of a strawberry. I hurried up the stairs, Willow at my side and Dex behind me. Bruner moved to the side to let me pass. When Dex reached the top of the stairs, I heard Bruner say, "Who's the chick, man?"

I didn't wait to hear what Dex said in reply. Instead, I led Willow inside and back up to my room. Which was, fortunately, unoccupied.

Fifteen minutes later the house was empty, except for Hannah, Avery—who was spending the night—and me. It was amazing how quickly everyone cleared out as soon as the threat of the police was raised. The guys who'd brought the keg in took it away with them.

"You get kicked off the team if you're caught drinking," Avery explained to me as she collapsed on the sofa in the living room. The house was a mess—half-empty beer cups were littered on every available surface, magazines and plants were tipped onto the ground, the smell of sweat and smoke hung in the air. Avery reclined back, kicking off her shoes and wriggling into a more comfortable position. She didn't seem to have any intention of helping with the cleanup effort.

"What team?" I asked, picking up a few of the cups littered about.

Avery shrugged. "Football. Soccer. Cross-country track. Take your pick," she said. "A few years ago the entire cheerleading squad was disbanded after they got busted drinking at homecoming." She closed her eyes. "God, I am so buzzed," she said, her speech slurring.

I left her and went into the kitchen to throw out the stack of cups. Hannah was there, already cleaning. I dumped the half-empty cups into the sink, while Hannah picked garbage up off of the floor. It was truly stunning how filthy the house had gotten in such a short period of time.

"Thanks," Hannah said as I tossed a stack of cups into the garbage.

"No problem," I said. "This place is a mess, though."

"Yeah, it got a little out of control. I only invited a few people over. Twenty, tops. And I specifically said no alcohol. And then this happened." Hannah waved a hand at the mess. "Oh, well. I'll have all day tomorrow to pick up before Mom and Richard get home. And Avery and the twins said they'd help," Hannah said. She looked at me then, and I could tell that she felt awkward. "Miranda . . . would you do me a favor and not tell my mom or your dad about the party?"

Hannah was asking me for a favor? I looked around, wondering if the earth had actually stopped spinning on its axis.

"Please?" she said softly, her pretty blue eyes pleading in a way that reminded me of Willow when she was angling for a doggy treat. "Mom would be furious if she found out. She told me not to have anyone over."

"Don't worry. I won't say a word," I promised.

"Thanks," she said. She smiled tentatively at me.

"No problem," I said.

"So . . . I saw you go outside with Dex," Hannah said as she turned to wipe up the kitchen counter with a damp sponge.

I couldn't help it—I blushed again. I had to figure out a way to stop doing that.

"He was helping me find Willow," I said. "Someone let her out of my room, and she got out."

"Is she okay?" Hannah asked, actually sounding concerned.

I nodded. "Yeah. We found her," I said, enjoying the way *we* sounded. *We*. Dex and me. The two of us *together*.

Hannah frowned suddenly. "Listen, I hate to tell you this, but I think you should know something," she said.

"What?" I asked.

"Dex has a girlfriend. Wendy. You know, the model. They got back together," Hannah said.

I wasn't prepared for how this news would hit me. My stomach actually hurt, as though I'd been punched. No, it was worse than that: I felt like I'd been punched in the gut, and then while I lay moaning on the floor, doubled up in pain, someone wearing very pointy shoes began to kick me. Surprisingly, it was worse—far worse—than watching Emmett and Hannah get together. Maybe it was that Emmett had always just been a fantasy. Deep down, I'd always known nothing would really happen between us. But Dex? Dex and I had zing. Or, at least, I thought we had.

After all, hadn't he been about to kiss me outside? Or . . . had I just imagined that? I could feel doubt surging up inside of me. No one had ever kissed me before, so really, how would I know what it was like to be almost kissed? Maybe he really was just brushing a leaf out of my hair. After all, if he had been planning to kiss me, wouldn't he have done so back when we were alone on the beach? And he hadn't.

That was just it: He hadn't kissed me. But then he wouldn't, would he? Not if he had a girlfriend. A gorgeous, model girlfriend. I suddenly felt incredibly stupid. What had I been thinking? Of course Dex wouldn't be interested in someone like *me*, when he was dating a model.

I was just very, very glad I hadn't asked Dex to be my date to the

Snowflake. Obviously, he'd have said no. And how mortifying that would have been, watching him stammer out his rejection, while his face creased with pity. I shivered with horror at the thought.

"Oh. Well, that's good. For Dex, I mean," I said, turning so that Hannah wouldn't be able to read the disappointment on my face.

"I'm sorry," Hannah said, more kindly than I'd have thought her capable of.

"It's no big deal," I lied. "I'm really tired. I'm going to go to bed. I'll help you clean up in the morning, okay?"

I got back to my room and text-messaged Charlie to tell her I wouldn't be coming over after all. And then I curled up in bed, my arms wrapped around my pillow, trying not to think about Dex, or our zing, or the kiss that wasn't, or—worst of all—about Dex holding his girlfriend in his arms, and lowering his lips to hers. . . . No. That I didn't want to think about, I decided, taking in a deep breath and then puffing out my cheeks as I blew it back out.

It took me a really, really long time to fall asleep.

# Chapter 23

$$\frac{\partial r}{\partial u} = \frac{\partial X}{\partial u}\, i + \frac{\partial Y}{\partial u}\, j + \frac{\partial Z}{\partial u}\, k$$

$$\frac{\partial r}{\partial v} = \frac{\partial X}{\partial v}\, i + \frac{\partial Y}{\partial v}\, j + \frac{\partial Z}{\partial v}\, k$$

If it weren't bad enough that I was yet again in the position of having fallen for a guy whom I didn't have even the slightest chance with, I still didn't have a date for the Snowflake. I knew Felicity had a date; her boyfriend was coming down from Yale for the weekend, and she wouldn't shut up about it. And even Morgan had Snake.

At least Charlie and I were in the same boat. The fact that she didn't have a date, either, made it bearable that I was still going stag.

"Why don't we go to the Snowflake together?" I suggested to Charlie over lunch. "It'll be cool. Who needs guys anyway?"

"Don't mind me," Finn remarked.

"Come on; it'll be great. We're liberated, self-assured women, completely comfortable being on our own. We don't need boys to have a good time," I enthused. Finn started to open his mouth, but I cut him off. "Present company excluded, of course."

"Sorry, Miranda, but I have a date," Charlie said apologetically.

Finn and I both stared at her.

"You do?" I asked.

"Who?" Finn asked.

"Mitch," Charlie said.

"Mitch? Mitch from Grounded? When did that happen?" I asked, feeling a bit put out that she hadn't bothered to mention this momentous news to me.

"This morning," Charlie said. "I stopped at the coffee shop on the way to school to grab a muffin, and Mitch was there, and we got to talking, and somehow the conversation turned to the Snowflake, and—long story short—he asked me to go with him." She finished with a shrug, and took a bite of her ham-and-cheese sandwich.

"But he doesn't even go to our school," Finn said hotly.

"So?" Charlie asked.

"So you have to actually be a student here before you can ask someone to the Snowflake. And no offense to Mitch, but I don't see him getting into Geek High anytime soon," Finn said. He was glowering at Charlie, and dropped his sandwich on his plate for emphasis.

"I suppose, technically, I should have been the one to issue the invite, but it doesn't really matter who asked whom," Charlie said, reasonably enough.

"Of course it matters," Finn said irritably. "In fact, his asking you doesn't count. It's not an official date."

Now it was our turn to stare at Finn.

"Who appointed you arbiter of whether a date is 'official'?" Charlie asked, making bunny fingers around the word *official*.

"Me, that's who," Finn said. He scowled at her and folded his arms over his chest.

"Why are you getting so worked up about this?" Charlie asked, her forehead puckering in confusion.

"I'm not worked up. Look, I have to go," Finn said. He stood up, tucked his laptop under one arm, and stalked out of the cafeteria.

"What," Charlie asked, watching him leave, "was that all about?"

I shrugged. "I have no idea," I said. Although I thought maybe I did have an idea . . . just not one Charlie was ready to hear.

And besides, I had other things to worry about. Like, how I was now probably, in all likelihood, the only person in the entire freaking school who didn't have a date to the Snowflake. Immediately I had a vision of Dex at the beach, his face flooded with moonlight, standing so close to me that I could see that his eyes were so pale as to almost be gray. . . .

*No,* I thought, firmly pushing the image from my mind. *I'm through getting crushes on guys I don't have a shot with. If I'm going to find a date for this stupid dance, I have to start being realistic.*

I glanced around the cafeteria, checking out the male population of Geek High. It was slim pickings. There was Sanjiv (*no*) sitting with Kyle Carpenter (absolutely *not*). At the next table, Emmett was sitting with Isaac Hanson (cute enough, but the last I heard he was dating Jena Worth) and Peter Rossi (Felicity's ex, and annoyingly cocky). Two tables over Marcus Jackson (spits when he talks) was eating lunch with Jonathan Barker (reasonably attractive, if you overlooked the unibrow) and Christopher Frost (incapable of normal conversation). I sighed. I was just going to have to suck it up, pick a guy, and ask him . . . and then pray that he wouldn't say no.

Sanjiv had scheduled the next Mu Alpha Theta practice on the same afternoon that the *Ampersand* was holding its informational meeting for interested sophomores. Attendance at the meeting was mandatory if you wanted to work on the magazine. And competition for the two spots they held open for sophomores was fierce. The two who made it in would have the best shot of running for editor in chief when the journal held its elections at the end of junior year. Everyone wanted to be EIC of the *Ampersand.* It won a ton of national awards every year, and was a plum extracurricular to list on your college applications.

"I can't stay long," I told Sanjiv when I got to Mr. Gordon's room for practice. I figured I'd stick around for thirty minutes, and then head over to the *Ampersand* meeting. The first Mu Alpha Theta competition was still months away, not until January. It wasn't like we were down to the wire.

But Sanjiv looked aggrieved. He pursed his lips and fixed me with a cold stare. His Adam's apple moved up and down in his thin throat. "The practice is scheduled to run for two hours," he said. "And as team captain, I have to insist that everyone stays for the entire practice."

I folded my arms. "And just exactly when were you named team captain?" I asked.

"It was decided at the first meeting. The one you missed," Sanjiv said.

"He was the only one who wanted the job," Leila Chang told me.

"Why? You want to be captain?" Kyle Carpenter asked with a sneer.

You know, I don't like Kyle. He's one of those people who's incapable of speaking without sounding confrontational. Also, he sneers. It's his all-purpose expression.

"No. I don't want to be captain," I said irritably.

"It sounds like you do," Kyle said. "In fact, it sounds like you want to be in charge of everything. The Snowflake, the Mu Alpha Theta team. What's next? Headmaster of Geek High?"

"Oh, no, you've uncovered my master plan," I said. "Today, it's the Mu Alpha Theta team. Tomorrow, the school. And then, with a little luck and my army of evil robot warriors, I plan to take over the world."

Leila Chang and Nicholas Pruitt both sniggered at this. Kyle sneered. Sanjiv pressed his lips together until they were rimmed with white.

"I just think that everyone on the team should make practice a priority," Sanjiv said.

Sanjiv was so tightly wound, it was only a matter of time until he snapped. I truly feared for his future coworkers in the actuarial department at an insurance company. Sanjiv's goal was actually to be a code breaker at the NSA, but I was pretty sure he wouldn't make it past the psychiatric exam. They'd ask one of those morality questions that don't have a good answer, like, *Your friend tells you he's planning to kill someone. Do you (a) agree to help him, (b) do it yourself to make sure it gets done correctly, or (c) refuse to kill anyone, but help him bury the body?*, and

Sanjiv would panic and overthink it, and finally choose *(b) do it yourself to make sure it gets done correctly*, and that would be the end of his NSA aspirations.

"Maybe we should get started with the practice," Mr. Gordon suggested mildly.

And so we did. Today we were—at my suggestion—finally doing oral drills. We focused on logic problems, which, to be honest, weren't that challenging for me, but it was fun to watch Sanjiv twitch and Kyle turn red with fury whenever they came up with the wrong answer, and Mr. Gordon had to gently correct them.

In the end, we practiced for only an hour, which I had to admit was a reasonable compromise, although I spent the whole time fidgeting and glancing at my watch, desperate for the practice to come to an end. Of course, Sanjiv didn't want to compromise at all, but Mr. Gordon couldn't stay any later. The Gordons belonged to a dinner club that met once a month. Tonight was Italian night, and Mr. Gordon had to get home in time to make meatballs.

When the hour was finally, mercifully up, I threw my books in my knapsack, jumped to my feet, and hurried out the door. Maybe, just maybe, I could catch the tail end of the *Ampersand* meeting.

"Bye, everyone. Great practice," I called out over my shoulder.

"I'm the team captain. I should be the one who says that," Sanjiv protested. He paused to clear his throat. "Great practice, everyone!"

I rolled my eyes and pushed out the door. I was halfway down the hallway when I heard someone calling my name.

"Miranda! Hey! Miranda, wait up!"

I spun around. Nicholas Pruitt was hurrying after me, his knapsack cradled it in his arms like a baby. I waited for him to catch up. When he did, his breath was coming in quick gasps. Nicholas hadn't yet hit his growth spurt, so he barely came up to my shoulder. He was also painfully thin, with narrow shoulders and eyes that were small and bright, like a bird's.

I waited for a moment for him to speak, but he just stood there, staring mutely at me.

"What's up, Nicholas?" I asked him, trying not to sound impatient. The *Ampersand* meeting, I thought helplessly.

But Nicholas just continued to stand there, not saying a word, while his face slowly turned the color of a ripe tomato. I peeked at my watch.

"I really have to get going," I said apologetically.

"Oh . . . okay. Well. I was just wondering . . ." He paused and sucked in a deep breath. I stifled the urge to scream with frustration. Why couldn't he just say what he had to say and let me go to my meeting? "Will you . . . will you go to the Snowflake with me?" Nicholas finally blurted out.

It was awful. I just stood there, rooted in place, as the invitation hung there between us. Go to the Snowflake with Nicholas? But . . . but . . . he looked like he was about twelve years old. Wait. *Was* he twelve? I'd assumed he was fourteen, like most freshmen, but it was entirely possible that he'd skipped a few grades somewhere along the way.

"Um," I said.

"It's just . . . if you don't have a date yet . . . I'd really like it if you could . . . you know. Go with me," Nicholas continued. He shifted nervously, and I was distantly aware of how much more painful this was for him. He was experiencing my discomfort times ten. Times a hundred.

And the thing was . . . what could I say? If I said no, I already had a date, and then showed up on my own . . . well, that would hurt his feelings.

But if I said yes . . . then I would have to go to the dance, the first real dance of my high school career, with a freshman midget. Okay, so Nicholas wasn't really a midget, but still, I had a good eight inches on him. If we danced, his head would be level with my chest. Especially if I wore heels.

This wasn't how it was supposed to happen. Your first dance is supposed to be *romantic*. You're supposed to go with the sort of guy who makes you feel all tingly and shivery inside. The kind of guy who you're hoping will kiss you at the end of the night. A guy you have zing with.

But, then again, I'd been in Nicholas's shoes every time I stared at Emmett, or fantasized about kissing Dex. I'd been the one who wasn't noticed. The one who didn't rate attention. And as much as I didn't want to go to this dance with Nicholas, I also didn't want to make him feel like I had when I watched Emmett pick Hannah up for their first date. Or fruitlessly waited for Dex to kiss me on the beach . . . only to find out later that he had a stunning girlfriend. I didn't want to be *that* person, the one who makes someone else feel like they're less-than just because they don't look like they walked out of a J.Crew catalog. Because you know what? There are lots of really great people out there in the world who don't look like models. Funny people, smart people, nice people. And why should they be discriminated against just because they don't possess the freakish genes that we've randomly decided as a society are preferable? What's so inherently great about a girl who's six feet tall and has starved herself down to a size two?

No. I needed to make a stand for Nicholas, a stand for all of the less-than-perfect people out there. A stand for all of the geeks.

I drew in a deep breath, and then forced myself to smile down at him. "Sure. That would be fun."

It clearly wasn't the response Nicholas had expected. He gaped up at me, while his expression shifted from scared, to hopeful, to, finally, delighted surprise. His face flushed an even darker shade of red, and his brown eyes opened wide.

"Really?" he asked.

"Really," I said.

"Wow. That's just . . . *wow*. That is so great," Nicholas said, breaking out in a wide smile. "*So* great. I guess it's a date."

*It's a date. Oh, no.* What had I just agreed to? I was going on a date with a freshman midget. It was true . . . I was really never going to be *that* girl. The movie girl. The one who shakes out her hair, and loses the clunky glasses, and gets the cute guy. Instead, I was going to be the girl who went to the geek prom with a guy who looked like he was still a good three to four years away from hitting puberty. This was actually my life.

"It's a date," I repeated faintly. Then I shook my head and remembered: the *Ampersand* meeting. "I'm sorry, but I really have to run."

"Okay, sure. Talk to you later," Nicholas said, still grinning broadly.

I turned and ran down the hall . . . but it was too late. By the time I got to the *Ampersand* office it was empty and dark, and the door was locked. I'd missed the meeting. There went any hope I'd had of being on the magazine staff this year. I leaned forward, pressing my head against the glass panel insert on the door. It felt cool against my hot forehead.

*Great*, I thought. *That's just* great.

# Chapter 24

$$a(S) = \iint\limits_{T} \left\| \frac{\partial r}{\partial u} \times \frac{\partial r}{\partial v} \right\| du\, dv$$

It was the annual fund-raising picnic for Great Greys, and—true to his word—Dad drove Willow and me down to West Palm Beach to attend the festivities. The event was over an hour away, so we left early and got to the park just as it was starting. Several tents were set up in and among the flower beds, shade trees, and fountains shooting jets of water into the air. There were greyhounds *everywhere*—walking on leads, lying down in the sun, dressed up in costumes. I had Willow's and my Calvin and Hobbes costumes for the competition stashed in a bag, and planned to change just before the judging started. As pleased as I was with how our costumes had turned out, I didn't want to have to spend the entire day dressed like Calvin.

"So what should we do first?" my dad asked. "Head over to the silent auction, or check out the food?"

"The silent auction," I decided. "They always have a ton of greyhound gear there, and Willow really needs a new leash."

I lifted her old nylon leash to show him. It had once been pink, but was now a decidedly gray shade with fraying ends.

"The auction it is," Dad said.

We headed over to the silent-auction tent. Items up for auction were arranged on long, rectangular folding tables. A clipboard had been placed in front of each lot, where interested browsers could write down their bids. The auction closed at noon, and whoever had the highest offer on the list at that time won. I'd learned from past experience that there were some ruthless snipers out there, people who ran around at the very last minute and outbid everyone else. So for now, I was content to browse the merchandise, looking at the various leashes up for auction. I quickly settled on the one I wanted—a gorgeous martingale leash made of soft red leather. I held it up to Willow's neck, and it looked stunning against her brindle coat. Willow didn't seem overly impressed. She just yawned and then began to pant, her wide pink tongue lolling out of her open mouth.

"This is the one I want," I said, showing it to my dad.

"That's nice," he said. "Shall we write down a bid?"

I shook my head. "Not this early. Someone will just one-up us."

"That's the whole point of an auction," Dad said. He picked the pen up, and with a flourish wrote down a number that was twenty dollars higher than the one above it.

"Dad, that's too much!" I said.

"It's a fund-raiser. The money's going for a good cause," Dad said.

"Oh . . . well, thanks," I said. "It's nice of you to support the group."

"It's important to you," Dad said, capping the pen and putting it back down on the table. "That makes it important to me, too."

Was that really true? I wondered. Or was he still just feeling guilty over how distant he'd been in recent years?

Then again, he had come to the fund-raiser with me.

*He's trying,* I thought. *Maybe people really can change. Or, at least, change back into who they used to be.*

"You know, the last few years there's been a woman here who sells doughnuts. She fries them right there in front of you, and they're amazing. Do you want to try one?" I asked.

My dad smiled at me. "I would love a freshly fried doughnut. Lead the way."

We found the doughnut seller in the food tent. I ordered a powdered sugar, while my dad got a plain one, sprinkled with cinnamon.

"This is the best doughnut I've ever had," he said.

"Told you," I said.

We spent the rest of the morning wandering around, admiring greyhounds and chatting with their owners, and browsing through the greyhound-themed merchandise sold by various vendors. For lunch, we washed down sausage sandwiches with cups of sweet tea, and then went back for a second round of doughnuts. Every half hour or so we'd check back at the auction tent to see if we still had the top bid for the red martingale leash. Every time we were overbid, Dad wrote down a new bid.

"Willow is going to get that leash if it's the last thing I do," he said fervently.

I hadn't known my dad could get so competitive over an auction. It was probably a good thing he hadn't yet discovered eBay.

Just before the costume parade began, I left Willow with Dad and went into the bathroom to change into my Calvin costume. I pulled on a red-and-black striped shirt, black shorts, and a short, spiky blond wig. I'd thought about wearing roller skates, but then remembered that last year Willow had gotten a little spooked during the parade, and had tried to dash off the stage. I didn't want to be on wheels should she decide upon a repeat performance.

"Ta-da," I said when I came out of the bathroom.

"Perfect!" Dad said. He tousled my wig hair. "You look just like Calvin."

"Now for Willow," I said. She had a furry tiger headpiece that went on like a hood and snapped under her neck, and furry booties. Willow submitted to being dressed with dignity, and didn't even fight me when I slid the fake tiger tail over her normal, thin greyhound one.

"How do we look?" I asked my dad, making Willow turn around with me, so he could see us from all angles.

"Like champions," Dad said. "I haven't seen anyone with a costume that's half as good."

"I don't know," I fretted. "There was a Donald and Melania Trump pair that looked pretty good. The wedding dress the greyhound was wearing was amazing. She even had a veil on."

"No, your costumes are definitely better," Dad said encouragingly. "I think this is your year to win."

The loudspeaker suddenly let out an ear-shattering squawk of feedback that caused everyone to cringe and cover their ears. "The costume parade and judging is about to begin. If you are entered in the contest, please line up by the fountain," a disembodied voice announced.

"That's us," I said. "Come on, Willow. I mean, Hobbes."

"Good luck," Dad called after us.

Willow and I didn't win the costume contest. We didn't even place. Unsurprisingly, Donald and Melania—whose doggy wedding dress, I learned, had been designed and hand-sewn at a swanky bridal shop on Palm Beach—took first place. Second place went to an owner and greyhound dressed as salt and pepper shakers, and third to a pair of mermaids.

"You were robbed. Your costumes were far better than the salt and pepper shakers. And those didn't even look like mermaids. I thought they were supposed to be fish," Dad grumbled when I met up with him after the contest.

"It's okay," I said, shrugging. "I probably would have voted for the Donald, too."

"If it makes you feel any better, I have a consolation prize for you," Dad said. He pulled out the beautiful red tooled martingale leash from behind his back, and held it out to me.

"We won the auction?" I asked, delighted.

Dad nodded. "I had to practically fight a woman for it," he said. He nodded at a short woman with frizzy blond curls and a white greyhound, who was scowling at my dad across the park. "She tried to sneak in at the last minute and outbid me. But I managed to top her just before the clipboards were picked up," Dad bragged, looking so pleased with himself that I had to laugh.

"Thanks, this is great," I said, slipping the new leash over Willow's head. It looked perfect.

I glanced around. People were starting to pack up and load dogs into cars.

"I guess it's time to go home," I said, pulling my itchy Calvin wig off my head.

"Okay," Dad said. "Let's go."

As we turned and headed toward his car, my dad looked down at me almost shyly.

"Thanks for letting me come with you," he said.

"No, thank *you*," I said. "If you hadn't driven me down, I wouldn't be here."

"I was glad to," Dad said. He paused before continuing. "We don't spend enough time together."

I bit my lip. We'd had such a nice day together, it seemed a shame to ruin it with a snide comment about the *reason* we hadn't been spending much time together. After all, I wasn't the one who'd disappeared to marry a cold-blooded demon.

"It's my fault," Dad said, as though reading my mind. "I know that. And I know that you're still angry with me. But I want to make it up to you."

"Thanks," I said, touched. "That means a lot to me."

Dad reached down and took my hand in his, and gave it a squeeze. We hadn't held hands in years, not since I was a little girl. And for just a brief moment, I remembered how safe it had felt to reach up and slip my small hand in his larger one. I hesitated, and then I squeezed his hand back.

# Chapter 25

$$\iint\limits_{r(T)} f\, dS = \iint\limits_{T} f[r(u, v)] \left\| \frac{\partial r}{\partial u} \times \frac{\partial r}{\partial v} \right\| du\, dv$$

Test time was, as usual at Geek High, crazy busy. Everyone was putting in as many hours of studying as they could, some even pulling all-nighters. I've tried all-nighters, but I normally make it until only about three a.m., at which point my brain shuts down and I end up passing out face-first right on my textbook.

Some of my classes, like astronomy, were only a semester long, which meant we were taking the course final during exam week. Other courses, like mod lit, were yearlong, and so we were prepping for the midterm. Either way, the tests were important, and would count as a major chunk of our grade. Which meant one thing: a total, schoolwide freakout. Sanjiv even canceled our Mu Alpha Theta practice sessions in honor of the exams.

"I have way too much to do," he said when he gave us the news that this would be our last practice of the semester. His Adam's apple was bobbing in his throat, and his left foot was tapping nervously. "I was up all night last night studying for Early American History. But it was worth it. I think I'm going to seriously ace that exam."

"Thanks for sharing, dude," Kyle Carpenter said snidely.

And for once I agreed with Kyle. Here's the thing about the Geek High student body: When we get stressed, we do our best to freak each other out. It's basically just an attempt to transfer our own anxiety onto someone else, and it's remarkably effective. Here's how it goes:

> *Student One:* Did you read that chapter for Latin on the conjugation paradigm? That was tough. I barely got through it.
>
> *Student Two* (voice panicky): *What?* We have to know *that* for the test?
>
> *Student One:* You didn't know that?
>
> *Student Two:* No! Oh, my God, I'm going to fail!
>
> *Student One* (looking more cheerful): Don't worry. I'm sure you'll do fine.

See? The downside is that even if you do manage to successfully freak someone else out, thus making yourself feel better, that good feeling lasts only until someone else comes along, intent on freaking you out. So I've found that the best policy is just to stay away from everyone.

Studying at school was completely out of the question. First of all, the Geek High library is an open echo chamber of a room. All it takes is for one person to start whispering to a friend behind the stacks, and *poof*, there goes any hope you might have had of concentrating on your work.

So Charlie and I studied at Grounded every afternoon after school. This worked pretty well. Or, at least, it did when Finn wasn't around.

"Hey, how long do you think I can balance this pencil on the end of my nose?" Finn asked, sliding into the open seat at our table, paper coffee cup in hand. "I bet I can keep it there for a full minute. Anyone want to bet me?"

He carefully set the pencil down on the end of his beaky nose.

Charlie looked at him with exasperation. "First of all, we're studying. Obviously." She gestured at the open pile of books and notebooks and empty coffee cups she and I had accumulated on the table before us. "And second, since I saw you stick your gum on the pencil, my guess would be that you can keep it on your nose until you decide to peel it off. So, no, I don't want to bet you."

Finn made a face at her and unstuck the pencil, leaving behind a little blob of pink chewing gum on the tip of his nose. He scratched it off with his fingernail.

"Why are you such a stress case?" Finn asked.

"Um, hello? Exams?" Charlie said, rolling her eyes at me.

Finn shrugged. "So?" he said.

Finn didn't believe in studying. Or maybe it would be more accurate to say that he simply didn't care what sort of grades he got. Although, annoyingly, he always did well. Even without studying.

"Finn, go away," Charlie said firmly.

"Okay, fine. Let me just finish my tasty hot beverage," Finn said. And then he began to slurp his coffee. Far more loudly then was absolutely necessary.

Charlie and I exchanged a look. I could tell that she was about to blow.

"I'm going to close my eyes and count to ten," Charlie said to me. "And if he's still sitting there when I'm done, I'm going to kill him." She shut her eyes. "One . . . two . . . three . . ."

"Does she really think I'm afraid of her?" Finn asked.

"Four . . . five . . ."

"Because I'm totally not," he said.

"Six . . . seven . . ."

"Not even a little," he continued. Although I noticed he was starting to edge off his seat.

"Eight . . . nine . . ."

"Later, chickadees," Finn said, fleeing. As he hurried out of the coffee shop, he looked back over his shoulder at me, and called out, "Check out geekhigh.com when you get a chance! Very interesting post today."

"*Ten.*" Charlie opened her eyes, and smiled serenely when she saw Finn was gone. "Now. Where were we?"

"Quasars," I said. "An astronomic source of electromagnetic energy with a very high redshift, as a result of Hubble's law."

"Hubble's law, Hubble's law. What's that again? Oh, here it is. 'The redshift in light is proportional to a galaxy's distance,' " Charlie said, reading from her notes. She looked up at me, a little wild-eyed. "Now, how on earth am I going to remember that?"

"Ha!" I said.

Charlie frowned. "What?" she asked.

"You made a pun. How on *earth* are you going to remember the *quasars*," I said.

Charlie closed her eyes and shook her head. When she opened her eyes again, she fixed me with her evilest of evil eyes. "*Miranda*. How can you joke at a time like this?"

*Yeesh,* I thought, ducking my head to avoid making eye contact. Charlie was scary when she got like this. I'd be glad when exams were over, once and for all. Well, over until next semester, anyway.

I pulled my laptop closer and surfed over to geekhigh.com. And this is what I read there:

**HOT ITEM**
*What math whiz and resident Geek High party planner is being escorted to the Snowflake by a younger man? Will one plus one equal romance? Stay tuned . . .*

I snapped my laptop shut and stood up.

"What's wrong," Charlie asked, looking up at me distractedly.

"Nothing," I said. "I just have to go find Finn. I'm going to find him . . . and then I'm going to kill him."

"Oh," Charlie said, returning to her astronomy book, and waving distractedly at me. "Good luck with that."

* * *

Our exams took place during the second week in December. Normal classes were suspended, while the tests were held every morning and afternoon. The week passed by in a blur of coffee, blue books, and stress. All in all, I felt okay about how I did. I was pretty sure I'd done well on my history, astronomy, mod lit, and math exams. I was less confident about my performance on the Latin midterm, and was pretty sure I'd flubbed a question on the differences between the Impressionists and the Postimpressionists on my art appreciation final.

"At least it's over," I said as Charlie and I left the art appreciation exam on Friday afternoon. "Now all I have to do is get through the Snowflake tomorrow, and I'm off to London on Sunday!"

"I'm so jealous." Charlie sighed. "I wish I could go with you. There's a Frida Kahlo exhibit at the Tate Modern that I'd give anything to see."

"I wish you could come, too," I said. I was getting a little nervous about my overseas flight. It was the longest trip I'd ever undertaken, and I was doing it on my own.

"Hello, girls," Finn said, appearing behind us. He squeezed himself in between Charlie and me, and draped an arm over each of our shoulders as we walked down the school corridor. "How are my little stress cases doing? Would you like to join me at Grounded for a celebratory latte? On me."

"We can't," I said.

"Why not?" Finn asked. "Exams are over! We're footloose and fancy-free!"

"No, we're not. We have our final Snowflake committee meeting right now. Remember?" I said, poking him in the ribs. "You're coming too."

Finn, who's very ticklish, flinched. "Hey, cut that out. I'd love to stay for the meeting, but unfortunately I have a pressing engagement elsewhere," he said.

"Liar. You just said you're going to Grounded," Charlie pointed out.

"Yes, and, while I'm there, I have to update a certain Web site. I haven't had a chance to post all week, what with the grueling test schedule and all," Finn said.

At this, Charlie and I both rolled our eyes. Finn had spent every moment that he didn't have a test playing the online adventure game he was currently obsessed with. Finn spent so much of his time gaming, I wasn't sure when he found the time to dream up his own games.

"You're coming to the meeting," Charlie told him flatly.

"I brought snacks," I lied, hoping to entice him. You can convince Finn to do just about anything if you promise to feed him.

Finn perked up at this. "Snacks?" he asked hopefully.

I rooted around in my knapsack until I found a roll of Butter Rum Life Savers.

"Here you go," I said, handing him the roll.

Finn looked crestfallen. "They're open," he complained critically, as he examined the Life Savers. "And there's fuzz on them."

"Just the one on the end," I said. "Toss that one. The rest should be fine."

"That's okay," Finn said, popping the first Life Saver into his mouth. "I sort of like the fuzz. It gives the candy an interesting texture."

"You," Charlie said, "are disgusting."

"Want one?" Finn asked, holding out the candy to her.

She swatted it away. "Come on. We're going to be late."

"We're ready," I announced, once everyone on the Snowflake committee had gathered for our final meeting in Mr. Arburro's social studies room. "Completely and totally ready."

"What about the food?" Morgan asked.

"Charlie and I are going to the grocery store this afternoon to pick up chips and soda and stuff. Oh, and guess what I found at that candy store at the mall? Black and white M&M's," I said proudly. "We're going to fill a giant punch bowl with them."

"Has anyone checked with the band to confirm they're coming?" Charlie asked.

"Of course they're coming," Morgan protested. "Snake's my date, after all."

The band. This was the one major problem we'd had while planning the Snowflake, and, try as I might, I could not wring one extra dollar out of Headmaster Hughes to hire a real band. A *good* band. Instead, we had to go with the free band, headed by Morgan's guitarist boyfriend, Snake. And it was a risk . . . a *big* risk.

I'd met Snake a few weeks earlier, when Morgan, Felicity, Charlie, and I had auditioned his band one afternoon after school. The audition took place in Snake's parents' garage, which was damp and dank and smelled like gasoline. Snake was thin, and sported a pierced eyebrow, a pierced nose, a pierced tongue, and an elaborate tattoo of (what else?) a snake wrapping up around his thin arm. He greeted Morgan with a wet kiss involving a lot of tongue, while the rest of us stood and watched, all completely revolted by the sight.

Finally they broke apart, Morgan giggling and wiping spittle off her mouth, and Snake's band, Snake House, played for us. They were . . . not awful. Which is not to say they were good. Because they weren't.

"Can you do more covers?" Felicity suggested, after the band finished a particularly jarring number, which sounded as though each musician were playing a different song.

"We don't do covers," Snake said haughtily. He pushed a handful of greasy black hair out of his eyes. "We're, like, artists."

"That's right, dude. We're artists," Doug, the lead singer, agreed. He balled his hand in a fist and raised it triumphantly in the air.

Felicity and I shared a worried look. We might not agree on much, but there was one thing she and I had in common: We weren't at all happy that Snake House was going to be playing at the Snowflake.

But, since they were the only band who would play for free, Snake House was in. And now, as the committee went over the final details for the dance, I tried to push out of my mind my concerns over just how much Snake House would suck. Maybe, set against the elegant black and white balloons and old Hollywood photographs, and lit by the thousands of twinkle lights we planned to string up around the gym, and the general glamour of everyone getting dressed up, Snake House would rise to the occasion and, for at least one night, they'd sound like Coldplay.

But, then, maybe that was setting my expectations just a wee bit high.

"So, we're all going to meet here tomorrow morning to decorate, right?" I said.

Finn raised his hand. "No can do," he said.

Charlie narrowed her eyes. "And why not?" she asked.

She sounded more annoyed than I thought she should be. After all, this was Finn. It was a minor miracle he'd shown up for any of the meetings. I'd never expected that he'd actually sacrifice a whole morning to decorate the gym for the dance. But, then, they'd been fighting more than usual lately . . . actually, ever since Charlie had announced that she was going to the Snowflake with Mitch. I was pretty sure that was the main reason behind the contention, and equally sure that neither of them would admit to it.

"I have something to do," Finn said, shrugging.

"So you're flaking," Charlie said, rolling her eyes. "Big surprise."

"If you must know, I have to pick up my tux," Finn retorted.

"Who are you taking to the dance?" Felicity asked Finn curiously.

"He doesn't have a date," Charlie said, sounding so scornful, I looked at her curiously. Sure, she could be sharp with Finn at times, but she was hardly ever mean about it.

"Yes, I do," Finn said loftily.

Finn had a date? I hadn't known that. He certainly hadn't mentioned anything about it to me. In fact, I'd just assumed that Finn wouldn't even show up at the Snowflake. It wasn't at all his sort of scene.

"Who?" Charlie asked suspiciously.

"Leila Chang," Finn said.

"Really?" I asked. Leila was a year older than us, and I'd thought she was going out with someone at Orange Cove High.

"Yup," Finn said. He grinned and looked pleased with himself. "She asked me," he said smugly.

"Way to go, Finn," I said.

But Charlie was glaring at him, looking even angrier.

"What's wrong, Charlie?" I asked her.

"Nothing," she said. Or, rather, snarled. She looked meaningfully at her watch. "Come on, Miranda; we should go. My mom will be here in a few minutes to take us to the grocery store."

"Okay," I said, standing and packing up my stuff. "I'll see everyone tomorrow morning. And don't worry . . . everything's going to be perfect. I promise."

# Chapter 26

$$\frac{\partial R}{\partial s} \times \frac{\partial R}{\partial t} = \left(\frac{\partial r}{\partial u} \times \frac{\partial r}{\partial v}\right) \frac{\partial(U, V)}{\partial(s, t)}$$

Except that everything wasn't perfect. Far from it. In fact, on the day of the Snowflake Gala, everything that possibly could go wrong, did.

*Everything.*

It started early in the morning, while I was still asleep. I was dreaming about the dance. Only in my dream, I was there with Willow as my date, not Nicholas, and everyone seemed to think this was totally normal and acceptable. A sharp rap on my door jarred me awake just as Headmaster Hughes was crowning Willow and me king and queen of the Snowflake . . . which was especially weird, since we don't even have a king and queen of the Snowflake. I lifted my head off my pillow and blinked sleepily. Willow stirred on her bed, but then yawned and instantly fell back asleep.

"Come in," I croaked in a voice still hoarse with sleep.

The door swung open. Peyton stood with a pinched expression on her face, and the cordless phone in her hand.

"Miranda, your headmaster is on the phone wishing to speak to you," Peyton announced.

This woke me up. Quickly. Headmaster Hughes was calling me at home? There was nothing good about that. It was creepy and weird and just plain wrong. I sat bolt upright and reached out for the phone.

"Thanks," I said, as Peyton crossed the room to hand it to me.

"It smells like dog in here." Peyton sniffed. She shot Willow a dirty look, and then turned on her heel and stalked out. I sighed. I swear, Cinderella's evil stepmother seemed positively warmhearted when compared to mine.

"Hello?" I said uncertainly into the phone.

"Miranda. C. Philip Hughes here."

*Gulp*. It *was* the headmaster. I wondered what the C stood for, and why Headmaster Hughes didn't use it. Cornelius? Cornwall? Curmudgeon? It would take a braver girl than I to ask him.

"Um, hi," I said.

"We seem to have a bit of a situation here," he said.

And then I suddenly remembered, the knowledge tumbling into place: Tonight was the Snowflake Gala. I was in charge. Everything had to be perfect.

"What's wrong?" I asked.

"A pipe burst in the boys' locker room. It flooded the auditorium. Building maintenance said there's no way they'll have it dried out in time for tonight."

So that was that, I thought as I climbed out of bed and padded out of my bedroom, Willow yawning at my heels. The Snowflake was off, postponed until a later date. Or, maybe if I was very lucky, permanently canceled. After all, this was the answer to all of my problems, right? Well. Not all of my problems. Certainly not the ones involving my parents or stepfamily or the pitiful state of my love life. But at least I wouldn't have to worry about the Snowflake sucking and everyone hating me for it. And I also wouldn't have to worry about Nicholas trying to kiss me, a situation I very much wanted to avoid.

But in a weird way, I was actually a little disappointed, too. I don't know why exactly. Maybe deep down, I was actually looking forward to the Snowflake.

"Is everything okay, honey?" Dad asked, looking concerned when Willow and I came into the kitchen. Dad, Peyton, and Hannah were all sitting around the breakfast table, reading the paper. Madonna was sitting in Hannah's lap, and she twitched her tail and narrowed her eyes when she saw Willow, but Willow took the moral high ground and ignored the Persian . . . although, then again, maybe she just didn't see the cat. A platter of halved bagels and flavored cream cheese sat in the middle of the table. Dad and Hannah were eating; Peyton was merely sipping at her black coffee.

"Yeah, everything's fine," I said, swallowing back a sigh.

"Why did your headmaster call?" Dad asked.

"Remember the dance that we were supposed to have tonight? The one I was in charge of planning?" I said.

Dad nodded.

"Well, it's been canceled. The auditorium flooded, and there's nowhere else we can have it," I said.

"Oh, that's too bad," Dad said sympathetically.

"Canceled?" Hannah exclaimed, looking up from the style page.

I blinked, surprised that she cared, before I remembered: Hannah was going to the Snowflake as Emmett's date. Or she would have gone with Emmett, had the gym not flooded.

Hannah frowned and snuggled Madonna up to her chest. "But I bought a new dress and everything."

I shrugged. "I'm sorry. It's just bad luck."

"Why don't you move the dance somewhere else?" Hannah asked.

"There's no way we could find a place that's big enough on such short notice," I said. I dumped dry dog food into Willow's bowl, and then sat down at the kitchen table. I selected a cinnamon-raisin bagel off the platter, and smeared it with cream cheese.

"Maybe you could hold it at Orange Cove High," Dad suggested.

Hannah shook her head. "That won't work. There's a football game tonight, and they're having a pep rally in the gym beforehand," she said. She put Willow down and took a small bite of her bagel. "No one goes but freshmen, of course, but the football players and cheerleaders at least have to be there. I know—how about the Yacht Club? They have a really big room they rent out for banquets, right, Mom?"

Peyton shook her head dismissively. "There's no way the Oar Room is free. You have to reserve it more than a year in advance," she said. "There are women in this town who book it for their weddings before they even get engaged."

"Besides, even if it was available, I doubt the school would pay to rent a room somewhere," I interjected.

"You could at least call and check, Mom. It would be the perfect place. It's right on the water," Hannah persisted.

Peyton and I both stared at Hannah. Peyton was probably horrified that her daughter was trying to talk her into doing a favor for me, while I was simply flabbergasted. It was completely unlike Hannah to do anything to help me. Was she really that eager to wear her new dress? Although, now that I thought of it, Hannah had been nicer to me lately, ever since her party. I'd kept my word and hadn't told Dad and Peyton about it. I wondered if Hannah was just trying to stay on my good side so that I wouldn't spill her secret . . . or if her feelings toward me had actually thawed out. It was hard to tell.

"That's a great idea, Hannah," Dad enthused. "Why don't you give them a call, Peyton? And if it's available, I'll cover the cost of renting it."

"You don't have to do that, Dad," I protested.

"You've put a lot of work into planning this dance," Dad said. "The show must go on, right?"

"Well . . . I suppose there's no harm in checking," Peyton said, shrugging. "But I wouldn't get your hopes up."

"Um, thanks, Peyton," I said. What a bizarre start to the day. First Hannah was being nice, and now Peyton was going to do me a favor.

Not to mention the wake-up call from Headmaster Hughes. What next? Would Willow and Madonna suddenly put aside their differences and become best buddies?

Peyton nodded curtly at me. She stood, walked over to the built-in telephone table located at the end of the kitchen counter, and flipped through her address book until she found the number for the Yacht Club. She picked up the phone and dialed.

"Hello, Rachel, this is Peyton Wainwright-Bloom. I know how unlikely this is, but I was calling to find out if there was any chance the Oar Room is free tonight." Pause. "Really?" Pause. *"Really?"* Pause. "Mmm-hmmm. I see. Yes. Well, that's . . . Yes, we would. Thank you. I'll call you back with the details."

Peyton hung up the phone, shook her head once in apparent disbelief, and then turned slowly toward us. "I can't believe this, but it's actually available. Samantha Sweeney was supposed to have her wedding reception there tonight, but the couple broke their engagement off just last night and canceled the wedding. So the room is all yours, Miranda."

"Excellent!" Hannah cheered.

"That's fantastic," Dad said.

"Wow," I said. "Thanks, Peyton. That was really nice of you."

Peyton nodded again, still looking a little confused. Being nice to me was so antithetical to her nature, it seemed to have thrown her for a loop. She even sat down and took a bite of a bagel before she'd realized what she was doing and quickly dropped the bagel back on her plate in horror.

"I guess I'd better go call Headmaster Hughes back and tell him the good news," I said.

Headmaster Hughes was pleased that I'd found an alternate location on such short notice, and he said he'd send out an e-mail to all of the students and teachers letting them know about the change in plans. I sent text messages to my committee members, filling them in on what had happened and asking them to meet me at the Yacht Club to decorate instead of at the school. Morgan texted back and said she'd take care of letting Snake and his band know about the location change.

I had just finished dressing and was about to ask my dad to give me a ride to the Yacht Club when Hannah appeared in my room.

"Hey," she said.

"Hi. Thanks for your help," I said.

"No problem," she said, wandering into my room, looking around. I realized she hadn't been in here since I'd moved in. She picked up my photos and looked at them, and then trailed a hand along the stack of books we'd read in mod lit so far that semester. I saw her eyes rest on the mostly packed suitcase propped open in the corner of my room. I was leaving for London tomorrow, and was just about ready to go. All I had to do was decide which books I was taking with me.

"So what are you wearing tonight?" she asked.

"The dress I wore to my mom's book party last year. I have it on in that picture there," I said, gesturing toward the photo of Sadie and me in our tiaras that I'd finally moved from the dresser drawer to the top of the dresser with my other photographs.

Hannah stared down at it, grimaced, and then gave a decisive shake of her head.

"No," she said. "You can't wear that."

"What's wrong with it?" I asked. The dress looked pretty inoffensive to me—a simple, knee-length sheath with cap sleeves and a round neck.

"It's just so boring. And it doesn't show any skin at all. No, you need to wear something sexier, something with more pizzazz," she said.

I shook my head and shrugged. "It's the only black dress I have. And I don't have time to go out and get anything else. I'm going to be at the Yacht Club all day today decorating."

"Don't worry; I'll handle it. What size are you? A six?" Hannah asked.

I frowned and nodded. "Yes, but—"

"Don't worry. Leave it to me." Hannah said, bouncing out of the room looking more cheerful. "Oh! I forgot to tell you. Remember how I told you that Dex and his girlfriend got back together?"

Like I'd forget. "Yeah?"

"I was wrong. They didn't. She got back together with the guy she was dating *before* Dex." Hannah frowned suddenly. "Oh, shoot. You could have asked him to go to the dance with you."

I felt like laughing and crying at the same time, but settled for shrugging and making a face. "Right. Like he'd have wanted to go with *me*."

"Why wouldn't he? You guys seem like you get along well together," Hannah said, absentmindedly twirling a lock of pale blond hair around one finger. "Oh . . . I also meant to tell you something else. It turns out Avery *did* take Mom's sweater. You know, the TSE one that went missing?"

This news was so surprising, it actually made me forget about Dex for thirty seconds. "Really? How do you know? Did she tell you?"

Hannah rolled her eyes. "She wore it to school. Can you believe that? Like I wouldn't notice. She tried denying it at first, but she finally broke down and admitted she'd taken it. We're so not friends anymore," she said, shaking her head.

"Wow," I said. "Did you tell Peyton?"

Hannah nodded. "I did. So she knows it wasn't you," Hannah said. She turned and started to walk out of my room. "And don't worry about the dress thing. I'm going to take care of it for you."

I stood there, reeling for a moment as I absorbed all of this news. So Peyton knew I hadn't been the one to steal her sweater. There was no chance she'd actually apologize for accusing me . . . but maybe that was why she had called the Yacht Club for me. Maybe that was as close to apologizing as Peyton would get.

And then I thought of Dex. And while I was glad that he wasn't dating the model, the news sort of depressed me at the same time. I had thought that maybe the reason he hadn't kissed me the night of Hannah's party was because he was seeing someone else. But now I knew that the only reason he hadn't kissed me . . . was me. Obviously he didn't have the same feelings for me that I had for him.

Not that this should surprise me. The star athlete and the math whiz? Like that would ever happen.

# Chapter 27

$$\iint_S \left(\frac{\partial R}{\partial y} - \frac{\partial Q}{\partial z}\right) dy \wedge dz + \left(\frac{\partial P}{\partial z} - \frac{\partial R}{\partial x}\right) dz \wedge dx + \left(\frac{\partial Q}{\partial x} - \frac{\partial P}{\partial y}\right) dx \wedge dy$$
$$= \int_C P\, dx + Q\, dy + R\, dz$$

I spent the rest of the morning and early afternoon dealing with one crisis after another. First there were the balloons. We'd ordered equal numbers of black and white balloons, but the party store had mistakenly given us black, white, red, and silver, and we didn't have time to go back and swap them out. Then, the glamour posters of Audrey Hepburn, Marilyn Monroe, Elizabeth Taylor, Lana Turner, and other Hollywood stars, which had been blown up to fit on the gymnasium walls, ended up being way too big for the much smaller Oar Room. We had to prop them against the walls at an angle, just to get the movie stars to fit. And then we found out that the Yacht Club had a rule against bringing in outside food, but we didn't have a budget to order food through them, so the only way we'd have a snack table was if we sneaked the food in.

"No problem," Finn said. He'd shown up after all, although I wasn't so sure that was a good thing, since he and Charlie continued to snipe at each other. "I'll smuggle in the snacks. You can count on me."

That was at least one detail I didn't have to worry about. When it came to breaking the rules and defying authority, Finn was a pro.

And when I finally got home that afternoon, exhausted and my fingers aching from tying off balloons, I had even more bad news.

The phone was ringing as I walked in the door.

"It's for you," Hannah called out, tossing me the cordless phone, which I took back to my room.

"Hello," I said, kicking off my sneakers, and hoping upon hope that it wasn't Felicity calling to notify me that someone had inadvertently opened a window in the Oar Room, allowing all of the balloons to escape.

"Hi, Miranda, it's Nicholas," a miserable voice bleated.

My date. And, sure, Nicholas wasn't the guy of my dreams, but that was okay. We were just going as friends, after all, and he was nice. I was sure we'd have fun together. Well ... pretty sure.

"Hi, Nicholas," I said, keeping my voice upbeat. "What time are you planning on picking me up?"

And by *you*, I meant *your mom*, since Nicholas had already informed me that she would be our chauffeur this evening.

"That's just it ... I'm not going to be able to go tonight. I have chicken pox," Nicholas said miserably. He sounded like he was about to burst into tears. "I'm so, so sorry. I feel terrible about canceling on you at the last minute."

"It's okay," I said soothingly.

"No, it's not. I was really looking forward to going, and it was going to be our first date, and now it's ruined."

*First* date?

"Really, it's okay," I said, starting to realize that as mortifying as it would be to show up at the Snowflake dateless, that might actually be better—much better—than Nicholas thinking that this was going to be a romantic date, and not just two friends going together.

"I got you a corsage and everything," Nicholas said, and then his voice broke. "Do you want my mom to drive it over to you? She said she would."

"No, that's okay. Really. You just ... get better soon," I said.

When I finally got off the phone with Nicholas—he insisted on apologizing seven more times, and I think he had actually started to cry by the time we hung up—I slumped back on my bed, lying down on the plush white comforter. I was so tired, all I wanted to do was sleep until it was time for my plane to take off the next day.

What I did not want to do was peel myself up off the bed and start getting ready to go to the Snowflake. And now that my date had canceled, why did I have to go, anyway? I was only in charge of planning the dance. And I'd done just that—I'd planned it. Everything was taken care of; all of the details were sorted out. And as for anything that might go wrong . . . well, there were four other people on the committee who would be there to deal with last-minute problems.

And yet . . . I couldn't bail, as much as I might like to. The Snowflake was my responsibility, and I had to go and make sure that everything ran smoothly. Even if it did mean showing up without a date. And even if during the slow songs, I'd have to stand by myself off to one side, looking like a complete loser. Although, come to think of it, what were the chances that Snake House knew any slow songs? Everything I'd heard them play was loud, fast, and incoherent.

"Knock, knock," Hannah said, opening my door. Her eyes sparkled, and she was grinning. "Are you off the phone?"

"Yup. Come on in," I said.

"First you have to close your eyes!"

"What?" I asked.

"Close your eyes!" she insisted.

So I did. I heard a plastic rustling noise as Hannah padded in.

"Okay. *Now* you can look," she instructed me.

When I opened my eyes, I saw Hannah standing at the foot of my bed, holding up a dress. A *beautiful* dress. It was simple—black, strapless, and knee-length—but very elegant and very sophisticated.

"Wow," I breathed. "Is that what you're wearing tonight?"

"No! It's what *you're* wearing!" Hannah announced. Her grin grew even broader.

I looked from the dress to Hannah and then back at the dress again. "You got me a dress?" I asked, stunned.

Hannah nodded. "I borrowed it from Tiff. She wore it to the senior prom last year. She went with this total dork, and she only said yes because she wanted to be able to say she went to the prom as a freshman," Hannah said.

"And she doesn't mind if I borrow it?" I asked.

"Not at all. It's not like she'll ever wear it again," Hannah said. "You can't wear the same prom dress twice."

I got up off the bed and took the dress from Hannah. I held it up in front of myself and turned to look at the reflection in the mirror, wondering if it would transform me into a princess. It didn't. I just looked like me standing behind a really pretty dress.

"What are you going to do with your hair?" Hannah asked.

"I don't know. I'll probably just wear it like this," I said, brushing my shoulder-length hair back with one hand.

"Like that?" Hannah sounded horrified. "You can't wear it like that. Look, I'll just do it for you."

"What will you do?" I asked, trying not to sound as suspicious as I felt. Because although she was acting incredibly—and bizarrely—nice to me, I didn't have the best track record with Hannah. I hoped this wasn't some elaborate practical joke that would end with my hair standing straight up on end, looking like I'd been electrocuted.

"Have you ever tried straightening it?" she asked. I shook my head. "I think that would be the best thing to do. I'll blow it out for you, and then run over it with my straightening iron. Trust me; it'll look great. Very chic."

"Thanks, but . . ." I trailed off.

"But what?" Hannah asked.

"Why are you being so nice to me?" I blurted out.

Hannah looked down at her pink-polished toes for a moment, and then shrugged. "I don't know. I guess . . . well . . . I should have told Peyton about Avery taking her sweater. I should have told her that first night she accused you of taking it," Hannah said.

"But you didn't know then," I said. I had no idea why I was trying to excuse Hannah's behavior. She just looked . . . so sorry.

"I had a pretty good idea it was her. Or, at least, I should have," Hannah confessed. She looked up at me, her lovely blue eyes contrite. "I'm really sorry, Miranda."

*Wow*. Hannah, who I'd always thought hated my guts, was apologizing to *me*. It was too weird for words.

"Well . . . thanks," I said. "I really appreciate that."

There was an awkward pause.

"And if you really don't mind, I'd love some help with my hair. I'm hopeless with it," I said.

Hannah brightened. "Oh, good! It'll be fun. And your date will die when he sees you all glammed up."

"Actually, my date just canceled," I confessed. "That was him on the phone. He has the chicken pox."

Hannah wrinkled her nose. "Chicken pox? Isn't that what little kids get?"

"I guess he never had it before. It's okay, though. I'm not that upset. We were just going as friends," I said. Or, at least, I was just going as a friend. Better not to think about what Nicholas had thought it was.

Hannah looked thoughtful. "Hmmm," she said.

"What?" I asked.

"Oh, nothing. But date or no date, you're still going to look great tonight," she assured me. "I have some Stila lip gloss that will look amazing on you. Come on; I'll show you," she said.

And as I followed her to her room—which featured an enormous canopy bed swathed in armfuls of tulle and an art deco vanity—I wondered . . . was this what it was like to have a real sister? And then I thought about Charlie and her two older sisters, who were both now in college, and how they'd all have screaming fights one day over something completely stupid, and then the next day would be best friends again. Sisters always seemed like they had such a love/hate relationship . . . and I'd always wished I had a sister to love/hate.

"Here it is," Hannah said, whipping out a tube of lip gloss and dabbing a berry pink streak of it on the back of her hand. "Try it on!"

"Okay," I said, taking the lip gloss from her. I slicked the gloss over my lips, and then pouted for Hannah. "What do you think?"

"Fab-u-lous!" Hannah pronounced. "When I'm done with you, you won't look like a geek at all. You won't even recognize yourself."

"Um, thanks. I think," I said.

But I laughed. Because here's the thing: Hannah and I certainly didn't love each other. Maybe we never would. But maybe, possibly, we could learn to like each other. And that might be as close to having a sister as either one of us would ever get.

# Chapter 28

$$\text{curl } F = \left( \frac{\partial R}{\partial y} - \frac{\partial Q}{\partial z} \right) i + \left( \frac{\partial P}{\partial z} - \frac{\partial R}{\partial x} \right) j + \left( \frac{\partial Q}{\partial x} - \frac{\partial P}{\partial y} \right) k$$

Three hours later, I stood in front of the mirror in my room, staring at my transformed self. I'd been buffed, tweezed, polished, and glossed, and my hair had been straightened into submission. And while I didn't look like a completely different person, I certainly looked different from the normal me.

*I'm pretty,* I thought, amazed. It was the first time I'd ever thought that about myself. But I *was* pretty. My eyes—lined and mascaraed— looked large and luminous, and my brown hair fell in a sleek, shiny cascade to my shoulders. My lips were full and amazingly pouty with Hannah's berry lip gloss. And the dress . . . it was the sort of dress a movie star would wear. And it fit perfectly, skimming over my chest and torso before flaring out into a knee-length skirt.

"You look *amazing,*" Hannah said.

She had appeared in the door, and as I turned to look at her, my mouth dropped open. Because if I was pretty, Hannah was *gorgeous.* She was wearing a floor-length white satin dress that looked like it had been designed just for her. The fabric hung slinkily along her perfect curves, with a modest rounded neckline and an entirely immodest low-cut back. She was wearing her hair up in a smooth French twist, and had done her face up in what she called her Marilyn Monroe look—lots of mascara and creamy red lipstick.

"*Wow!*" I said.

"You like?" Hannah asked. She pirouetted. "Is the back too slutty?"

"No, it's perfect. Just slutty enough," I said, meaning it as a compliment. Hannah smiled, understanding what I meant.

Just then, the doorbell rang.

"That's probably Emmett," Hannah said. She smoothed her dress down and giggled. "I don't know why, but I feel a little nervous."

I shook my head. "You have nothing to worry about. Well. Other than that Emmett's probably going to pass out when he sees you."

"You think?"

"Definitely. Just be careful. He'll hit his head on the marble floor, get a concussion, and you'll end up spending the night at the ER. It could be bad," I said.

Hannah laughed again, and pleasure lit her face. Clearly, the idea of Emmett finding her so breathtaking that he'd actually keel over thrilled her. It made me wonder . . . did Hannah have any idea of how lovely she really was? Or was she one of those girls who truly wasn't aware of her own beauty?

"Do you want to ride with us to the dance?" she offered.

"No, that's okay. Dad already said he'd drive me," I said. Even if I was over Emmett, it didn't mean that I wanted to sit with him and Hannah, a third wheel to their romantic date.

"Okay. I'll see you there, then," Hannah said. She smiled one more time, and then she was gone, leaving behind a cloud of floral perfume.

When my dad dropped me off at the Yacht Club, I felt nervous, too. Not about seeing anyone in particular, but about showing off this new side of me to the people who had grown accustomed to seeing me every day in my normal, slightly disheveled, frizzy-haired state. It made me feel vulnerable, almost like I was a new foal, still unused to my legs. (Although that may have had more to do with the fact that I was wearing high heels for the first time, and could hardly walk across the room on them without tripping.)

"Here you go, Cinderella," Dad said.

"Cinderella?" I asked.

"That's right. Just think of my car as your own personal pumpkin coach," Dad said.

Except that there wasn't a Prince Charming waiting for me inside, I thought. But I quickly shook off that gloomy thought. It didn't matter. I was going to have fun on my own tonight.

"Thanks for the ride," I said.

"Have I told you how great you look?" Dad asked.

Even though I knew that he was obligated to compliment me, I still blushed.

"Yeah. You did. In fact, you've told me ten times," I said. "You're embarrassing me."

"Good. I wouldn't be doing my job as your father if I didn't embarrass you. So what time should I pick you up?"

"I'm not sure. Can I call you?"

"Of course. Do you have your cell phone?"

I patted the little bejeweled bag, also a loan from Hannah. "Right here. Cell phone, lipgloss, credit card. All the needs of a modern girl encased in a purse the size of my hand. Life is truly miraculous."

Dad laughed, and I opened the door to climb out. Just before I shut the door, my dad leaned over across the seat.

"Hey," he said. "Have a great time."

"Thanks," I said, smiling. "I think I will."

Dad drove off, and I turned to walk toward the Yacht Club. I wasn't the first one there. Other students had started slowly streaming in. I saw Finn up ahead, dapper in his rented tux, walking with Leila. She looked adorable in a black-and-white striped knee-length dress. Sanjiv was there with a girl I didn't recognize. He was talking to her animatedly, his Adam's apple bobbing up and down in his throat. Alex Bendell and

Guy Parkinson, both seniors and Geek High's resident golden couple, arrived holding hands.

*That's a good sign,* I thought. The senior class always skipped the Snowflake. If Alex and Guy showed up, that meant other seniors were probably coming as well.

"Well, here goes nothing," I said to myself. And then I took a deep breath and walked into the Oar Room.

The decorations looked especially nice, I thought. We'd strung balloons up everywhere—bobbing along the ceiling, tied in bunches as center-pieces on the tables, wound around pillars. I was glad that we'd used the red and silver balloons that had been sent by mistake. The red popped out and the silver shone against the black and white balloons. And the movie-star posters looked fabulous, giving the room an elegant air, as though it weren't just a high school party, but a Hollywood soiree.

There was already a good turnout, from a pack of runty freshmen grouped together against the wall to the cluster of seniors who were join-ing Alex and Guy in the center of the room. It looked like everyone was already having a good time. Faces were flushed with excitement, and friends were chattering. I waved at Hannah, who was hanging out with Emmett, Emmett's best friend, Isaac, and Isaac's girlfriend, Jenna. Han-nah grinned and waved back at me.

There was just one thing missing . . . there wasn't any music. Where was Snake House? Their instruments were there, set up in the far corner next to the dance floor. But I didn't see any of the band members.

"Oh, good, you're here, Miranda."

I turned and saw Felicity bearing down on me. She was wearing a short, tight, sparkly black dress, and her hair was piled on her head, se-cured with chopsticks. Felicity's face was screwed up in a frown.

"We have a big problem," Felicity said. "Bigger than big. Hugely big."

. . .

Felicity, Morgan, Charlie, and I convened in the ladies' room five minutes later. (Finn couldn't join us because of the locale, but he was busy anyway, surreptitiously putting out the snack bowls filled with candy and bags of chips). Charlie had dyed her hair purple for the night, and wore a vintage fifties black tulle dress. Charlie, being Charlie, pulled it off beautifully. Morgan, on the other hand, had made the mistake of wearing a long, puffy, bridal-looking white dress that made her look even more square and squat than usual.

"Morgan, where is the band?" Felicity asked severely.

"I don't know," Morgan bleated. "Snake came with me. And the drummer and bassist showed up. But none of them know where Doug is."

Doug was the lead singer of Snake House. If you could call what he did singing. He was really more of a lead wailer.

"Does he know that the venue changed?" I asked.

"I think so," Morgan said. "I mean, I told him, but . . . I'm not one hundred percent sure he was listening."

"Morgan!" Felicity said, her eyes narrowing into angry slits. "It was your job to notify the band!"

"Can't you call him now?" Charlie asked.

"He doesn't have a cell phone," Morgan said miserably. "He thinks they're fascist."

"How can a cell phone be fascist?" I asked. "It's an inanimate object."

"Well, it is sort of fascist," Charlie said. "In an oblique way."

"You guys! This is serious!" Felicity said, rounding on us. "We can't have a dance without a band."

"We have most of a band," Charlie said reasonably. "We're just missing a singer."

"Well, that's sort of a major part, don't you think?" Felicity snapped.

"Well . . ." I said, looking at Felicity.

"What?" she said.

"We *do* have a singer," I said.

"Who?" Felicity asked, narrowing her eyes with suspicion.

"*You*," I said.

Felicity stared at me for a moment, her mouth falling open. "No way. I can't do that," she finally said.

"Why not?" Charlie asked. "It'll be very Blondie meets the Sex Pistols."

"I am a classically trained opera singer," Felicity insisted. "I can't sing with a rock band."

"Singing is singing," Charlie said. "Just don't do any of those weird, high-pitched screechy noises. I think it might freak out the crowd."

"*Charlie*, you're not *helping*," I hissed.

"Look, you're going to have to think of something else. I can't do it," Felicity said. "I mean, I have a date. My boyfriend—you know, *Justin* from *Yale*—is here."

"You have a boyfriend who goes to Yale?" Charlie asked in mock surprise. I elbowed her. Taunting Felicity, while fun, was not helpful at the moment.

"I'm supposed to leave Justin all alone while I sing? He'll look like a loser just standing there by himself," Felicity said.

"Hey!" Morgan said, rounding on her friend.

"What?" Felicity asked, crossing her thin arms over her low-cut dress.

"Snake's going to be performing while I'm alone. Does that make me look like a loser?" Morgan asked hotly.

Charlie and I exchanged a look. Under any other circumstances, a Felimonster-Toady catfight would be a real hoot to watch, but, unfortunately, right now we had to stay focused on the task at hand.

"Felicity, you have to do it. Because if you don't, we won't have a band. No band means no music, and no music means that everyone is just going to leave," I said.

"Besides, just think how cool you'll be as Rocker Girl," Charlie said, with a flash of brilliance. When dealing with Felicity, you could never go wrong playing to her ego. "It'll be totally hot. *You'll* be totally hot."

"Well . . ." Felicity said, considering. We all waited hopefully while she deliberated. Finally, Felicity looked at Morgan. "Does Snake House know any Jessica Simpson songs?" she asked with a resigned sigh.

# Chapter 29

$$\iint_S (\text{curl}\, F) \cdot n \, dS = \int_C F \cdot d\alpha$$

**A**s it turned out, Felicity wasn't awful. In fact, she was pretty good, if a bit tentative as she launched into her first song, ABBA's "Dancing Queen" (Charlie's suggestion, of course).

Snake House, on the other hand, struggled to all play the same song at the same time. But most of the crowd was having so much fun, they didn't seem to notice. Charlie even dragged me out on the dance floor when Felicity and Snake House broke into a recognizable cover of the Killers' "Mr. Brightside." I danced with Charlie and her date, Mitch—who looked surprisingly cute out of his Grounded uniform—and even Morgan joined us. I could see Finn dancing with Leila . . . if you could call it dancing. Mostly Finn was just jumping up and down in place, and looking like a total goofball. Even Christopher Frost was there with a date; I saw him leading mousy Angel Baker—a freshman and two-time winner of the state spelling bee—out onto the dance floor.

I tried not to dwell on the fact that even Christopher had a date, while I did not, and instead comforted myself with the knowledge that everyone seemed to be having a ball. Even Felicity eventually got over her inhibitions, and seriously got into her role as Rocker Girl. She started to shimmy her hips and make eyes at her boyfriend, Yale Justin, as she sang.

"Look out, world," Charlie shouted in my ear. "Next thing you know, Felicity will be auditioning for *American Idol*."

"I seriously wouldn't be surprised," I said. "You know she'd love the attention."

When Felicity and Snake House transitioned into a slower-paced rendition of Coldplay's "Green Eyes," and all of the couples began pairing up, I turned to leave before I found myself in the embarrassing predicament of being the only partnerless person on the dance floor. Even Morgan had a partner; she was dancing with Yale Justin, although he didn't once take his eyes off of Felicity. And, actually, Morgan didn't take her eyes off of Snake, either. It was almost sweet, I thought.

"Miranda, don't go," Charlie said. She tried to grab my hand to keep me from leaving the dance floor.

"I don't have a partner," I said, feeling myself turn red.

"You can dance with Mitch and me," Charlie offered sweetly. And even though Mitch didn't look thrilled by this idea, he nodded gamely, holding out his hand to me.

"Sure," he said. "Come on."

I shook my head. "No, it's okay. I'm thirsty anyway. I'm going to get a soda."

I turned and walked away before Charlie could talk me out of leaving. I held my head high, and tried not to let it bother me that I was alone. At a dance. While the most romantic song ever written was being played. Standing in a glamorous room full of balloons and twinkle lights, with an amazing view of the river out of the tall glass double doors that lined one side of the room. Nope. I didn't mind at all.

I got my soda and stood to one side, fanning myself with the little jeweled bag and trying to look relieved at being able to take a break, as I watched the dancers. Emmett and Hannah were holding each other close, her head tucked against his shoulder. Charlie was trying to talk Mitch into attempting a goofy sort of a waltz. Finn was rocking stiffly back and forth from one foot to the other, with his hands firmly planted on Leila's hips. Tate Metcalf was spinning Padma Paswan around in a circle. A few of the chaperones were dancing too. Mr. and Mrs. Gordon were gliding along, as were Headmaster Hughes and Miss Tilley, my Latin teacher.

And suddenly, I *did* mind being there alone. I minded a lot. Sure, Nicholas wouldn't have been my dream date, but at least I would have had someone to dance with during the slow songs . . . instead of having to stand by myself off to one side, feeling like the world's biggest loser. I set down my plastic soda cup and headed for the doors that led out to the deck overlooking the river. At least out there I could be alone, and away from all of the nauseating coupledom.

I opened the doors and stepped out onto the wood porch that wrapped around the Oar Room. I was immediately cooled by the brisk breeze blowing off the water. It was such a beautiful night—the sky was cloudless and dark, except for the moon, which hung low and round off in the distance. The stars were easily visible above, a canopy of tiny lights. And off in the distance, two boats were making their slow progress toward each other along the water. One looked like a party boat, from the lights strung along it from bow to stern.

I walked over to the wooden railing and leaned against it, breathing in the salty air, and tried to focus on the positive. The Snowflake was a success, after all. Everyone was having a good time, and—at the very least—no one was bored to tears by a string of dry academics droning on and on about the need for accelerated programs at the university level, or some other such drivel that we were supposed to care about, but of course didn't. So I wouldn't be the most reviled student at Geek High. In fact, my fellow students might even appreciate what I had accomplished, with the help of my committee, of course.

And who needed a boy to have a good time anyway? Not me. No. I had Girl Power. I'd proven to myself that I could go to a dance on my own, hold my head up high, and have a good time. Feeling better with this pep talk, I took in a deep breath and straightened up. The slow song would be over soon, and then the band was due to take a break, so I'd just hang out with Charlie, Finn, and the others, and have a fine time while I was at it. I turned, and even took a step toward the doors, before I saw him, framed in the doorway. The lights of the dance glowed behind him, sparking against the golden-red highlights in his hair. And I couldn't help inhaling a sharp breath of surprise, as the zing hit me.

It was *Dex*.

# Chapter 30

$$\iiint\limits_{V} (\text{div } F)\, dx\, dy\, dz = \iint\limits_{S} F \cdot n\, dS$$

"Hi," Dex said, stepping forward onto the deck. He was wearing a blue blazer over a white shirt and crisply ironed khaki pants. A striped tie hung around his neck. His hands were stuffed casually into his pants pockets.

"Hi," I said. "What are you doing here?"

And then suddenly I realized: He must have come as someone's date. Disappointment crashed over me. This was too much to deal with. It had been hard enough watching Emmett and Hannah fall for each other. But I couldn't bear seeing Dex pull some other girl into his arms, holding her close as they danced. I just couldn't. I gripped my purse a little more tightly, thankful that it contained my cell phone. As soon as I could get away from Dex, I'd call my dad and have him pick me up.

But then Dex said, "I came to find you."

I had to work really hard to keep my mouth from dropping open in shock.

"You came . . . to find . . . *me*?" I asked slowly, wanting to make sure I'd heard him correctly.

Dex nodded.

"But how did you even know I was here?" I asked.

"Hannah. She called me this afternoon, and told me that your date had fallen through," Dex said. "She asked me to meet you here."

"She did?" I asked.

He nodded and smiled crookedly. His entire face seemed to suddenly glow luminously. I smiled back at him, not able to help myself, even as my mind churned with questions. Why had Hannah called him? And why had he come? Was he supposed to be my date? And did he even *want* to be my date, or was he just doing Hannah a favor?

"Sorry about my clothes," Dex said. "It was too late to rent a tux, and these are the dressiest clothes I own." He picked up his tie and grinned at it self-deprecatingly. "Except for the tie. That's my dad's."

"You look"—*amazing, incredible, eminently kissable*—"fine," I finished weakly.

"Thanks," Dex said. He stepped forward, so that he was standing only an arm's length away from me. My pulse began to drum loudly, and my stomach fluttered with excitement. He was so close now. So very, very close. I could see how pale his eyelashes were. So pale they were almost silver. I hadn't noticed that before.

"You look really pretty," he said softly.

And then he reached out and lightly touched my newly smoothed hair. I had to hold my breath so as not to do something incredibly embarrassing, like squeaking with excitement.

Dex gently tugged on a lock of hair. "Your hair's different."

"I straightened it," I said, the words sounding creaky.

"It looks nice," Dex said. He moved forward again, and for one heart-stopping moment I thought he might actually be moving in for a kiss . . . but then he stepped past me and looked out at the river. The lights from the Yacht Club were reflected on the water, glowing there as though there were lights submerged beneath. The two boats off in the distance had now passed each other, and were chugging off in the opposite direction. Dex turned suddenly to face me, leaning back casually against the railing.

"So what happened to your date?" he asked.

"Who, Nicholas?" I asked. "Oh . . . he wasn't really a date. I mean, he *was*, but . . . well. We were just going as friends," I said.

"Did *he* know that?" Dex asked, so perceptively I blushed.

"I'm not sure," I admitted.

"So what happened to him?"

"He has chicken pox," I said.

Dex whistled. "Bad luck," he said, and he looked at me with a bemused expression that made me think he knew just how brokenhearted I hadn't been that Nicholas had canceled on me. Which nettled me, because, really, it wasn't like I'd wished chicken pox on the poor guy. I crossed my arms and glowered at Dex, which made him grin.

"That's more like it. I hardly recognize you when you're not frowning at me," he said cheerfully.

I rolled my eyes, but I did uncross my arms. "Seriously . . . why did you come tonight?" I asked, trying to keep my temper in check.

"I already told you. Hannah said that you needed an escort," Dex said. As though this explained everything . . . when, in fact, it explained nothing.

I raised my eyebrows. "You just came here tonight as a favor to Hannah?" I asked, while hoping, hoping, hoping that this wasn't true.

Dex didn't speak for a long moment. "No. I'm not doing Hannah a favor," he finally said, his voice soft.

He stepped closer to me, so close I had to tip my head back to look up at him. He lifted one hand and rested it gently on the back of my neck, and with his other hand he gently brushed a stray lock of hair away from my cheek. That was when I stopped breathing. I looked up at him, looked right into his pale blue eyes, and then suddenly Dex leaned forward . . . and kissed me.

If I could have melted into a Miranda-shaped puddle right then and there, I would have. Because the kiss? Was *amazing*. His lips felt warm and deliciously soft pressed against mine, and the feel of his hands—one pressed against my neck, the other gently cupping my cheek—caused goose bumps to spread over my bare arms and shoulders. And all I could think was, *Oh, my gosh . . . Dex is kissing me. Dex! Is kissing! Me!*

And then way, way too soon, he pulled back and looked down at me again.

"That's why," he said softly.

"Oh," I said, feeling a little dizzy. He smelled so good, like soap and clean clothes fresh from the dryer.

"I've been wanting to do that for a long time," Dex said. "I wanted to that night on the beach when we were looking for your greyhound."

"Why didn't you?" I asked.

Dex smiled, looking almost shy as he smoothed another strand of hair behind my ear. "I wasn't sure you wanted me to."

"I did!" I exclaimed. "I thought you didn't want to kiss me!"

Tentatively I reached forward and touched his cheek. And I realized how seriously wrong I'd been that day I first met Dex. I definitely *did* have a thing for redheads.

And then Dex leaned forward . . . and he kissed me again. And I stopped thinking altogether as the zing took over.

Dex held my hand as we walked back into the Oar Room together. I wondered if I looked any different. I certainly *felt* different. I was no longer Miranda, Loser in Love and Poster Girl of the Late Bloomers. I was Miranda, Kissed by Dex McConnell! The excitement filled me like a bubble until I thought I would actually float away with happiness.

Felicity and Snake House were playing another ballad. Or, at least, Felicity was singing a slow song—John Mayer's "Daughters." Snake House sounded like they were playing some other song entirely.

"Do you want to dance?" Dex asked.

I nodded, and, still holding my hand, Dex led me out to the dance floor. He rested his hands on my waist, and I wrapped my arms up around his neck, and then we were swaying together, holding each other close. My first kiss, followed by my first slow dance. And, even better, both had been with Dex. Dex, with his glittering pale eyes and slow smile. Dex, who had taken up permanent residence in my thoughts ever since I'd first laid eyes on him back in September. It was all so unreal . . . so amazingly, incredibly, blissfully unreal.

I came out of my happiness haze just long enough to look around the dance floor. I first noticed that Charlie's and Finn's dates, Mitch and Leila, were dancing together. I frowned, and glanced around, and then I saw that Charlie and Finn were dancing together, too. Finn was joking around about something, and Charlie was laughing up at him. I smiled. It was nice to see the two of them getting along for a change. They'd been so hostile toward each other recently. Just past Charlie and Finn, Hannah and Emmett were dancing together. Her head was resting on his shoulder, and his hands were curled around her waist. They looked contented. I was glad, truly happy for them.

The song came to an end, and Felicity leaned forward into the microphone and said, "We're going to take a short break now." And everyone clapped and cheered for the band. Felicity looked flushed and hot, but she smiled her thanks and gave a little curtsy before heading off the stage and into the arms of her boyfriend, Yale Justin.

Dex and I stepped apart, and we stood grinning at each other for a moment. He finally glanced around, eyeing the refreshment table, which was currently being mobbed by everyone streaming off the dance floor.

"Would you like a soda?" he asked me.

"Yeah, that would be great," I said.

"Stay here. I'll be right back," Dex said.

I watched him go, wondering if it was possible to actually burst open from happiness.

"Miranda!"

I turned to see who was calling me. It was Mrs. Gordon. She was wearing a white sweater and a long black skirt, and looked really pretty.

Her hair, which usually was half-in, half-out of a bun, even looked nice hanging loosely around her shoulders.

"Hi, Mrs. Gordon," I said.

"Did you get my e-mail?" she asked.

"No, I didn't. It's been sort of crazy today getting everything ready. I haven't had a chance to check my e-mail," I said apologetically.

"Actually, I'm glad that I get to tell you in person. I have some fantastic news," Mrs. Gordon said. She smiled broadly, and her brown eyes were warm with pleasure. "I found out yesterday afternoon . . . you made it! They chose your story as a finalist for the Winston Creative Writing Contest! You're going to the finals in D.C.!"

"What?" I asked, not sure if I'd heard her right. "Did you say . . . *Wait*. I'm a *finalist*? My story actually got picked?"

Mrs. Gordon nodded. "Congratulations," she said, leaning forward and giving me a quick hug. "Let's get together after the winter break to go over the details."

"Great . . . thanks," I said, feeling a little disoriented. But even so, a huge smile stretched across my face.

First Dex, now the writing contest . . . it was a lot of good news to take in all at once. Or maybe, it was just that I wasn't used to good news. I hadn't had a lot of it lately. First Sadie leaving, and then my run-in with Headmaster Hughes.

Speaking of whom, where did he go? I wondered.

Then I saw him standing off to one side, chatting with the astronomy teacher, Mr. "Call Me Doug" Keegan. As though he could sense my eyes on him, Headmaster Hughes's baldhead swiveled toward me, and he looked at me appraisingly. And then he nodded courteously, signaling his pleasure with how the Snowflake had turned out. I grinned back at him. Even though I was still annoyed that he'd blackmailed me into rejoining Mu Alpha Theta, I couldn't be mad at anyone tonight, the most perfect of nights. Not even at the headmaster.

"Here's your soda," Dex said, returning to my side and handing over a Coke.

"Thanks," I said. "And . . . thanks for coming to find me tonight."

"Don't mention it," Dex said, grinning. "I'm glad I came."

Just then, music began to blare. I looked up and saw that Finn had plugged his iPod into the band's sound system. The room was instantly filled with Fall Out Boy, playing at top decibel.

"Do you want to dance?" Dex asked, tipping his head toward the dance floor, which was filling up again, and holding his hand out to me. He was still smiling at me, and the smile carried up to his pale blue eyes.

I hesitated. I just wanted a moment to take it all in: the dance, the enchantingly beautiful room, all of my classmates swirling around in their black and white gowns, the good news about the writing contest, my trip to London tomorrow. And, of course, Dex. Dex coming to find me . . . Dex holding me close as we danced . . . Dex kissing me in the moonlight.

Dex's eyebrows arched up in a question. He was clearly wondering what I was waiting for. I beamed at him.

"Absolutely," I said. "Let's dance."

If you loved *Geek High*,

be sure to look out for Miranda Bloom's

next adventure…

# Geek Abroad

available from NAL Jam

Read on for a sneak peek….

"We've received permission to land, and will shortly be making our final descent into London's Heathrow Airport. Please put your seats and tray tables in their upright and locked positions. . . ."

A shiver of excitement ran down my back. We were going to land! Soon I'd be in London! The only question was, where would Sadie and I go first? The Tower of London? Madame Tussauds wax museum? The London Eye? I clasped my hands together, so excited that I could hardly sit still.

"Excuse me." I felt a tap on my right arm and turned. It was the frazzled mom. "Would you mind holding my baby for just a minute? I have to run to the bathroom before we land," she said pleadingly.

"Oh . . . Um, sure," I said. Babies had never been my forte, but the mom looked so exhausted and strung out, I didn't have the heart to refuse her.

She gratefully handed over the baby, unbuckled her seatbelt and dashed off toward the toilets. I held the baby gingerly out from me, my hands hooked under its armpits. We stared at one another for a long moment until the baby finally grinned, exposing a toothless gummy mouth. Charmed, I grinned back. And just then, as I was smiling away, the baby—in what can be described only as a horror movie–like moment—

opened its mouth and ejected a stream of foul, neon green vomit right down the front of my T-shirt.

Speechless, I stared down at my now-dripping shirt, and then back up at the baby. He kicked his chubby legs and emitted a loud, satisfied burp. The farting businessman next to me actually had the nerve to pinch his nose and lean away. Granted, the baby vomit was pretty vile smelling—who knew someone so small and cute could produce something so revolting?—but considering that the businessman had been befouling the cabin for the past seven hours, I didn't think he was in any position to complain.

The baby giggled suddenly, and stuffed one round hand into his mouth. I sighed and smiled ruefully back. There was no point in holding a grudge. And besides, for once in my life everything was perfect. I wasn't going to let a little bit—okay, a *lot*—of baby vomit get me down now.

"Miranda! Yoo hoo! Over here!"

I craned my neck and looked from side to side . . . and then I saw Sadie. She would have been hard to miss, considering that she was wearing a dramatic scarlet ankle-length wool cape that made her look like a matronly version of Little Red Riding Hood. Sadie was beaming and waving at me, standing just past Customs and ignoring the grumpy passengers who had to step around her. She'd changed her hair since I'd last seen her. The long blond curls were gone, replaced by a smart, sleek dark brown bob. Actually, she looked fantastic, like the after picture in one of those makeover shows my stepsister and all her friends are addicted to.

I rushed to Sadie, pulling my wheeled suitcase behind me, and she caught me up in her arms. She smelled so achingly familiar—a mixture of coffee, mint toothpaste and Joy perfume—that I almost dissolved into tears. Sadie pulled me close, and the wool of her cape felt scratchy against my cheek.

"Hi, Sadie," I said, my voice muffled.

"Hello, darling," Sadie crooned. "It's so wonderful to see you!"

"You too," I said. And then, because I couldn't help myself, I added, "Nice cape."

"Do you like it?" Sadie asked, delighted. She pulled back and spun around so that the cape circled out for a moment. "I thought it was divine."

"It's very"—I searched for a neutral adjective—"red," I finished lamely.

"Exactly!" Sadie beamed. "It's putting me in the mood for Christmas." Her expression suddenly shifted into a frown. She held me by my shoulders and looked down at my vomit-covered shirt, her nose wrinkling. "What's that? It smells like . . ."

"Baby vomit," I said. "I'm a casualty of modern air travel."

Sadie hustled me into the nearest bathroom, electing to wait for me outside and away from the smell. Once I'd changed, and stuffed the vomit shirt in my suitcase, I rejoined Sadie. She linked her arm through mine, and I had to walk quickly to keep up with her, while dragging my suitcase behind me.

"Christmas in London is going to be magical! Just think of it, darling! It will be so Dickensian!" Sadie enthused.

"Dickensian?" I repeated. "You mean, like Scrooge and Tiny Tim and bah-humbug?"

"Well, not the bah-humbug," Sadie said. "I was thinking more along the lines of roast goose and mince pies and waking up to snow on Christmas morning! We've never had a white Christmas before."

That was true enough. We lived in Florida, where it was normally warm enough to wear shorts on Christmas Day. Every year, we wrapped twinkle lights around the palm trees in our front yard.

"So other than being vomited on, how was your flight?" Sadie asked, as we joined the throng of people filing out of the airport through large automatic doors.

I gasped as the frigid air hit me, as though I'd walked smack into an iceberg. It was *freezing* out. The wind was blowing so coldly, it felt like it was rattling my bones under my skin. As we queued for a cab—even the taxis were cool here, all black and boxy—I unzipped my suitcase, pulled out my coat and quickly slipped it on.

"Long," I said to answer Sadie's question. Suddenly I felt really, really tired. I checked my watch. No wonder: it was two in the morning at home, and I'd been too excited to sleep on the plane. Just thinking of it made me yawn—a long, cold, shaky yawn.

"You must be exhausted," Sadie said, patting my arm. "We'll get you home, and you can take a nice nap."

"But I don't want to nap," I said. "I'm only going to be in London for two and a half weeks! If I'm going to see everything I want to see, I have to start today. I just don't know where to begin."

But then I yawned again, and this time my eyes watered from the cold, causing my vision to go blurry for a moment. I rubbed my hands together and stamped my feet, trying to warm up, and wished I'd brought a heavier coat with me. Maybe Sadie's Little Red Riding Hood cape wasn't so crazy after all.

"There will be plenty of time to do everything," Sadie promised me, as we finally reached the front of the line and climbed into one of the big black taxicabs.

"Maybe I'll just power-nap now," I said, leaning back against the gray leather seat. "Then I'll be all rested up and ready to get started."

Sadie leaned over and squeezed my hand. "Good idea. I'm so glad you're finally here," she said fondly.

"Me too," I mumbled, wondering what my first glimpse of London would be as we drove into the city. Would we pass by Big Ben? Or Tower Bridge? Or maybe even Buckingham Palace? But before I could ask Sadie, who was leaning forward to give the cabbie detailed instructions on where we were going, my eyelids drooped closed. I was zonked out before the cab pulled away from the curb.

# About the Author

Photo by Marie Langmore

**Piper Banks** lives in South Florida with her husband, son, and smelly pug dog. You can visit her Web site at www.piperbanks.com.